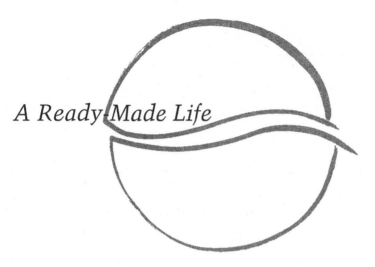

A Ready-Made Life

A Ready-Made Life

EARLY MASTERS OF MODERN KOREAN FICTION

Selected and Translated by

Kim Chong-un and Bruce Fulton

UNIVERSITY OF HAWAI'I PRESS, HONOLULU

This book has been published with the support of a grant
from the Korean Culture and Arts Foundation.

Library of Congress Cataloging-in-Publication Data
A ready-made life : early masters of modern Korean fiction / selected and
    translated by Kim Chong-un and Bruce Fulton.
        p.   cm.
    ISBN 0-8248-2015-0 (cloth : alk. paper). — ISBN 0-8248-2071-1
(pbk. : alk. paper)
    1. Short stories, Korean—Translations into English.   2. Korean
fiction—20th century—Translations into English.   I. Kim, Chong-un,
1929–   II. Fulton, Bruce.
PL984.E8R43   1998
895.7'30108—dc21   98-16635
                                                                         CIP

University of Hawai'i Press books are printed on acid-free
paper and meet the guidelines for permanence and durability
of the Council on Library Resources.

Book designed by Kenneth Miyamoto
Printed by The Maple-Vail Book Manufacturing Group

www.uhpress.hawaii.edu

Contents

v

Translators' Preface

This is a collection of Korean short fiction predating 1945. Our selection of that year as a chronological boundary is based not only on its importance in modern Korean history—it marked the liberation of Korea from Japanese colonial rule—but also on the Korean literature community's convention of demarcating the Korean literature of the present century into "modern" *(kŭndae)*, or pre-1945, and "contemporary" *(hyŏndae)*, or post-1945.

Korean fiction of the pre-1945 period is ill served in translation, both in quantity and quality, and the need for a representative anthology covering those years has long been felt. But rather than attempting a definitive, canonical collection, we have selected stories on the basis of their appeal to us, their brevity (the title story notwithstanding), and their unavailability in English translation. To our knowledge, only two of the stories have appeared previously in English, and both of them exercise such a hold on us that the temptation to attempt a new translation could not be withstood. Above all we have tried to reflect in our selection the great variety of styles and stylists in early modern Korean fiction.

We wish to thank Ju-Chan Fulton for reviewing drafts of several of the stories, Paul La Selle for commenting on the title story, and an anonymous reviewer for the University of Hawai'i Press for comparing our translations word for word with the original Korean versions and detecting some of the miscues that are inevitable in any work of translation. The usefulness of Kwon Youngmin's *Hanguk kŭndae munin taesajŏn* (Encyclopedia of modern Korean authors) in preparing the biographical notes is gratefully acknowledged. We also wish to thank the editors of *Korea Journal, The World & I, Korean Culture,*

Morning Calm, Kyoto Journal, Korea Fulbright *Forum,* and *Korean Literature Today,* in which earlier versions of several of these translations appeared.

Thanks are also due to the Korean Culture and Arts Foundation, which assisted us with a translation subsidy; and to the Northeast Asia Council of the Association for Asian Studies for a travel grant that enabled us to work together.

Finally, we are grateful to the late Marshall R. Pihl, mentor, colleague, and friend, who was a constant source of encouragement during the lengthy development of this project. We dedicate the book to his memory with great affection.

KCU
BEF

Introduction

KIM CHONG-UN AND BRUCE FULTON

Few modern literatures have developed as rapidly as that of Korea. At the end of the nineteenth century many Korean writers still wrote in Chinese, the classical literary language, though the admirably precise native script, *hangŭl*, had existed since the mid-1400s. But by the 1920s Korean fiction writers had begun producing works in *hangŭl* that, while bearing noticeable similarities in style to Western fiction, were unmistakably Korean in tone, theme, and outlook. And by the 1930s Korea had produced several masters of the short story form. How did this rapid development come about?

The history of early modern Korean fiction, extending from the late teens to Liberation from Japanese colonial rule, must be seen first and foremost in light of the nation's colonization by Japan from 1910 to 1945. Japanese rule offered a not always consistent blend of oppression and enlightenment whose legacy is still debated. It seems clear, though, that the Japanese presence played a significant role in modern Korean literary history, in that the modernization movement that swept East Asia beginning in the late 1800s was centered in Japan. The lure of modernization drew many young Koreans to Japan for their higher education, and it was there that many aspiring writers— indeed many of the writers represented in this anthology—became acquainted with Western forms of literature, which were widely available in Japanese translation. Hwang Sun-wŏn, for example, Korea's preeminent short fiction writer, read such authors as O. Henry, Maupassant, Turgenev, Balzac, Flaubert, Dostoyevsky, and Hemingway, in addition to the Japanese authors Shiga and Dazai, while studying at Waseda University. Perhaps more important for the future of modern Korean fiction, young Korean intellectuals saw for the first

1

time, in Natsume Sōseki and others, the possibility of creative writing as a profession. Returning to Korea, they quickly put these experiences to use, founding literary magazines and publishing there and in newspapers as well.

Interpretations of these early developments, and of the origins of modern Korean literature in general, tend to follow two almost antithetical lines. The great majority of Korean literature specialists in Korea emphasize the native elements of modern Korean literature. They stress the literary contributions of Pak Chi-wŏn and other *shirhak* (practical learning) scholars of the 1700s. It was those writers and scholars, they argue, who represent the origins of modern Korean literature and modern Korean thought. Other Korean scholars, most of them trained in Western literatures, emphasize the influence of the Western tradition. A more persuasive view is that modern Korean literature derived to an important extent from both native and foreign traditions. As Marshall R. Pihl has noted:

> In seeking formative influences on writers of early modern [Korean] fiction, like Ch'ae Man-shik and Yi Kwang-su, we must consider not only historical influences (Confucian didactic materials in Korean, vernacular written fiction, Buddhist narratives, and oral literature) but also contemporary experiments in Korean composition (Bible translation; reports, editorials, sketches, and anecdotes in early newspapers; and textbooks for modern education). In addition, we must also look at the growing impact of foreign literary culture, particularly Japanese (or Japanized), and judge its role in the rapidly changing state of Korean writing during the era of early experimentation and the ensuing take-off of the 1920s.[1]

The reality of the Japanese occupation, which was driven home by the brutal imperial policies that led to Korea's March 1, 1919, Independence Movement, had the effect of popularizing *hangŭl* as a vehicle for literary expression by Koreans. After crushing the independence movement, imperial Japan tried a new tack—the so-called Cultural Policy. In this climate of relative freedom of artistic expression, Korean literature began to flower. But with the outbreak of the Pacific War, colonial policy once again became oppressive. During the latter years of the occupation, when Japan banned materials writ-

---

1. Marshall R. Pihl, "Narrative Technique in Korean Fiction, 1860–1940" (paper presented to the annual conference of the Association for Asian Studies, New Orleans, 1991), 3.

ten in Korean, and when some Korean writers took the fateful step of writing in Japanese, the very act of writing in *hangŭl* was a courageous political statement and an affirmation of artistic freedom.

The rapid development of short fiction in early modern Korea is due in large part to its status as the genre of choice for those fiction writers who saw themselves as champions of pure literature. Novels were commonly serialized in newspapers but were disdained by the pure literature school as hack work turned out by didactic writers. In any event, distinctive short story stylists had appeared in numbers by the 1930s, and they wrote in a variety of styles. At least two of them, Yi Sang and Ch'ae Man-shik, are still among the most modern of modern Korean writers in terms of their artistic imagination and free-wheeling narrative style. The accomplishments of the early modern writers may be seen in the ironic fact that many of these impecunious authors turned out short gems instead of padding their stories to get more money (Korean authors were and still are paid by the manuscript page); whereas today financially secure writers write long, discursive stories that often cry out for editing. It is an incalculable loss to modern Korean fiction that so many early modern writers died young: Hyŏn Chin-gŏn at forty-two, Yi Sang at twenty-six, Na To-hyang at twenty-five, Kim Yu-jŏng at twenty-nine, Yi Hyo-sŏk at thirty-five, Ch'ae Man-shik at forty-eight.

Korean short fiction of the 1920s tends to be strongly realistic, reflecting both the familiarity of most authors with the realist traditions of French and Russian literature, and the mood of a people whose hopes for self-determination had been crushed. The establishment of the Korean Artist Proletariat Federation (KAPF) in 1925, tolerated by the Japanese because it served to divide Korean nationalists, proved a further stimulus for the production of realist fiction, and especially works that reveal class consciousness, such as Yi Ki-yŏng's "A Tale of Rats," included in this volume.

In 1935 the KAPF was forced to disband. Already by then, virtually any reference in literature to socialism or to inflammatory political issues was being blue-penciled into oblivion by the colonial censors. Under these circumstances many Korean short fiction writers concentrated on refining their craft and sharpening their creative imagination. The result is some of the best Korean short fiction of the century, most of it produced in the mid-1930s. Yi Hyo-sŏk's "When the Buckwheat Blooms," written in Korea's literary golden year of 1936, is an example of structural perfection. Another frequent type of story was the character sketch, often depicting a misfit, as in Kim Tong-ni's "A Descendant of the *Hwarang*" and Yi T'ae-jun's "An Idiot's Delight." Other writers produced stylized stories that bore little resemblance to contemporary Korean realities. Kim Tong-in's "The Photograph and the Letter," for instance, is interesting for its subversion of gender stereotypes. Other stories reconsidered the effects of Korea's Confucian heritage. Chu Yo-sŏp's "Mama and the Boarder," one of the best-loved of all Korean stories, is a poignant account, told from the point of view of a six-year-old girl, of a young widow prevented by Confucian dictates from remarrying. Other early masters returned to the Korean countryside for inspiration. Kim Yu-jŏng's "Wife," a brilliant first-person narrative, is written almost completely in pure Korean vocabulary, a striking achievement in that some 50 percent of the Korean language consists of Sino-Korean words. Hwang Sun-wŏn, sometimes unfairly pigeonholed as a rural writer, did produce splendid works with rural settings, among them the tragicomic "Mule."

Like all good literature, the best of early modern Korean fiction is susceptible to multiple readings. The most obvious interpretation of many early modern stories is that their oppressiveness and gloom conceal an anticolonial subtext. But these early works can also be read as the collective record of a people whose life choices in general were severely restricted, not just by colonization, but by education (either too little or too much, as the title story shows), and by a highly structured society that left little opportunity for misfits. In this respect, many Koreans in the occupation period were restricted to a "ready-made life." More recently, and especially since South Korea's democratization movement in the late 1980s, when domestic restrictions on Marxist writings were lifted, Marxist readings have become popular. Freudian readings are also useful; Hwang Sun-wŏn, for one, has acknowledged his familiarity with Freud, and it is highly probable that Yi Sang, Kim Tong-ni, and Ch'ae Man-shik drew artistic inspiration from Freudian thought as well. Finally, though, in this age of rampant critical jargon, we should not forget that the stories in this book, like all good literature, can be read simply for enjoyment.

Two groups of early modern Korean writers deserve special mention: the *wŏlbuk* writers (those who moved from the U.S.-occupied south to the Soviet-occupied north after 1945) and women writers. Writings by *wŏlbuk* writers were banned in South Korea until the late 1980s and democratization. In the years since, scholars and readers are rapidly becoming acquainted or reacquainted with the wealth of writing by such authors as Yi T'ae-jun, Yi Ki-yŏng, and Pak T'ae-wŏn, who combine pointed social observation with accomplished style.

Women writers played an important role in the development of the modern Korean short story. Kim Myŏng-sun's "Ŭishim ŭi sonyŏ" (A suspicious girl, 1917), for example, is among the very first modern Korean stories. Like their male counterparts, young Korean women intellectuals studied in Japan and participated in the formation of Korean literary journals and their associated circles. There is reason to believe, though, that the patriarchal nature of Korean society in general and of the Korean literature field in particular restricted the range of themes open to women writers. Significantly, early modern women writers such as Kim Myŏng-sun, Yi Wŏn-ju, and Na Hye-sŏk, who advocated freedom of lifestyle and flouted Korean social conventions, were ostracized and their careers curtailed. Kim was hounded into insanity, Yi became a nun, and Na turned to painting. Other women writers, such as Kang Kyŏng-ae and Paek Shin-ae, died young. Ch'oe Chŏng-hŭi, represented in this anthology, and Pak Hwa-sŏng were two of the few women who lived long enough to remain active after Liberation.

Most of the authors in this anthology lived and flourished before 1945. Of the remainder, two in particular made the transition to contemporary fiction and enriched it immeasurably in the course of their long careers. Hwang Sun-wŏn went on to become Korea's greatest short story writer, an author whose protean range defies categorization. And Kim Tong-ni came to be regarded by many as the Korean writer best able to express in his fiction that which is thought to be uniquely Korean. Ch'ae Man-shik survived for a short time into the post-Liberation era, producing satiric sketches as well as muted, soul-searching accounts of the dilemma of the artist in a colonized society. (While Hwang Sun-wŏn was evading the colonial authorities at his family home and continuing to write fiction that had to wait years to see the light of day, Ch'ae was being accused of not taking a more active role in opposing the Japanese.)

In the rush for globalization and the fervor for a Nobel Literature Prize in 1990s Korea, the works of these and other early masters tend to be downplayed. This is unfortunate, for contemporary Korean fiction writers have much to learn from that group of writers in terms of economy of expression and command of the Korean language. It is to be expected that further study, reading, and exposure of pre-1945 Korean fiction will solidify its standing as the foundation of contemporary Korean fiction.

A Society That Drives You to Drink

Hyŏn Chin-gŏn

Hyŏn Chin-gŏn was born in Taegu in 1900 and was educated there and in Shanghai. He later worked for the *Shidae ilbo* and *Tonga ilbo* newspapers.

Hyŏn first appeared in print in 1920 with the story "Hŭisaenghwa" (Sacrificial flowers), published in the literary journal *Kaebyŏk*. This story was soon followed by other works of fiction, such as "Pinch'ŏ" (The destitute wife, 1921) and "T'arakcha" (The degenerate, 1922), that, like the story translated here, depict the forbidding problems faced by an intellectual class whose society struggles to modernize. "Unsu choŏn nal" (A lucky day, 1924) and "Pul" (Fire, 1925) are perhaps his two best-known stories. The former, as darkly realistic a story as any in modern Korean fiction, juxtaposes a husband's windfall and his wife's death. The latter depicts a teenage wife driven to distraction by brutalities suffered on her wedding night. Both can be read as allegories of occupied Korea.

In 1926 Hyŏn collected these and other stories in his *Chosŏn ŭi ŏlgul* (Faces of Korea). These slices of life in colonial Korea are peopled almost uniformly by individuals oppressed by forces beyond their control. This volume established Hyŏn as one of the fathers of Korean realist fiction, along with Kim Tong-in and Yŏm Sang-sŏp.

"A Society That Drives You to Drink" (Sul kwŏnhanŭn sahoe), also included in *Chosŏn ŭi ŏlgul*, first appeared in *Kaebyŏk* in 1921. It is a passionate, if overstated, account of enlightened minds trying to overcome factionalism and other vestiges of traditional Korean society. It also reveals the plight of the great majority of Korean women who went unschooled and thus could not benefit intellectually from their country's modernization.

"*Aya!*" Scowling, she interrupted her solitary sewing with this weak outcry. The needle had stabbed beneath her left thumbnail. Her thumb trembled faintly and cherry-red blood appeared beneath the white nail. She quickly extracted the needle and pressed down on the wound with her other thumb. At the same time, she gingerly pushed the sewing down into her lap with her elbow. Then she let up on her thumb. The area showed no color; perhaps the bleeding had stopped. But then from beneath the pallid skin the crimson oozed forth once again in a flowery network and a drop of blood no larger than a millet grain welled up, barely visible, from the wound. Nothing to do but press down once more. Again the bleeding seemed almost stanched, but if she relaxed the pressure it soon resumed.

She would have to bandage the wound. Pressing down on her thumb, she looked into her wicker sewing basket. A scrap of cloth suitable for the purpose lay beneath a spool of thread. She pushed the spool aside and tried to take the cloth between her little fingers. But it remained caught beneath the spool, as if glued there, and for all the world she couldn't grasp it. The two fingers could only scrape helplessly against the cloth.

"Why can't I pick you up!" she finally cried, on the verge of tears. And then she glanced about the room, as if looking for someone who could help. But no one was there except, perhaps, for phantasms of her own making. Outside it was dead still but for the dreary, steady drip of water from the faucet. Suddenly the electric light seemed to brighten. It glinted from the glass face of the wall clock, and the hour hand, pointing at one o'clock, glared menacingly at her. Her husband still hadn't returned.

She could scarcely believe they'd been married seven or eight years already. But if she were to calculate the time they'd actually spent together, it might not amount to a single year. For as soon as they had married, upon his completing high school in Seoul, he had gone to Tokyo to study. And there he had graduated from college. How anxious, how lonesome she had been during that long period! In spring she would breathe in the scent of the laughing flowers, in winter hot tears would cover her icy pillow. How she missed him the times her body ached, the times her soul despaired! But all this she endured stoically, indeed welcomed. For one day he would return. This thought consoled her, gave her courage.

What was her husband doing in Tokyo? Well, he was studying. But what did that mean? She wasn't really sure. Nor did she need to bother herself to learn. Whatever it was, it was supposed to be the best, the most valuable thing in the world. It was like the goblin's spiked club that granted all wishes, as related in that tale from the old days: if he wished for clothing, then clothing would appear; and

the same with food, money. . . . Her husband could wish for anything—no request was impossible—and he would return with it from
Tokyo. Occasionally she saw his relatives wearing silk clothing and
gold rings. It was an eye-opening sight, one that made her envy them
deep down inside, but later she would think, "When my husband
returns! . . ." And she would cast a look of contempt at these luxuries.

Finally he was home for good. A month passed, and then another.
But his activities seemed inconsistent with her expectations. He was
no different from those who hadn't studied. Well, actually there *was*
a difference: Others made money; her husband, though, spent money,
his family's money. It seemed like he was always gadding about somewhere. And when he did stay at home, he was usually lost in a book
or else he was up half the night writing something.

That must be how you make the magic club—this was how she
interpreted it.

A couple of more months passed. Her husband's work seemed un-
changed. The only obvious difference from before was that he now
and then heaved a great sigh. And his face was all tensed up, as if
something was troubling him. His body seemed to droop more with
each passing day.

What's bothering him? his wife wondered. And she too grew troubled. She made various attempts to restore what was wasting away.
She tried as best she could to add tasty dishes to his meals, and she
made things such as oxtail soup. But it was all in vain. Her husband
took little food, saying he had no appetite.

Several more months passed. Now he was always at home. And he
was so irritable. He kept saying he was aggravated.

Once, as dawn was approaching, she half awoke and groped for
him. But all she clutched was the flap of his quilt. Sleepy though she
was, she felt a pang of disappointment. She opened her drowsy eyes,
as if looking for something she had lost. There sat her husband, head
down on his desk and clasped between his hands. As the haze lifted
from her mind, she realized his shoulders were heaving. He was sob-
bing. The sound echoed in her ears. Instantly her mind cleared and
she sat up. She went to his side and gently patted him on the back.

"What's the matter, dear?" she asked in a pinched tone.

But he said not a word.

She reached for his face and felt warm tears.

Another month or two passed. Her husband frequently went out
again, as he had upon returning from Tokyo. When he finally came

home late at night, his breath stank of liquor. This was a recent development.

And on this particular night, he still hadn't returned. From early in the evening she had entertained all sorts of wild thoughts as she awaited him impatiently. To speed up the tedious passage of time, she had resumed her sewing. But even this work hadn't gone as she had wanted. Now and then her needle had gone astray, and finally she had pricked her thumb.

"Where could he be all this time!"

In her annoyance, she forgot the stinging sensation in her thumb. For an instant, the images and fantasies she had been entertaining once again surfaced in her mind. Dishes of tasty food on a white table-cloth embroidered with rare and wonderful flowers flashed before her eyes. And then a scene in which several of his friends offered each other drinks and gulped them down. The disgusting spectacle of some *kisaeng* bitch enticing her husband with a flirtatious smile. Her husband chuckling like a moron. And then, all of it disappearing, as if behind a black curtain, and in their place a meal table in disarray; bright light glancing off liquor bottles; that *kisaeng* girl, one arm propping herself up on the floor, doubled up and almost choking on her laughter. And finally there appeared her husband sprawled in the street, weeping.

Suddenly the gate rattled and a thick voice cried out: "Open up!"

"I'm coming!" she blurted, and out she went to the veranda. Her slippers, put on too hastily, scuffed along as she rushed across the courtyard. The inner gate wasn't yet bolted for the night, and the servants in their quarters beside it were always fast asleep by then, so she hurried to the outer gate herself. Her slender hand, white in the darkness, took the bolt and worked at it. The gate opened.

The chill of the nighttime breeze settled against her face. No one was there! Not a single human shadow to be seen. Only the deep blue night shrouding the faint white of the alleyway.

She lingered, a look of astonishment on her face. And then she hurriedly shut the gate, as if to prevent a devil from entering.

So it was the wind, she told herself as she caressed her cool cheeks. With a sheepish grin she retraced her steps.

But I'm sure I heard him. . . . Maybe I just didn't see him. . . . I wonder if he was lying on the ground where I couldn't see him. . . .

These thoughts brought her to a stop at the inner gate.

Maybe I'll take another look. . . . No, no, no, it was all in my head. . . . But what if? . . . No, no, no, it was all in my head.

Vacillating like this, she reached the veranda, like someone sleep-walking. And then the queerest thought flashed through her mind like lightning: do you suppose he came in without my noticing him?

Sure enough, she thought she heard sounds coming from their room. Surely someone was moving about in there. Like a child about to catch a scolding from a grownup, she tiptoed to the door. Reaching toward the threshold, she smiled in spite of herself; it was the smile of a child asking forgiveness for a mistake. Ever so carefully she opened the door. The quilt seemed to be moving.

Look at him, all wrapped up, trying to fool me, she told herself. She sat down and kept still, as if sensing something awful might happen if she touched the quilt. But finally she lifted it. The white sleeping mat was all she saw.

"What! He's not back?" she cried out tearfully. She seemed finally to have accepted the fact.

It was well past two in the morning when he returned. There was a thud, followed immediately by someone calling "Missus! Oh Missus!" She awakened thinking she was still sitting up, but found herself sprawled on the quilt. So sound asleep had she been that the elderly maid, herself a heavy sleeper, had had to open the outer gate. Then and there the wife's dreamy wanderings came to an end and she gathered her wits. She rubbed her face once or twice and was out the door.

Her husband lay on his side on the veranda, a leg hanging over the edge, head nestled in the crook of his arm. His breathing was raspy.

The old maid yanked his shoes off, then stood up, a scowl furrowing her swarthy face.

"Come, sir, get up and go inside, please."

Barely able to move his tongue, he mouthed an answer: "All right." But he didn't budge. The lids of his vacant, sleepy eyes gently drooped.

His wife rubbed her eyes.

"Come, sir, get up," said the maid. "Go on inside now, please."

This time there wasn't an answer. Instead he reached out a hand. "Water, water—cold water," he mumbled.

The maid quickly poured water in a bowl and thrust it beneath the nose of the hopelessly drunken man. But he made no effort to drink it. It was as if he had forgotten his own request.

"Won't you drink, sir?" the maid reminded him.

"Mmm, all right," he said. Finally he propped himself up on one arm and lifted his head. The bowl was emptied in a gulp. Again he slumped down.

"Oh, bother! There he goes again."

The maid reached out as if to rescue a child about to fall into a well.

"That's enough—you can go back to bed," said the husband in a vexed tone.

The wife too, standing uncertainly, wished the maid would leave. She was eager to take hold of her husband and help him up, but felt incapable of doing any such thing with the old woman watching. Although they'd been married seven or eight years now, in terms of the time they'd been together she was still a newlywed.

"Go back to bed"—these words, intended for the maid, died on her lips. If only the old woman would go inside.

But the maid had different ideas. "Let me help you up." Forcing a smile, she stubbornly stepped up onto the veranda. She seemed to take it as her proper duty that she must carry the master to his room when he had had too much to drink.

"Come now, come on," she said, giggling and looking up at the mistress. She placed a hand against the small of his back.

"All right, all right, I'll get up."

He stirred, and sure enough he slowly rose. He clomped unsteadily across the veranda toward the room, threatening to topple over at any second. He slid the door open with a bang, then went inside. His wife followed. The maid, after tsk-tsking at the threshold of the inner gate, disappeared whence she had come.

The husband stood crookedly, like someone leaning against a wall. His head drooped, as if he were pondering something.

Anxiously observing the throbbing veins of his bony temples, his wife approached. She took his suit jacket collar with one hand and his sleeve with the other.

"All right, let's take your jacket off," she said in a gentle voice.

Suddenly he slid down the wall to the floor, almost knocking her over in the process. There he sat, outstretched legs pushing away the edge of the quilt.

"Why are you acting like this? I ask you to take off your jacket and you won't do it," she cried out plaintively. Sitting down herself, she again took hold of his jacket. "It's getting wrinkled—will you please take it off?" But with the drunken man glued to the wall like a dead weight, it proved impossible. After a prolonged effort she let go and sank back.

"Good lord," she said in vexation. "Who in the world is making you drink like this?"

"Is someone *making* me? Hah!" Apparently the question was not to his liking. Even so, he repeated it: "Was someone *making* me?" Then he said, "Would you kindly find out who it was that made me drink?" He guffawed. But it was a hollow, despairing laugh.

His wife laughed with him, then took hold of his jacket again.

"Come on now, off with your clothes. We can save the talk for later. Get a good night's sleep, and tomorrow morning I'll talk with you."

"What do you mean? Why put off today's business till tomorrow? If there's something to say, then let's come out with it!"

"*Yakchu*'s made you drunk now, but tomorrow you'll be clear-headed."

"What? *Yakchu*'s made me drunk?" He wagged his head back and forth. "No. No one's drunk. I'm just acting up. I feel bright and sober now. Just the frame of mind for talking . . . any kind of talk . . . so out with it."

"Well, all right. Why is it you drink *yakchu*, when it doesn't agree with you? Look at what it does to you," she said, mopping the cold sweat from his forehead.

The drunken man shook his head.

"Uh-uh, no, that's not what I expected to hear." He fell silent, then seemed to recall what had been said a short time earlier. "That's right—you were asking if someone was making me drink? Or if I drank because I wanted to?"

"No, you don't drink because you want to. Shall I tell who or what I think is driving you to drink? Well . . . first of all I thought it was anger that drove you to drink, and second, maybe the fashionable people drove you to drink." She produced a gentle smile. Looks like I hit the mark, she seemed to be saying.

Her husband smiled bitterly.

"Afraid not. You thought wrong. Anger didn't drive me to drink, and it wasn't the dandies either. It was something else. You worry that I'm obsessed with the dandies, that they're always driving me to drink. Well, it's a needless worry. I don't have any use for the dandies. The only thing that's useful to me is booze. Booze swirls around in my guts and makes me forget—that's the only thing I get out of it." Suddenly his tone changed, and he said with deep emotion, "What is it that makes a man paralyze a capable and promising mind with alcohol?"

He heaved a great sigh, sending a sour liquor smell throughout the room.

These words were difficult for his wife to understand. She remained silent, mouth clamped shut. She felt as if an invisible wall separated them. This was the bitter experience she had whenever she and her husband engaged in a drawn-out discussion; it had happened quite a few times.

Her husband smiled helplessly.

"Here we go again," he snorted. "You don't understand, do you? I shouldn't have asked you in the first place. Of course you don't understand. I'll try to explain. Now listen carefully. What's driving me to drink isn't anger and it isn't the dandies. It's this society—our Korean society—that drives me to drink. It's my good fate to have been born in Korea—if I'd been born in another country, would I be able to get booze? . . ."

What did he mean by *society?* His wife still didn't understand. At any rate, it must be some drinking establishment or something uniquely Korean that you wouldn't find in any other country.

"You don't have to visit that 'society' place every day, even though it's in Korea."

Her husband produced another grim smile. And then he said in a tone so clear he truly seemed unaffected by alcohol:

"It's so damned frustrating. When you're a member of that society it doesn't matter if you visit it or not. You think I'm driven to drink only when I go out, but I won't be driven to drink if I'm home? No, it's not like that. And it's not as if someone from our society is out there waiting for me to come out, so he can latch onto me and pour drinks down me. . . . How can I put it? . . . This society that we Koreans have established can't help but drive me to drink. . . . How so? I'll tell you. Let's suppose we organize a club. Now the fellows that get together in this club—to hear them talk, it's the people, the society, that comes first. There isn't one of them who wouldn't give his life for that cause. And yet in just two days—you know what happens in just two days?"

He raised his voice a notch and counted off one and then two on his fingers.

"They argue over who gets credit, they fight over who gets what position—'I'm right, you're wrong; I've got more power than you do' —and night and day they tear into each other, they try and destroy each other. What comes of all this? What's accomplished? And it's not just clubs that are like this—it's companies, it's associations, everything. . . . All the groups we lowly Koreans have organized are fragments of this society and they are all alike. What's there to do in a society like that? The fellow who tries to do something is a fool. The fellow who has his wits about him throws up blood and dies— nothing he can do about it. And if he doesn't die, then he's left with absolutely nothing but booze. There was a time when I decided to do something, and I gave it a try. It all went up in smoke. I was a fool. . . . I don't drink because I want to. These days I'm used to booze, but when I was first drinking, I practically killed myself— remember? A person who hasn't gone through the suffering of being drunk can't possibly understand. The splitting headache, the stuff you drank coming back up. . . . Even so, it's better than not drinking, because you're not suffering mentally even though you're hurting physically. The only thing you can do in this society is be a lush. . . ."

"Please don't talk like that. Surely you can be something better than a lush!"

She blurted this out in agitation, gazing at her husband with feverish eyes. In those eyes, her husband was the most divine man in the world. Accordingly she had believed he would turn out better than anyone else. She knew, though only dimly, that his goals were farsighted and high-minded. He had been a gentle man, and she realized vaguely that turning to drink was not something he had wanted but rather a means of venting his anger. He couldn't keep drinking forever, though. Else he would end up ruining both himself and his family. And so she couldn't help wishing she could dissipate his anger as quickly as possible, so that he'd return to his old gentle self. And she was sure this would happen someday. Starting today, starting tomorrow. . . . But the previous day he had gotten drunk. And he was in the same condition today. Each passing day proved her expectations more mistaken, and weakened her confidence in those expectations. Plaintive longings sometimes oppressed her, and when she saw her husband's face growing haggard, she couldn't keep such sentiments in check. And so it was hardly surprising that she'd become agitated just now.

"You just don't understand. God, what's a man to do! What I'm trying to say is, you can't stay sane and live even a day in this society. You'll throw up blood and die, or you'll throw yourself into the river and drown. You feel choked, you feel suffocated, dammit!"

Scowling in an agony of impatience, he clutched at his chest like a madman.

Ignoring him, she shouted back, her face redder, "So you drink, and you don't feel suffocated?"

Her husband looked dumbstruck at her, stunned by her words. The next instant a shadow of unspeakable distress fell over his eyes.

"I was wrong, wrong, wrong. Wrong to confide in a simpleton like you. I just wanted a bit of sympathy from you—but I was wrong," he lamented. "I'm so damn frustrated!"

Saying no more, he bolted to his feet and opened the door.

Instantly she regretted her mistake. "Why are you going out?" she said anxiously, grabbing the back of his jacket. "Where are you going at this time of night? I made a mistake. I won't talk like that again. We can talk tomorrow morning."

"I've heard enough. Let go of me. Let go!"

Pushing her away, he tottered to the edge of the veranda, slumped down, and began putting on his shoes.

She followed and took him by the arm.

"For goodness' sake, why are you doing this? I said I wouldn't talk like that again."

But he brushed her hand aside. His own hands were trembling and he seemed ready to burst into tears. "What's the matter with you? Go away!" he snapped, breaking free. He clumped to the inner gate and was gone. The bolt on the outer gate clanged.

Left at the edge of the veranda, she called out several times for the maid, but in vain. Her husband's footsteps grew distant in the still of the darkness and finally were gone beyond the alleyway. The night wore on in desolate silence.

"He's gone . . . gone!" she cried while she strained to listen, as if determined never to lose the sound of his footsteps. But her voice was that of someone who had lost everything: not only the sound of his footsteps but her mind, her spirit, as well. She felt empty, body and soul. Her eyes stared blankly into the murky haze of the night, seeking the poisonous shape of that "society" her husband had spoken of.

The chill, dreary breeze of the early-morning hour raked her chest. The raw sensation brought her sleepless, tired body to the breaking point. Her face, pallid as that of a corpse, quivered and twitched.

"Why does this wicked 'society' drive him to drink?" she whispered in despair.

The Lady Barber

NA TO-HYANG

Na To-hyang (pen name of Na Kyŏng-sŏn; he is sometimes referred to as well by another pen name—Na Pin) was born in 1902 in Seoul. After an abortive attempt at studying literature in Japan, he returned to Korea, where he made his literary debut in 1921 with the story "Ch'uŏk" (Remembrances). The following year he allied himself with the literary journal *Paekcho*, which published his story "Chŏlmŭni ŭi shijŏl" (A young man's life). Thus began a productive but short-lived life of letters. By 1926 heavy drinking and a peripatetic lifestyle had begun to take its toll on Na's lungs, and he died the following year.

Na's works reflect a youthful romanticism, evident in "The Lady Barber," but at the same time a keen eye for the social realities of his time, as in "Mullebanga" (The watermill, 1925). Among his other well-known stories are "Chagi rŭl ch'atki chŏn" (Before she found herself, 1924), "Pŏngŏri Samyongi" (Samyong the mute, 1925), and "Ppong" (Mulberries, 1925). "The Lady Barber" (Yŏibalsa) was first published in 1923 in the literary journal *Kaebyŏk*.

He took his cotton pajamas to the pawnshop and came away with a single fifty-sen silver piece. Recently minted, it had a hefty feel. As he clutched the serrated coin, he felt as if he were suddenly rid of the bothersome melancholy that had clung to his face like a tangled cobweb.

He crossed Ochanomizu Bridge and passed the girls' high school nearby, then turned down a side street bordering Juntendo Hospital and headed for Hongo. He looked into every single window he passed along the way, and there beneath the straw hat that had yellowed in the sun was the reflection of his shaggy hair. It lay in snarls like a bramble thicket, reminding him of John the Baptist; soaked with sweat, it resembled a frog hopping about in the monsoon rains.

"Time for a haircut—no way around it," he muttered. Again he removed his hat and patted down the hair that crept every which way beneath his ears, then returned the sweaty-smelling thing to his head.

He stopped at a building with a sign reading "Certified First-Class Barbershop." But, determined as he was to have his hair cut, he couldn't muster the courage to enter such a place.

To have his hair cut there would have cost him all his money. But after moping about for several hours before going to the pawnshop and managing to obtain the modest sum of fifty sen, he didn't relish the idea of spending the entire amount within the hour. If he could keep just ten sen, perhaps the sound of it jingling in the corner of his pocket would help fill the emptiness in his mind.

He left the classy barbershop with its electric fan whirring so proudly and impressively, its scintillating sterilizers framed in stainless steel, and walked on. The breeze from Tokyo Bay bathed his forehead with warmth, but the intense heat radiating from the ground made him feel like an animal in a boiling cauldron. A sprinkling cart passed by, but before the drops of water could run off they were absorbed into clumps of earth that resembled earthworm leavings.

He wandered along, wondering if there weren't a third-class barbershop in the area. At these *tokoya*, as the Japanese called them, you could have your hair cut for twenty sen—and a haircut that cheap would be good enough for a struggling student like himself. He would then have thirty sen left over.

Thirty sen—more than what he would pay for the haircut. That thought was somewhat reassuring. And the idea of having thirty sen in his pocket reminded him of the business at hand.

Coming upon a *tokoya* with two lone chairs and a zinc washstand, he looked inside.

The proprietor sat half asleep, nodding off in fits and starts, his head lurching like a watermill pestle in a drought. One hand held a newspaper, the other a fan with which he swatted flies.

He took heart at this scene and swaggered inside.

"Hello!"

His greeting brought the barber to life. Apparently embarrassed at having been caught napping, the man sprang to his feet and, bowing repeatedly, offered his customer straw sandals to wear inside.

"Right this way, please!"

The barber stood like a lamppost behind the other chair.

He hung his hat, then removed his suit jacket. As he sat down he glanced at the prices listed on the wall. Just as he had thought, a haircut was twenty sen. He could rest easier. It's always best to be sure, if you're short on money. Just as he would make sure to have his ticket in hand before boarding the streetcar, he now checked his pocket for the money he had received with the pawnshop ticket. Inadvertently producing the pawn ticket would have been embarrassing, and so he wedged the coin into a separate corner of his pocket before leaning back in the barber chair.

Various thoughts passed through his mind as the clippers crisscrossed his scalp. Needless to say, he could use his thirty sen in any number of ways. But this small sum had to be put to the most effective use possible. He'd been urged to pay his food bill at the boarding house, now three months overdue, or risk being turned out any day. But his family in Korea had no money to send. He'd probably have to approach someone with a story to come up with ten yen at least. The image of his best friend, who lived in Shibuya, came to mind as the clippers chattered. The first thing he'd have to do was go see this guy and grub dinner and twenty or thirty yen. That's right, he thought —his grandfather always wires him money on the last of the month, so he must have received it today! I'll have to feed him a line—say I'm expecting money from my mother's family in a few days, and I need to borrow from him in the meantime. Yeah! But it's too far to walk to his place; I'll need ten sen to get there and back on the streetcar. And the remaining twenty sen? Well, since it's so hot, I'll buy myself a shaved ice—that'll be ten sen. And tomorrow morning—or maybe tonight—I'll use the other ten for a bath.

But as he thought about the copper coins left over after the haircut, the clippers suddenly yanked at his hair. He'd been enjoying this game of budgeting, and now, rudely roused, he found himself back in the barber chair, his reverie gone.

He was riled, and it was all he could do to contain his urge for revenge. But then he realized he couldn't very well get up and slap the fellow, nor could he openly reprimand him.

Instead he shouted, "Ouch! That hurts!" and scowled.

"Oh my," the barber said with a bow. "I'm so sorry." He did look somewhat apologetic.

But that was all. When he looked carefully into the mirror, he saw on the barber's face what might be called a look that said "sorry" and a bow. This was an apology, perfunctory though it might be, but he wanted to see an expression of genuine regret in the man's eyes. Somehow, the fellow's bow had left him completely dissatisfied. He wanted to retaliate then and there for having his hair ripped out. He couldn't wait.

Then an opportunity presented itself. With a slight prompt of the hands, the barber tried to turn his customer's head to the side.

Now's my chance, he thought. He turned in the opposite direction. And when the barber wanted him to lift his head, he lowered it, and vice versa. In this way he made a point of giving the barber a hard time. He looked in the mirror, and there was the fellow scowling, evidently trying to suppress his anger.

The barber set down his clippers, dusted himself off, and heaved a sigh of relief. Then, as he brushed the young man's hair, he took a look at his face, as if to see just what sort of fellow he was dealing with.

Just then came the melodious voice of a woman from the living quarters to the rear of the shop: "Please come and eat."

The voice alone suggested its owner was beautiful. In this dismal, chaotic existence of his, it was a siren's song. His blood tingled, his heart jumped; he was floating on air.

"Eat?" the fellow answered as he dusted off his clippers. His arrogant tone revealed the way he acted toward his wife.

"Give this gentleman a shave."

This was said indistinctly, and it took him a few moments to understand. Why would the barber ask his wife to give a customer a shave? Well, maybe it's possible, he thought. He had heard, after all, that quite a few Tokyo barbershops employed women to cut hair, but he had never dared hope to have the good fortune to be served by one.

The fellow disappeared, and out came the little woman. Let's check her out in the mirror! Expectation and anxiety coiled and uncoiled in his mind. Was she comely? Pockmarked? What if she turned out homely? How wonderful if she were attractive. But it was useless to speculate about another man's wife.

Her face came into view in the mirror. Wow! She couldn't have been more than twenty-three or twenty-four, and those eyes. . . . Her mouth, nose, and cheeks were almost as fine. Her hair wasn't unsightly, nor was it attractive, but no matter. She had a slender waistline with a slight curve, and a generally svelte figure. She was too lovely for her husband, and if he were asked if he'd want to live with her, well, he'd have to think twice before saying no.

She picked up the straight razor. Absorbed with her features, he

now realized her hands were pretty as well. How dangerous yet marvelous that hand looked. It was as if a freshly caught whitefish had
taken a razor in its mouth and begun flopping about. As the hand
came closer, he closed his eyes. Rather than watch that pretty hand
with the razor approach his cheek, what a wonderful sensation to
feel the sudden touch with his eyes firmly closed. In contrast, the
lathering of his face had been somehow unpleasant. He smelled her
woman's odor, so like mother's milk, and felt her body heat on his
back. Her hand touched his face where he thought it would, and her
warm, warm fingers applied a gentle, steady pressure. He could almost
see through his closed eyes her face moving back and forth above his.
She stroked his cheeks, feeling for the stubble, then rubbed them till
they were putty in her silky hands, her fingers dancing all over his
face like the still-living severed tail of a lizard. Her breath tickled his
nose like burning incense, her fleshy thighs brushed his, and she came
so close to him when she pinched his eyebrows, he thought she
would sit right down in his lap. He wanted so badly to open his eyes,
he couldn't stand it. Her eyes examining his pores and the openings
of his ears with such care—how they sparkled, bathing his spirit with
clear springwater. And her scarlet lips, just inches from his—how
they invigorated and inflamed his tired blood. Still he kept his eyes
closed. It was the first time he'd felt rapture at the sight of a woman
wielding a razor. As the woman neared the end of her task, he couldn't
have described how much he wanted her to continue. He didn't like
the idea of that fellow finishing his meal and showing up again, but
what could he do about it?

She finished shaving him, then washed his face and applied powder.
She smiled sweetly, perhaps at the sight of the white powder on his
swarthy skin.

The sight of her biting her lip to stifle the smile nipped at his heart,
and he ached with bashfulness. But he didn't mind. Instead, he
responded with a big grin.

The woman burst into laughter. "Why are you smiling?" she asked
as she removed the towel from his shoulders. He detected a touch of
derision in the politeness of her speech.

"All finished?" he asked as he stood up. As he turned to her, she
laughed again.

"Why are you laughing?" He tried to sound casual, but deep
inside he was all in a tizzy. She didn't respond, merely kept on smiling. Crazy girl, he thought. It was time to pay her. But to leave then
and there would have been a letdown.

He couldn't understand that smile. She intrigued him. And so he tried to prolong the moment. He would have liked some booze, but instead he asked for a bowl of water. She went out back and brought it to him.

"What's so funny, anyway?" he asked between sips. He smiled back as if to tease her.

"Nothing. Nothing at all."

Playing the innocent, she managed to wipe away her smile, but her eyes betrayed a hint of laughter barely suppressed. He was overcome with an urge to seize her hand and say how pretty it was—or something equally brazen—but decided he'd do so instead at the next convenient opportunity.

"How much do I owe you?" he asked, knowing full well the answer.

"Twenty sen," she said with a bow.

He handed her the silver coin, and as soon as it dropped into her lovely palm, he donned his hat and prepared to leave.

"See you next time."

"What about your change?"

How could he accept it? The visit to his friend in Shibuya, the shaved ice, the bath, relief from his landlady's badgering—none of this mattered now.

"Keep it!" he said with an air of bravura. He turned for one last look at the woman, and there she was, giving him another smile. It just about took his breath away. And off he swaggered. He had established a special relationship with this woman, and there was no turning back; it was as if they had both been branded. Filled with an inexpressible sense of satisfaction, he strutted along, swinging his shoulders. Wait till he told his friend Kim at the boarding house! Briskly he strode off, wanting to be there as soon as possible.

The heat prompted him to remove his hat, and he passed his hand over his hair a couple of times.

"What the hell?"

He came to a stop, feeling as if he'd sunk his teeth into something bitter.

"Dammit all!"

He clenched his fists, then flung his hat into the distance.

"Thirty sen down the drain!"

With the tip of his index finger, he rubbed that spot on his head once more, that spot left bare by the home cure for his childhood epilepsy.

A Tale of Rats

Yi Ki-yŏng

Yi Ki-yŏng was born in the village of Hoeryong in South Ch'ungchŏng Province in 1896 and was educated in the city of Ch'ŏnan and in Tokyo. His first published work was "Oppa ŭi pimil p'yŏnji" (Big Brother's secret letter), appearing in *Kaebyŏk* in 1924. The following year he helped organize the Korean Artist Proletariat Federation (KAPF). In 1931 and 1934 he was arrested with other KAPF members. In the first instance he was released on probation; the second time, he was jailed for two years. In 1945 he participated in the founding of the Chosŏn Proletariat Writers Alliance. Shortly after Liberation he migrated to North Korea. Little is known of his activities since, apart from a novel, *Tumangang* (The Tuman River), published in Seoul in 1989.

Yi was a voluminous writer of fiction and criticism. The importance of his work is suggested by the fact that he probably received more critical attention during his lifetime than any of his contemporaries except Yi Kwang-su and Yŏm Sang-sŏp. In agrarian works such as the novella *Sŏhwa* (Rat fire, 1933), Yi portrayed the straitened circumstances of Korean tenant farmers. No less than Im Hwa, one of the most radical Korean socialist writers, praised the work as representing a new stage in the development of Korean literature. But it is another work with an agrarian background, *Kohyang* (The ancestral home), serialized in the *Chosŏn ilbo* in 1933–1934, that is still regarded as one of the finest Korean novels of the prewar era. *Ingan suŏp* (Lessons in humanity, 1936) is a satirical novel about the aspirations of intellectuals in a colonized land.

"A Tale of Rats" (Chwi iyagi), first published in *Munye undong* in 1926, has a familiar socialist line but the charm of a fable.

1

It's along about midnight of a nippy early-winter evening. All is dead quiet; surely the humans are wandering in dreamland. Yes, indeed, this is the time when rats everywhere are masters of the world.

In Yangji Village too the rats are stirring above the ceiling of Rich Man Kim's house.

Papa Rat calls his family to attention. "Want to run around a bit? Or maybe we ought to find some food—my stomach's growling."

"Food! Let's find some food!" say Mama Rat and the children.

And off they go toward the kitchen.

This family of rats lived for a time in Su-dol's house in the neighboring village before moving recently to Rich Man Kim's. Everyone called Papa Rat the Thunder Giant, for he was as fearsome as that terrible being. It wasn't just his glaring, protruding eyes or the long, thick whiskers extending far to the sides. It was also his strength: he was large as a puppy, could bound across your average ditch, and not even cast iron could stand up to his firmly rooted, closely set row of inward-arching teeth. Once he had alarmed his comrades by snatching at the whiskers of a cat dozing in the sun. But it was the time before that when in broad daylight he pissed on the face of Rich Man Kim during his nap that he had become the stuff of legend. And so his comrades grew even more fearful of him, and the Thunder Giant's wife bragged about how well she had done in finding a husband.

The Thunder Giant had four mouths to feed—apart from himself there was his aging wife and a son and daughter. His married daughters lived with the in-laws, and many other sons lived apart with their own families. Still other children had been killed by the cat, and many had lost their lives in rattraps.

As soon as they moved to Rich Man Kim's they tunneled straight into his shed, and from there they dug branch tunnels to his storeroom and cowshed. And so they could snitch as much rice and other grain as they could eat. But every so often when they hankered for something really tasty they raided the kitchen, as they were doing tonight. On one of those raids they had been spotted by Hook Nose, Rich Man Kim's eldest daughter-in-law, and had barely escaped her fire poker.

Speaking of narrow escapes, the Thunder Giant had ventured out to the main veranda the previous day and been spotted by Rich Man Kim. He scurried out to the courtyard, and when he realized he was about to be caught by the tail, he produced a loud squeak and sunk his teeth into the back of the rich man's hand. Fortunately the man let go and the Thunder Giant escaped with his life. Listening in wide-eyed surprise to this account, the Thunder Giant's wife grew deeply worried. What if he had been caught? Shouldn't they instead make late-night raids or else simply get along on the grain they already had?

"Hmph!" snorted the Thunder Giant. "There's no problem. You just try and live till the day I get caught," he boasted.

In truth the Thunder Giant was as robust as his word, though his wife was a feeble old thing. And so his children praised his daring even more. With a wide grin his daughter nestled into his lap.

"Father, when I have a daughter I'm going to find her a husband just like you!"

Mama Rat was lost to the world as she gnawed away at some grains of rice, but when she heard this she tittered.

2

When the Thunder Giant had proposed moving to Rich Man Kim's house the rest of the family were all opposed. More than anyone else, his wife harped on the dangers involved. It was a long way to Yangji Village; the trip wouldn't be safe for the little ones. More important, a rich man's house would probably have a cat and some rattraps. Did the Thunder Giant want to die before his time?

But the Thunder Giant would have none of it.

"Listen to you—you sound as if you're afraid of your own shadow. Who's to say a fire won't break out right here, this very night? The main thing is, we're going hungry because here, the humans themselves don't have enough to eat, and nobody's going to give us food. Besides, the people in this house are poor, and it wouldn't be right to consume what's theirs. So instead of wasting our time arguing about it like this, we're going to a rich man's house where there's mountains of grain. We don't have to feel guilty about taking food there. Why, they could feed us and still have something left over. Woman who doesn't have any sense—stop your fussing, and let's be off!"

In the end, these words of the family head convinced the others.

It was like the Thunder Giant had said. Now that they had moved, they could fill their stomachs. That was the best thing. True, there was the daughter-in-law with her poker, and the Thunder Giant's hair-raising experience with Rich Man Kim. But here they could find tasty food and scraps of meat. Even so, the Thunder Giant's wife found one thing unpleasant: Rich Man Kim's house was crawling with other rats, and every once in a while the Thunder Giant was unfaithful and returned home late. But she realized she was getting on in years, so what was the use of being jealous? And so she turned a blind eye to it all. As you might expect, she soon stopped burdening herself with various thoughts, and instead enjoyed a filling meal and a warm bed while looking forward to her children growing up healthy and free.

3

"Let's have some meat!" the children said one day, and off went the Thunder Giant for the inner kitchen. Rich Man Kim's house was thronged with people that day, and there was a general commotion. Some tasty food would be in the offing, guessed the Thunder Giant. And sure enough, when he arrived at the kitchen he was greeted with the aroma of meat. But it looked like all the meat had been stuffed into a cast-iron kettle, and that heavy lid wouldn't be easy to open. Yes, today's trip had been a wild goose chase, thought the Thunder Giant in utter exasperation.

There was nothing to do but return. But then it occurred to him to take a look into one of the rooms. Beneath the shelves he found the hole that led to the side room, and he ventured through it. The sliding door between the side room and the family room was open a crack, and there in the bright light of the room was Rich Man Kim, absorbed in counting his money.

The rich man was by himself. Had his good-for-nothing wife gone out again for a tryst? From the room across the veranda came the tattoo of fulling sticks on cloth together with the chirping laughter of girls who had probably stuffed their stomachs at supper and now were chattering away. Rich Man Kim, wearing his headgear with the ox-horn ornaments, was seated on the floor in front of a stack of bank notes and piles of silver and copper coins. He must have earned it all from selling rice amid the general commotion of that day.

Suddenly Rich Man Kim was seized by a coughing fit. It happened that the room lacked a chamber pot, so he slid open the far door and went out to the veranda, still coughing. As he stood at the edge of the veranda, clearing his throat and spitting, the Thunder Giant stole into the room, sank his teeth into the huge wad of bank notes, and scurried away.

His family had been patiently awaiting a windfall of pilfered meat, but when they saw what the Thunder Giant had brought them, their eyes opened wide in disappointment.

The Thunder Giant's daughter stepped forward.

"Father, what's this! What happened to our meat?"

"This is what they call money," said the Thunder Giant.

"What's it for? All I see is scraps of paper."

"Well, people who have 'em can get meat, rice, whatever they want to eat."

"You mean these scraps of paper have some way of making those things appear?"

"Yes, it's marvelous. It's just like the magic hat in the old fairy tale."

"And so you get food and stuff without giving up anything?"

"Sure! All you do is give this paper, and you get rice, meat, fabric —anything."

The daughter sat wide-eyed for a time, unable to swallow what she had just heard, then said, "Well, those scraps of paper can't turn into rice or meat, so how do you get those things by giving them paper? Are there really people that foolish, who would give you things in return for scrap paper?" She looked up at the Thunder Giant.

"Yes, there are. But there are also dullards like Su-dol who don't know that this money is like a magic hat, that it's created by clever fellows to take advantage of nitwits. And there those no-goods sit with their money, doing their stealing plain as day, and they call *us* thieving good-for-nothings. Those humans see a thief, and they have the gall to call him a 'thieving rat.' "

Until then the Thunder Giant's wife had been silently gnawing on rice. But now her head jerked up toward her husband.

"How come Su-dol's family are so poor, anyway? They do their farming every year."

The Thunder Giant stroked his whiskers in a dignified manner.

"It's because people with this thing called money have taken everything away from them and forced them to accept money in return."

"If that's the case, then it looks like we're not the only thieves around," said the Thunder Giant's son as he jumped up and down in delight.

"Son, we tend to be honest as far as thieves are concerned. In a rich man's house like this one here, it's no crime to take what they don't use. After all, we were born and given life, just like they were." The Thunder Giant turned to his wife: "Woman, why do you always say we're snitching food? I know it sounds terrible, but we're not snitching—we're taking! Since they won't give it to us, then what else are we supposed—"

"So from now on we'll be snitch—I mean, taking—food."

"That's right! But just this morning I saw that idiot Su-dol here. He was kowtowing to the old fart: 'Sir!' he begs him, 'we're starving. Can't you lend us five bushels of rice? We'll pay you back for sure, at high interest too.' Well, it'll never work! You know, this Kim is a stingy fellow, and you think he'll lend to someone like Su-dol? Not on your life! What I'd like to know is why Su-dol didn't just snatch the rice. Is he afraid of getting caught? Because that would be even better—in prison you get food and clothes free!"

The Thunder Giant spoke heatedly, even though this matter did not directly concern him.

"Giving in to someone who does wrong just makes it all the more likely that the wrong will be repeated. Hoping for generosity from someone like that is like wishing a crow would turn into a white crane. If it came to that, I'd rather kill myself! A lousy existence is hardly worth—"

"But here's what I heard Su-dol say once: 'There's no limit to what you'll think of doing if you go hungry for three days. But I don't think I'd ever turn to stealing'—them's his words."

"He's right! Yes, he is! You've got to give a person credit if he can starve to death without stealing. But we're not talking about stealing here. When you have nothing to eat it's not stealing to take from a family that's well off. Why, it's your rightful share for the work you've done. Why go to a thief and ask for something? Begging for food that's already been stolen—that's even worse than stealing!"

"I almost forgot," said the Thunder Giant's wife. "Su-dol's wife was in the kitchen a little while ago begging for rice. 'Young miss,' she says, 'we been without food for three days now. The little ones are starving. Won't you lend us just three little measures of rice? You can think of it as a good deed. Well, two measures. All right, just one measure. . . .' She begs in every possible way, but that Hook Nose has a sharp tongue: 'We don't have rice to give away. Now get out of here! No one asked you to go hungry. The two of you come around here so uppity—husband in the morning, wife in the evening. Get out!' And she drives her away. Su-dol's wife goes off with an empty basket, crying her eyes out. It's cold these days, but she's still wearing her summer bloomers, and they look like shredded rags. . . ."

"How could she!" said the Thunder Giant, his temper flaring. "That Hook Nose—ain't she some bitch! One of these days we're going to have to piss on her face. Woman, you piss on her face, too.

But Su-dol and his family aren't blameless, either. They won't snitch
—I mean, take—food and whatnot, like we do. Why do they have to
be so cowardly! Oh, those humans are so worthless and ignorant!
We rats are born handicapped, so there's a limit to what we can do.
But poor folks like Su-dol—they're people too, so why should they
have to put up with it? Rich Man Kim, that worthless creature, he
ought to be torn in half. If that kind of thing happened now and then,
those rich dogs would fling open their granaries without so much as
a peep. . . . But because everyone comes and grovels in front of those
no-goods, the sons of bitches get more and more arrogant. . . ."

"Poor Su-dol and his family! Even though we're animals, we've
never once gone hungry. And to think humans could go three or four
days without eating. . . . Gee, how are they supposed to survive?"

"Yeah, but the two of 'em seem to be doing a lot of sleeping together, if you look at how many children they've produced. I
hear Su-dol's wife got knocked up again and her stomach's big as a
mountain. In her situation she's going to have another kid? Those
morons—"

"But maybe that's the only joy they get out of life."

"Joy? Yeah, just like some of us rats have fun eating crab apples."

"Among the humans, are there families worse off than Su-dol's?"

"You can bet on it—here in Chosŏn alone there must be millions
of people, easy, who are like that."

"But them humans, do they still think they're supposed to be supe-
rior?" the Thunder Giant's daughter broke in, jumping up and down.

"Sure, they claim humans are the noblest creatures in the
universe."

"What's that supposed to mean?"

"It means people are the most noble of anything between heaven
and earth."

"Did you ever hear of anything so ridiculous? This human hell,
full of starving ghosts—"

Mama Rat and her son tittered once more.

With a forepaw the Thunder Giant stomped for silence, then
spoke again: "If there's ever a rat like that fellow Kim, a rat who fills
his belly while the rest of us starve, then watch out! He won't get
away with it—we'll tear him in half on the spot!"

"You know, I wouldn't let a fellow like that get away with it,
either!" one of the children heatedly exclaimed.

"Me neither!" said the other.

4

The Thunder Giant lovingly embraced his family, then began another dignified admonition. The others listened attentively.

"My precious children, when it comes time for you to go forth in the world, you must have your wits about you. Because when life in the world of people becomes as difficult as you see it now, life becomes just as difficult for us, too. If you're going to survive in this world, what it comes down to is this: without power you can't live. Your life becomes a living death. Su-dol's family are like that. A life without power is what people call incompetency. Now incompetency ain't something wicked; it's just a lack of power, and that's a fact. But since there's no life to speak of when there's no power, in the end you can't help but look at incompetency as a kind of crime—the crime of a person not being able to save his own life. No matter how evil a person is, as long as he has power he has life. Where there's life, it follows that there's also goodness, beauty, and truth—because power can sustain knowledge that's put to the good. . . . And so it's this power, this very power, that both of you must cultivate. Think about it: a bird flying in the air, a flower blooming in the garden—aren't both of them expressions of power? Symbols of power? Where there's life there's power. Let there be no more misunderstanding: power is something that must be used with knowledge that's put to the good. It absolutely cannot be used for personal greed. Children, do you understand?"

"Yes! I'm going to be powerful like Father, and be a great woman."

"And I'm going to be a great man," said his son.

The Thunder Giant gave them an affectionate pat on the rump.

"Now let's count the money! How much do we have here? The old fart's going to have a hard time stomaching this. One . . . two . . . three . . . ten in all. I tell you what—let's use this money to paper our den floor before we go to sleep tonight. This smooth, shiny money will make first-rate floor paper. You too, Mama, lay out one of those bills . . . and we'll set up a screen like this to keep out the draft . . . and the rest of the money we'll give to Su-dol."

"Hey, that's a great idea. Give him mine, too."

"There's a lot of money here already, so you don't have to give up your bedding. If we give them too much, Su-dol will faint. I'll bet he's never laid hands on so much money in his life. All right, we'll scrap the idea of a screen and give that bill to Su-dol as well. That'll make his share a total of six bills," said the Thunder Giant.

"But how are we going to get to Su-dol's?" worried his wife.

"Heck, I'll take it over right now."

So saying, the Thunder Giant rolled up the money, put it in his mouth, and was off.

His wife begged him to take care.

The Thunder Giant shot like an arrow to Su-dol's house, and there in the feeble lamplight flickering in their dark room he could see the children lying languid from hunger. He dropped the money on the floor, and immediately returned home.

When he arrived at the den he found his wife and children waiting up, along with a mound of rice that they had husked for him. And so they enjoyed a bedtime snack before snuggling into comfortable places on the spread-out bills.

The next day Su-dol's family awakened to find a windfall of sixty wǒn, and Rich Man Kim's entire household was in an uproar over the loss of a hundred wǒn.

The Rotary Press

YŎM SANG-SŎP

Yŏm Sang-sŏp was born in Seoul in 1897 and was educated there and in Kyoto and Tokyo. Like many of his contemporaries, he worked for various newspapers and literary magazines in Seoul. Later in life he taught at Sŏrabŏl College of Fine Arts. He died in 1963.

Yŏm, along with Kim Tong-in and Hyŏn Chin-gŏn, is often cited as the father of Korean realism. But he might be described more accurately as a specialist in psychological description. As scholar Kwon Youngmin has suggested, Yŏm's first three published stories—the oft-cited "P'yobonshil ŭi ch'ŏng kaegori" (The green frog in the specimen room, 1921), "Amya" (Dark night, 1922), and "Cheya" (New Year's eve, 1922)—are characterized by abstraction rather than description of contemporary Korean realities. "Imjong" (Deathbed, 1949) is a later example. His best-known novel, Samdae (Three generations, 1931), examines the dynamics of an extended, middle-class family in Seoul as well as the transition from a Confucian to a modernizing society.

"The Rotary Press" (Yunjŏngi, 1925) uses the straitened situation of the media in colonial Korea to sustain a tension that hinges on the arrival of money that will keep a threatened newspaper in operation. The story is like a chamber play in which a psychological drama is played out to the ticking of a clock. The central importance of time and money in the story is an apt commentary on the life of intellectuals in 1920s Seoul.

1

The clock ticking above A's head chimed once, softly. The sound drew the gaze of the small clusters of figures slumped in their chairs in front of A. Those people knew without looking that it was nine-thirty. A was relieved that it wasn't ten o'clock, but he was troubled by the prospect of having to wait another thirty minutes. He drew a cigarette from the pack on his desk and nervously struck a match, using more force than necessary. He inhaled and then watched list-lessly as the cloud of smoke issuing from his mouth drifted up toward the light.

He'll come in any case, with or without the money, A told himself. But why did he have to send us a telegram when he planned to arrive in an hour or two—and he's not that far away? A thought about how his mouth had dropped open in delight when he'd received the tele-gram a short time earlier—"will arrive at ten"—and again he won-dered anxiously if he'd misplaced his trust. He considered how he'd been waiting here like a dog. No doubt the man had sent the wire out of sympathy for A and the others at the newspaper office as soon as he saw the possibility of borrowing some money. But A could not relax, because the telegram had failed to mention that very thing—money. The fact that the man had wired the office to notify them of his impending return from Inchon could be construed as a sure sign the loan had come through. In which case A could put his mind at ease right off, and work could resume. But suppose it fell through for some reason: All hell would break loose. No quibble or subterfuge would be of any use then, especially with that drunken bunch of pressworkers running loose and harassing people. A's lips burned and his eyes felt feverish. He realized he had been worrying too much.

"Tŏk-jin, is Mr. P downstairs?"

"No, he isn't."

A jerked upright in his chair, wondering if P had slipped away too.

"Did he say he was going somewhere?"

"I think he might have gone to the station."

Once again the large room fell silent. A felt like he was sitting on a pincushion. He considered the situation: K, too, had seen the tele-gram, had been visibly relieved, and then had vanished. P had gone to the station, it seemed, but if he failed to meet the man with the money there, he'd probably make some lame excuse over the phone for not returning to the office and leave the job of pacifying the workers entirely to A. Once ten o'clock came and went, A would have no choice but to do all the dirty work single-handedly. Even so, A told himself, he'd first finish his article, and he took up his pen. Several of the others, arms folded, watched with interest the hand that held the pen.

The enervated silence of the office was suddenly broken by snor-ing. The rhythmic sound was like that of a saw blade passing through wood.

"What is *that?*"

A looked up, scowling, and tried to maintain his composure. The younger ones sitting around the dying stove chuckled at A's appearance, his unkempt hair making him look all the more startled. The snoring came from a dark recess of the office. Whoever it was, he was out of sight there, apparently lying on chairs behind the largest desk.

On it went, the wheezing and rasping, the rasping and wheezing.

A realized that the younger ones were laughing at the snoring, and not at himself, but he was irritated and hurt all the same and he flared up even more.

"Who's doing that? How could anyone sleep like that in this office?" he shouted, his face severe.

"Why, it's Sŏng-ch'ŏl. He's over there in the corner, sleeping like a log," said an older worker nicknamed Generalissimo, as if this was the most ridiculous thing he had ever witnessed.

A, as was his habit, clamped his lips together, snorted, and directed his gaze toward the top of the page of manuscript in front of him.

Once again a commotion rose from downstairs. P had barely been able to subdue those drunks, and now it sounded like they were throwing chairs around and bashing up the stove again. There was a constant stream of curses along with voices saying, "Stop that—are you out of your mind?"

A could stand it no longer. He flung down his pen and bolted to his feet. The young ones near the stove observed him with contempt. But contrary to their expectations, A didn't go downstairs. Instead he made a circuit of the desks, which were arranged like a square with one side missing. The *crack* of his horseshoe-sized heel plates on the wooden floor disturbed the cold air in the large, gloomy office. A piercing sound to some, for A it was almost refreshing.

The snowflakes falling since dinnertime had turned to sleet and the wind was rising. As the commotion downstairs subsided, the ruthless gusts shook the windows like an earthquake. Those in the office, engrossed in worries about getting home in the foul weather, hunched up to keep warm.

A felt a strong urge to go out and wander in the drizzling sleet. But he realized that if he left as well, it would give the appearance of running off. His noisy tramping around the desks quickened.

I might as well be a hostage—it's been three days now!

For each of those days A had been stuck here in the same fix.

"Damned clock! Are those hands crippled, or what? They're never going to reach ten!" someone said. The impatience of the workers was increasing as the prescribed time neared.

"This is getting fishier by the minute!" someone else snorted. "If nothing's happened by now, it's not going to happen in the next ten minutes. Should have sold the goddamn rotary press a long time ago and divvied up the money. Why drag things out? You don't get medals for a wild goose chase. I'll tell you, they sure know how to talk big."

"Listen you, they been stringing us along for two months now— what's another ten minutes? Even if there *is* no hope in sight!"

"Enough is enough. If nothing happens tonight, then anyone who sets foot here tomorrow is a son of a bitch."

The jeers and promises followed in quick succession.

A came to a stop near the stove and stood alone. His none-too-large eyes narrowed behind the thick lenses of his glasses. And then he noticed the guy in the traditional white calico topcoat and the yellowish kidskin shoes, stretching out his ugly-looking legs and muttering. The man returned A's gaze with a dirty look. A grew red in the face at this display of insolence. Straining to control himself, he returned to his desk. He tore off his topcoat and flung it over the chair like someone ready for a fistfight. Then he sat down.

A looked at his topcoat. He'd worn it only four or five days and already it was soiled and a seam had come open at the armpit. He was troubled by the thought of spending yet another night here in the office, then wearing the unsightly thing outside on the street the next morning. Bickering with the workers during the day, barely getting the newspaper out at night, and then sprawling in the night-duty room after midnight, still wearing the topcoat—this was how it had been.

Maybe I ought to go home tonight and see how the family's doing. It's been almost four months since I've brought home any money, and yet I'm wondering why my wife isn't taking care of my clothes?!

This thought reminded him that his family had run out of rice four days earlier.

Here I am running around, going hungry, shivering, staying up all night, and she probably thinks I'm having an affair with someone. . . . Supposing the money arrives tonight, could I set aside even one wŏn for myself? No way! People say I run the newspaper as badly as I run my household affairs, and you know something—they're right!

A recalled a comment made by a worker one day, a comment clearly meant to be heard by A: "You can't print newspapers on an empty stomach!"

They had a point, A admitted. But the steering committee that ran the newspaper had been elected by the employees themselves, who then proceeded to harass the committee members at all hours and make life miserable for them. And judging from what they wore and the money they carried around, they were much better off than A.

True, no matter how important a newspaper is, people have to eat. But they couldn't be allowed to kill the newspaper on account of hunger. And this was not a matter of vanity or ambition. Rather, once the Governor-General's Office revoked the paper's publication right, they would never reinstate it. This was a frightening prospect. A considered it his duty to the people and to society to keep that publication right—to keep the newspaper running—until a suitable owner turned up. Most of the regular workers were not thinking so far ahead, but there was nothing A could do about that.

From the various desks A gathered the manuscript left by the few remaining members of the editorial staff, put it in four separate envelopes, one for each of the newspaper's four pages, and set the envelopes in order on his own desk. If the man expected at ten did indeed arrive and the workers were given at least half a month's pay, then he would tell them they must get the newspaper out even if it meant working through the night.

The cynical looks of the groups around the stove were concentrated on the four envelopes. A, though, feeling a sense of triumph, lit a cigarette and sat down. He now felt confidently defiant, but more than just delighting in that confidence, he found himself in a rebellious frame of mind.

You guys say this is your last night. Well, this is my last night, too. The bottom line is that you and I have the same duties, the same responsibilities—right? Go ahead—try and shirk those responsibilities, and we'll see if I can stop you!

With such thoughts convincing him he could bully his way through, A managed to toughen his resolve until he felt there was nothing to fear even if by some chance the money didn't materialize.

The large, gloomy office, lit only in A's area by two dim light bulbs, lapsed again into a dismal silence punctuated by the drunken snoring, which added a bit of comic relief to the tense, veiled, seemingly endless confrontation between mind and mind, eye and eye.

"Five more minutes!" someone remarked, half derisively and half impatiently. All eyes converged on the clock above A's head. The commotion downstairs, which had subsided briefly, started up again. Feet thumped up the stairs, and the office door creaked open to admit the hubbub from below.

"Sir, what's going to happen now? You don't mean to make us wait till ten o'clock sharp, do you? Let's see, it's three minutes to. The money must be ready by now?"

The man who said this was Tŏk-sam, foreman of the pressworkers, who had lately been the self-appointed leader of all the fuss and commotion and was supposed to have smashed a dozen or so chairs in anger.

A looked him in the eye, not saying a word.

"Why don't you say something? Time's up—you have to produce. You've stalled us this long, and now you mean to tell us that with only three minutes left you won't give us the money when it's right there in your hand? I could just about . . ."

Swaying back and forth beside A, Tŏk-sam brandished his fists, which were the size of A's skull.

"What are these, anyhow? Boys, these must be the wads of money they promised!" said Wino, a buddy of Tŏk-sam's and a fellow troublemaker, thumping the envelopes of manuscript on A's desk with a sneer.

A stifled a response, not wanting to pick a fight.

Right, he thought. Three more minutes to go. Three more minutes, and ten wŏn will go into your pocket, and won't you be ashamed of yourself then. Three minutes before, you behave outrageously like this, and three minutes later when you have your ten wŏn, just don't let me see that big lump of a body of yours bowing and scraping in front of me.

A was tempted to fly into a rage and yell something like this. But he realized it wouldn't do to get into a shouting match and provoke the men further. Besides, if the money didn't arrive, they would become even more ferocious. And so the dressing down that A thought was in order shriveled on the tip of his tongue.

"So, it's not ready yet?" asked Tŏk-sam.

"What's not ready?" A tried to joke the matter away. "Whatever it is, I'm sorry it's late."

Tŏk-sam, momentarily befuddled, could only chuckle.

Taking advantage of this moment of relaxation, A allowed anger to enter his voice for the first time: "If you'd bother to think about it, you'd realize we're all in this together. Why do you have to be so harsh with me? The way you talk, it's as if we have the money and aren't paying you. Well, if you want to believe that, go ahead!"

So saying, A threw on his topcoat as if he intended to leave that very moment.

"Hey now, hold your horses. As long as we've come this far, why not pipe down and see things through to the end? How'd you ever manage to control yourselves till now if you're in such a rush?" said Generalissimo, who was the oldest of the machine-room workers and a decent man.

"*You* pipe down, Mr. Generalissimo," Wino interrupted. "And keep out of this."

Tŏk-sam then retorted to Generalissimo: "Look, man, maybe you have a golden calf at the end of your tether and live like royalty. Maybe you can sit back nice and relaxed. Not me! I can't afford to be generous like you. I feel like an anchovy that's been dried for three years. Look at my arms! They used to be strong, but they're pitiful now!"

He rolled up his sleeves, showing the steely arms he took such pride in. In truth, it was a good thing no one thus far had been "treated" by those arms. If a man like A were to get a taste of them, he'd be in for a cracked skull.

A, seeing the situation turn volatile once again, knew he couldn't maintain his hard-line approach indefinitely. But then he couldn't condone the men's violence and meekly wash his hands of the matter. He was caught in a dilemma.

"It won't do to keep acting like this, fellows. Let's try to be a little more patient. I know it's supposed to be ten o'clock, but the train may not arrive until ten after, and it could be ten-thirty by the time he gets here. Let's try to wait till then. What do you think Mr. A and the others are working so hard for? Everything they're doing is for your benefit, isn't it? And what are we all sitting here for anyway? Hoping for money? No—we want to get our work done."

This was the head of the proofreading section, and the senior man in the editorial department. In fact, A and this man were the only editorial members still in the office. This man hadn't seen any money in a long time either, and though he sensed there was no hope of obtaining a single copper for himself even if the money arrived, there he sat shivering, nose running, hungry because of the meals he'd skipped.

"Aha, putting us off another thirty minutes, is that it? Then why didn't you say ten-thirty in the first place? Seems you've decided to duck your responsibilities any way you can. For months the company's been making ten wŏn, maybe forty or fifty wŏn, but never over a hundred. Then all of a sudden you talk about a thousand wŏn. That's some nerve you got! It's ten o'clock. What now? Let's settle this thing one way or another. Mr. A, why don't you take in my wife and two kids and do what you want with 'em. Dammit all!"

As Tŏk-sam's subdued harangue came to an end, the clock struck ten.

"Now go on downstairs," A said in a friendly, persuasive tone. "Thirty minutes from now I'll start looking after your family. But until then let's keep nice and quiet—no more broken chairs. We'll take action before the night's out."

"So, I wait till ten-thirty, then go home in a blizzard, empty-handed and feeling like shit. No heat in our rooms, empty stomachs. . . . My family should all come here and die together, or something. . . . God!"

So saying, Tŏk-sam picked up a chair and pounded it once on the floor.

2

The wind whistled, rattling the windows. Once again the younger ones grew concerned about getting home, perhaps imagining their young wives tending a bubbling stewpot on a warm charcoal stove.

"Even if we come into some money," one of them objected, "printing the paper tonight is out of the question. We'll just make a file copy for the Governor-General's Office, and starting tomorrow we'll go regular."

All present shouted a chorus of approval. The rotary press had been still the last two days, and only the file copies, needed to maintain the paper's publication right, had been prepared, and those just barely.

A ignored this, waited for the pressworkers to go back downstairs, then called Generalissimo over and tried to discuss the situation: "Seems we still have some charcoal, so I'll have the stoves fired up. Then we ought to be able to open up the shop downstairs and get back to work, eh? And did all the type get reslotted yet?"

"Well . . ."

Generalissimo seemed to be at a loss. If they started working, as A suggested, things would be fine, but first he had read the faces of his co-workers to see which way the wind blew. And what he saw made him realize he'd be shouted down if he attempted to relay A's suggestion.

While Generalissimo was searching a few faces and fumbling for words, the man in the new calico topcoat spoke out against A:

"What are we supposed to do at this point? It's out of the question, even if the money turns up. Look at Sŏng-ch'ŏl, dead to the world—he couldn't stay awake any longer. And you can bet that Ch'un-shik, *if* he comes back, will be stinking drunk. You figure on doing anything without those two? No way," he sneered, glaring at A. The man was a loafer, and even among the chronic troublemakers it seemed that all he did was gather human trash around him.

"So, you'll take your money and head for the nearest bar? Well, suit yourselves."

As A scolded the men, he was thinking that the money must almost have arrived, and he strained to listen to what was happening downstairs. He had just sat down when he heard the sound of a ruckus below, followed by the thump of several pairs of footsteps coming up the stairs. Everyone looked expectantly toward the door, and in staggered Ch'un-shik and his gang, their faces ruddy.

Ch'un-shik swaggered up to A's desk. "Look at you sitting there so patiently on an empty stomach. Is that supposed to make everything turn out happy? Come on, let's lug that press away and sell it, or do *something.* . . . God—do you know what time it is, Mr. A? Do you?"

A scowled at him, and Ch'un-shik quickly retreated to the stove.

"Now look here," said Ch'un-shik provocatively, "you guys must have gotten paid. Did I get left out 'cause I'm late?"

"I'll bet you're drunk," said one of the others. "Who ever heard of not paying someone because he's late?" And then to A: "Give Ch'un-shik and the three of us our share, will you? . . . Shit, I'm not going home till I get my hands on some money—even if it's just a copper."

"Even if it's just a copper"—A could easily guess the situation of the man who had said this. It was obvious from his clothing that he was hard put. Still, A was aggravated by the man's drunken disorderliness and his interference, and his temper flared: "I don't know any more than you do!" Then he looked away.

"Well, who was it that said ten o'clock tonight? And where's Mr. —K, is it?—and Mr. P? You don't all three need to be here when the money arrives, right? All you do is whisper among yourselves, and all we get is a pack of lies. Now see here, for two months we been scraping along on the lies the three of you fed us. Well, those lies ran out fast, and now it looks like we don't have no choice but to starve to death."

Everyone laughed. And then Tŏk-sam appeared from downstairs, panting menacingly.

"You men, what's going on?" he said. And then, as if to placate the most drunken of the workers, he shouldered his way among Ch'un-shik and the others and approached A.

"Sir! I sat tight another thirty minutes like you said, and felt like I died and come back to life. Now, I want you to please take my family. The three of 'em's waiting downstairs. You've got to settle this once and for all, right now!"

It seemed from his slurred speech that Tŏk-sam had gone out again and found a place where he could drink on credit.

"We're just wasting time. I need to go home and sleep. My family's down there, shivering. Why don't you go down and see for yourself."

This brought laughter from several of the others. Tŏk-sam likewise chuckled.

A stood up to him: "What do you mean, wasting time? We're all hard up, every one of us. You're harping about this because you can't take it any longer? Well, there's nothing I can do, so you do as you please."

Eking out a living one day at a time on the occasional ten or twenty wŏn that trickled in must have put everyone's household economy in bad shape. Without a source of capital for the newspaper, though, all the workers should have been willing to share responsibilities. But they didn't give such notions a passing thought. Instead they surged in, a bunch at a time, persistent and tenacious, to mock and harass A and to belittle him for not being a vested owner. This was even more distasteful to A.

"Is that the best you can do? You make us wait all this while just to give us the same line you been feeding us all along? God!"

Tŏk-sam took a step toward A's desk, brandished his fist, then crashed it down.

"Look, you, what are you trying to prove?" Ch'un-shik, who had been silenced by Tŏk-sam's forceful manner, now spoke up. "Always waving that fist of yours around—big deal. Now *I've* got something to say." But then, hit suddenly by the liquor, he seemed to forget the words. Weaving back and forth, he gaped at A's face.

"What's the matter?" said Tŏk-sam before Ch'un-shik could speak. "Come on, out with it. Are you going to tell him instead of me? You had one drink too many, asshole!"

Disgusted by the other's lack of respect, he punched the dazed Ch'un-shik smack in the face with that proud fist of his.

Ch'un-shik snapped out of his stupor: "Hey, look at this son of a bitch. You haven't had a taste of my fist yet. The model worker— who do you think you're punching!" He tried to grab Tŏk-sam by the collar, but several of the others intervened, and he could only struggle futilely. By now even the people who had been sitting next to the stove like sticky rice cake had risen en masse to mill about in front of S's desk, pushing and grabbing, and suddenly the room was in utter turmoil.

A, arms folded, remained seated, looking like a still life.

"Tŏk-sam, you go on downstairs right now," Generalissimo said, ushering Tŏk-sam toward the door. "What do you think you're doing, slapping people around for no good reason?"

"Wait a minute!" said Tŏk-sam. "It's my turn to say something. That boy sticks his nose into what a grown-up is saying . . . and he can't even talk right."

As Tŏk-sam tried to loosen Generalissimo's hold on him and stagger back toward the others, someone came up the stairs shouting something. Tŏk-sam opened the door and looked down.

"Huh? What? He's here? Really? Then it's for real! Hey! It's here!" Tŏk-sam crowed, turning back toward the office. "What are you guys making so much noise for, anyway? You sound like a bunch of herons screeching for food," he scolded, suddenly a model of decorum.

"What's going on? What happened?"

"What happened! Money! We got money! So stop your bitching and get yourselves downstairs!" Tŏk-sam shouted, his spirits up.

The dozen or so men who had been milling about fell into a stunned, somber silence, mouths and hands frozen as if they'd been electrocuted.

"What's with the dumb looks? Open up your ears and listen! The money's here—the money from the Inchon office. We're all set. You can have yourselves a drink." Tŏk-sam then turned to A: "Sir, we done wrong. We'll go back to work now."

With a final display of bravado, Tŏk-sam led the others away in unison, leaving only the type pickers behind. The younger ones who had been making nasty remarks all along turned away from A and sat down near the stove, which was now ice cold.

"Would you give me that copy?" said Generalissimo, holding out his hand with a repentant look. "We should get started right away." His tone told A he was confident there would be no more resistance from the workers.

"Would you please not give us so much work?" implored one of the younger ones in a complete turnabout of manner. "Other times we've worked straight through the night on half that amount. In any event, it'll be past midnight by the time we finish reslotting the type."

"Come on now, get going," said Generalissimo, ignoring the appeal. "If you'd started earlier, you'd have your money by now and be on your way home for a good night's rest. This isn't a worker–employer dispute we got here, but that's what you fellows called it, and you made a stink about it right up to the end. . . ."

The others were on their way to the machine room when in walked S with the money from Inchon. As they passed by S they nodded at him as if he were a friend they hadn't seen for years. A smiled inwardly.

As A was about to sit down with P and S to discuss how to divide the money, Ch'un-shik reappeared. He seemed to have made yet another quick trip to a stand-up bar, for he still couldn't steady himself.

"Are we working tonight? They go upstairs already?"

"You're still drunk. Go over there and sleep it off for a few minutes, then get to work," A chided him.

"Quite all right," said Ch'un-shik. "No one's drunk. Did they start up?"

He was about to go upstairs when he heard Sŏng-ch'ŏl snoring. He tottered over to where the man lay.

"Who's this? Hey, Sŏng-ch'ŏl, what gives? Get up, now. One or two drinks, and you drop off. . . ."

A snorted in disdain at Ch'un-shik and went upstairs, where he saw that two of the type pickers were in the same drunken condition. The only thing he could do was replace some of the copy with free advertisements to reduce their workload. When he thought of the vicious insults he'd endured from that man Ch'un-shik, A was not inclined to help him. But he changed his mind.

3

A's eyes snapped open. He had been dead to the world, buried in a
chair in front of the stove, when the whir and thump of the rotary
press turning vigorously in the machine room downstairs awakened
him. It was the first time the press had been heard in three days. A's
head was still fuzzy from the drinks he'd had with S and P a couple
of hours earlier to ward off the chill, and his mouth had a metallic
taste. As sleep stole over him again, the noise from the press grew
hazy and distant. He felt like a baby being rocked to sleep while a
lullaby flowed into its ears. But then the noise stopped abruptly—
perhaps the press was being adjusted—and A awoke with a start and
sat up. It was four in the morning. All around him in a tight group
were snoring men who had stayed up into the night. A thought he
would wait for the machine to start up again, but then curiosity got
the better of him and he went downstairs.

The machine room was a mass of confused activity, some of the
men oiling the press, others leaping about like tigers as they rearranged
the lead plates. Tŏk-sam was a whirl of motion, obviously pleased at
being able to work his machine after three long days. He noticed A
and gave him a hearty welcome: "Sir, were you able to get some
sleep?" Then he presented A with a test sheet of the newspaper. They
inspected it together and then Tŏk-sam shouted to one of the pressworkers, "This here needs to go up a little.... And those parts are
getting too much ink."

A marveled at Tŏk-sam. Was this the same man who a few hours
earlier in a fit of mad passion had brandished his fists, smashed a
desk, and railed at A, asking the company to support his family?

A looked on with rapt attention and then, hearing the whir of the
press setting into motion again, found himself responding to the ela-
tion of the moment. The entire company, which had been slumbering
until now, seemed suddenly to have awakened. And the men, whose
hearts had been steadily turning cold, were now revived, their lips
moving, their hands in motion. In his mind A visualized these men
jumping to their feet, alive and kicking, and running about full of
energy. He realized the thousand wŏn that had arrived was no more
than a measly injection, good for a few days at best, but still he was
relieved.

A could contain himself no longer. Seizing Tŏk-sam's cudgel-like hand, he tearfully exclaimed, "You love our newspaper just as much as I do!"

So embarrassed was Tŏk-sam at this display of emotion that he didn't know what to say. And it was hard to make out A's words above the noise of the press. But the gist had not escaped him.

"I'm so sorry. Please forgive me for what I did yesterday."

As Tŏk-sam said this, tears welled up in his eyes as well.

"Forgive you? Don't be silly. When I see you men putting in so much effort after all you've been through, I feel so thankful. . . ."

Tears laden with emotion rolled down A's cheeks. And his smile had returned.

An Idiot's Delight

YI T'AE-JUN

Yi T'ae-jun was born in Ch'ŏrwŏn, Kangwŏn Province, in 1904. After studying for two years in Japan, he returned to Korea and took on a succession of
editorial positions at literary magazines and newspapers. Yi was an influential editor, and it is significant that when Kim Tong-ni, another great prose
stylist, made his literary debut, he chose to do so in the daily where Yi then
worked, the *Chosŏn Chungang ilbo*, rather than in the more prestigious *Tonga
ilbo*. By the time Yi moved from Seoul to North Korea in 1946, he had published some seventy stories, several novels, a collection of essays, three plays,
and an extensive body of criticism. Little is known about his life in the North.

Yi's spare prose style is shown to good effect in stories such as "Kka-
magwi" (Crows, 1936) and "Poktŏkpang" (The realtor's office, 1937). He wrote
frequently of the underclass in colonial Korea. Many of his characters are
failures, pessimists, or victims of nostalgia, unable to adapt to changing circumstances in their own lives or to the sweeping changes in modern Korea.
In one of his last stories, "Haebang chŏnhu" (Liberation, before and after,
1946), he attempts to come to terms with the complicity of Korean intellectuals with the colonial regime in the latter years of the occupation period.

The character sketch "An Idiot's Delight" (Talpam) was first published in
the journal *Chungang* in 1933.

"Just like the countryside," I said to myself as I pushed aside my
newspaper and lay down in bed. It was several days after we'd
arrived in Sŏngbuk-dong, on the outskirts of Seoul.

It wasn't my initial sight of the dark shapes outside our door, nor
was it the chittering of the stream or the sighing of the wind in the
pine trees that gave me this feeling, but rather the sight of that man
Hwang Su-gŏn.

With only a few words he had given himself away as a simpleton.
More than the hills near our new home in Sŏngbuk-dong, more than

46

the brooks and the shortcuts, it was this simpleton who filled me with the feeling that I was in rustic surroundings.

Of course there's no reason to presume that big cities lack simpletons. It's just that in an urban center you don't see them on the street. In the countryside, though, any sort of fool can go about free as the wind. And this is probably the reason simpletons are often in view there, giving one the impression that rural areas are the only places they're found. They often have the obtuse, artless look of people in ancient times, and to someone who enters a village for the first time, this look gives rise to a mood of unspoiled rusticity.

Anyway, it wasn't a week since we had moved to Sŏngbuk-dong that Hwang paid us a visit. It was about ten in the evening when I heard a shout from the gloom of our courtyard:

"Are you the folks who moved out here from the city?"

Dispensing with preliminaries, he jumped up onto the veranda and rushed over to the lattice door of my study like someone in a heap of trouble.

"I heard you folks are from the West Gate area."

The newspapers he was toting suggested he was a paperboy, though he wasn't wearing the uniform.

"Well, so you deliver the paper?"

"Oh, this—three days now I been searching for you folks across the way there. Darn!" He threw a paper into my study. "How come you folks bought such a tiny house, anyhow? I could of told you there's a lot of big houses with tile roofs down thataway...."

Somewhat taken aback by his audacity, I examined his features. What struck me about him was his cropped hair and his bulging, oversize head.

"Is that so? Well, anyway, thanks for taking the trouble to find us."

A contented smile suddenly framed his big eyes and his mouth. "Thanks for what? It's my job."

But instead of leaving, he craned his neck and inspected the study. Then, without any prompting, he introduced himself.

"Hwang Su-gŏn—that's me. I'm one of your neighbors."

I politely told him my name, and he produced another grin.

"You folks own a dog?"

"No. Not yet, anyway."

"Please don't."

"Why not?"

"I have to ask all the folks on my route not to," he quickly replied.

I found this rather intriguing, so I asked him again to explain.

"Well, there's a bank clerk in the next neighborhood back that has a dog the size of a pony. How's a fellow supposed to deliver a paper to a place like that?"

"What's the problem?"

"The thing'll sink its teeth into me."

I couldn't quite see that as a necessary consequence, and I smiled. This made Hwang even more animated.

"Damn dog. I'll learn him a lesson one of these days."

He brandished a fist, and I noticed that his hands and wrists were as small and slender as his head was large and bulging.

"You must have had a long day. Isn't it time you went home and got some rest?"

Hwang reluctantly got up and took his leave.

"Good night, Mr. Yi, sir. We don't live too far from you."

Although he now knew where we lived, it was after nine when he appeared the following evening.

"Here's your paper!" he shouted as he entered the front gate.

"Why so late?" I asked.

"Because." And then he changed the subject.

Originally he had worked at Samsan Primary School, some distance down the hill, he proceeded to inform me. But then he had some trouble with a teacher there. And now he was delivering newspapers, but he wasn't a regular carrier, only a helper. His family consisted of his parents, his older brother and his wife, a niece, and him and his wife—a grand total of seven. And his father's name was such-and-such, his brother's name so-and-so. His family name was Hwang; his given name was Su-gŏn, whose two elements meant "life" and "construct." But because *Hwang* means "yellow" and the word *sugŏn* means "towel," the children teased him by calling him Yellow Towel, and this was how he was known by all the families in Sŏngbuk-dong. All of this he related proudly.

Again it became necessary for me to break in:

"I think the neighbors are waiting for their papers."

He left reluctantly.

My wife would ask me what I was talking about with "that half-wit," but I must admit I enjoyed gabbing with him. I liked the enthusiastic way he talked about the most trivial things, and we could chatter on for the longest time without any effort on my part. And no matter how long he carried on, I was always left with a good laugh, which lightened my heart. So I always took the time to chat with him if I wasn't in the middle of something important.

Sometimes our exchanges proceeded in fits and starts—not because we couldn't answer each other's questions, but because we couldn't always find something suitable to talk about. But when it came to launching in on a new topic, he did a better job than I. It might be May or June, but he'd ask me if I liked pheasant—something people ate only in winter. A couple of my other favorites were, "When you're wearing a Western suit, what do you put on first, the jacket or the pants?" and "If a cow and a horse got into a fight, who do you think would win?" No matter what we talked about, he would come up with something quite original. I couldn't help but be impressed by the range of his remarks.

One day I asked him what he wanted to do in life.

"Piece of cake—I want to be a regular paperboy."

He was now making three wŏn or so a month for delivering twenty or so copies for the regular carrier. Naturally, the position of a regular, which paid upwards of twenty wŏn and brought you a uniform and bell from the company, was the most enviable thing in the world. All he'd have to do was ring that bell, he said, and he'd make his rounds in a jiffy, plus that dog at the bank clerk's house wouldn't faze him a bit.

"Why not shoot for president of the whole newspaper, or something like that? Then you could forget about being a regular paperboy, and you wouldn't have to worry about that dog, would you?"

Su-gŏn rolled those round eyes of his, thought for a minute, and said, "Indeed." For lack of worldly experience that thought had never entered his mind, he said, pounding on his chest the way other people might slap their knee.

But he soon forgot about the idea of president and fixed his sights on becoming a regular carrier. And then one day we heard him shout from the courtyard:

"Mr. Yi! Oh, Mr. Yi! I'll be a regular starting tomorrow. Just think, I'll wake up tomorrow morning and . . ."

I asked for particulars.

Sŏngbuk-dong had been made a separate route, he told me, and the next day he'd drop by so we could see him in uniform ringing his bell. "Keep your nose to the grindstone—it always pays off," he philosophized. Then he left in high spirits.

We were as delighted as if a good friend had achieved a great

success. We looked forward to seeing him swagger in the next
evening wearing his uniform and ringing his bell.

But he didn't return the next day. We waited until late in the evening,
but neither he nor the paper arrived. The following day was the
same. Finally, on the third day, long before sunset, the clamor of the
bell raced into our house.

"Let's have a look at this!" I said as I rushed outside.

But the figure in the uniform with the bell and the newspapers was
not Hwang Su-gŏn but rather someone I had never seen before.

"Did you take over for the other fellow?" I asked.

"Yes, I'm in charge of Sŏngbuk-dong now."

"Was the other fellow assigned somewhere else?"

"I'm not sure where they'd want a nincompoop like that," the
man said with a smile. "They were going to use him as a paperboy,
but it seems they changed their minds when they found out how
dumb he is."

"So he's not even a helper?"

"That's right. Sŏngbuk-dong is a route by itself now, and I don't
need help."

With a ring of his bell the man was off.

And so Hwang Su-gŏn no longer had occasion to visit us. I occasionally went into town, but his house didn't seem to be on my way,
because I never ran into him.

It was as if a close friend had been sent far away, or had failed in a
large-scale business venture, and I wouldn't be seeing him again.
Indeed, my heart ached. The world had treated Su-gŏn heartlessly,
and I resented that.

As Su-gŏn had said, he was well known throughout the neighborhood as Yellow Towel. I gradually realized that anyone who had lived
in Sŏngbuk-dong for any length of time would smile at the mention
of his name.

From my short association with him I had gathered he would be
full of humorous anecdotes about himself. There were numerous
stories from his days as an errand boy at Samsan School. Let me pass
along a couple that circulated among the neighbors. The one I found
most delightful was this:

If a visitor arrived when the teachers were in class, Su-gŏn would
offer him a seat, sit down across from him, and devote himself to

entertaining the guest in his own comic way. Once he had received an inspector from the provincial bureau of education and management in this fashion. The man was a Japanese, but Su-gŏn didn't know enough Japanese to perform his usual antic routine, and so he proceeded to practice what little Japanese he knew.

"*Sensei,* heh-heh, *ohayō gozaimasu ka,* heh-heh, *ame ga hurimasu. Yuki ga hurimasu ka,* heh-heh. . . ."

The official smiled the first time he heard this, but by the tenth or twentieth time he wasn't so pleased. The teachers kept waiting for the bell to end class, and finally one of them emerged from his classroom to find that Su-gŏn had forgotten this duty of his and was sitting directly across from his guest reciting, "*Ohayō. Yuki ga hurimasu ka.* . . ."

That day, Su-gŏn was soundly reprimanded by the teachers, and he promised not to repeat this behavior. But he wasn't able to break himself of his habit, and in the end he was discharged by the school.

The most unsettling thing to tell him was, "Your woman's going to run away from you."

One day a teacher had facetiously told him, "You know, ever since the old days, women have always preferred warm spring days like this for running away from their husbands. I heard a couple of ladies in the village down yonder flew the coop yesterday. I wouldn't be surprised if it happened in our neighborhood today. . . ."

Su-gŏn had stopped in the middle of his lunch and looked up at the teacher wide-eyed in surprise. That afternoon, wanting to go home early, he rang the school bell every twenty minutes instead of the usual fifty minutes. So the story went.

I had practically forgotten about Su-gŏn when one day he paid us a visit.

"Mr. Yi?"

I was delighted to see him.

"Any problems with the delivery of your paper, sir?"

He sounded as if he were now in charge of newspaper delivery.

"No. Why?"

"It always comes right on time?"

"Yes, every day—and three hours earlier than when you delivered it."

Hwang scratched his head sheepishly.

"Well, if it's ever held up, I'll go straight to the office and give them what for," he said, brandishing his puny fist. "You know what, sir?"

"What?"

"The errand boy who came after me at Samsan School—do you think he's stronger than me?"

"Well, I haven't seen him, so I can't say."

He smiled genially.

"I'm going to get that job back, and I got a few angles I'm playing," he said in an earnest tone.

"What angles, if I may ask?"

"It's a snap—I'll go to the school office every day and pester them to take me back. And you know what—the new guy is a lot bigger than me. And he's been grumbling about me. That means we're going to have a showdown. So I'd better see how strong he is."

He chuckled.

"Darn right," I said. "If you challenge him without sizing him up first, you'll catch a beating."

Su-gŏn came a step closer and gave me a confidential smile.

"You're right. So, last night I rolled a big rock up to the front gate of the school. This morning it was gone. But since I didn't see him, I can't tell if he rolled it like I did, or if he picked it up easy as can be. Dang!"

He scratched his head again. Then, as if he had suddenly thought of something, he clapped his hands.

"I almost forgot—the real reason I came was to tell you not to get a smallpox vaccination."

"Why shouldn't I?"

"Well, the pox is going around, and everybody's getting vaccinated. But if you're vaccinated against smallpox, you lose your strength," he said, rolling up his sleeve and showing me his vaccination mark. "Look at this. I was vaccinated, and now I'm not as strong as I used to be."

"Who told you all this?"

"I figured it out myself," he said with a grin.

"Yes?" I said, waiting for an explanation.

"Well . . . Pockmark Yun, who lives down yonder—he's strong as an ox. He was never vaccinated, you know. That new guy at Samsan School—he'll be a pushover if he's been vaccinated."

"I'm very grateful to you for passing on this clever idea."

He beamed contentedly and scratched his head.

"Are you still waiting for them to take you back at the school?"

"Naw. If I had some money, I wouldn't bother my head about being a worthless errand boy. With some capital I could walk tall and set up a shop in front of the school."

"What would you sell?"

"Well, until summer vacation I'd sell *ch'amoe* melons, and in the fall, roasted chestnuts, Japanese rice cakes, calligraphy paper, drawing paper—you name it. You know, the pupils there think more highly of me than they do the teachers."

That day I gave him three wŏn and told him to do as he said—to "walk tall" and set up a melon stand in front of the school. I told him not to worry about repayment if he couldn't turn a profit.

In great cheer, he rushed out the gate as if he were performing a dance. The next day he dropped by while I was out and left three *ch'amoe* melons with my wife, asking her to offer them to me.

But we didn't see hide nor hair of him the whole summer.

I heard later that he had set up his melon stand only to see the monsoon rains set in shortly thereafter. That's when melons lose their taste, and soon his capital was exhausted. But this development paled in comparison with the shocking news that his wife had abandoned him. She and Su-gŏn had gotten along well enough, but she could no longer put up with the ill treatment she suffered at the hands of his sister-in-law. If Su-gŏn had been a normal man, they might have been able to live in a house of their own someday, and she could have waited for that. But the prospect of living out her days under the sister-in-law's thumb had prompted her to leave.

Then one night a few days ago, Su-gŏn visited for the first time in about a month. He brought half a dozen bunches of large grapes. I noticed he hadn't bothered to wrap them in paper.

"For you, sir," he said with a broad smile.

Just then somebody came up from behind, grabbed him firmly by the collar, and dragged him off. Su-gŏn's dimwitted face turned pale, and he offered no resistance as he was led away. I guessed immediately that he had stolen the grapes from the vineyard. I followed the two men, stepped in between them as Su-gŏn was being beaten, and offered to pay for the grapes. While I was going through this, Su-gŏn managed to slip away.

I took the bunches of grapes home, set them on the table, and stared at them as I nibbled a few. For the longest time I rolled each of them in my mouth, as if to savor the fruit of Su-gŏn's warm-hearted naïveté.

Last night I returned late from downtown. I could see no lights as I passed through Sŏngbuk-dong; there was only the luxuriant moonlight brightening the road.

As I made my way up the hill near the vineyard, I heard a raspy voice.

"*Sa . . . ke . . . wa . . . na . . . midaka, tamei . . . ki . . . ka.*"[1]

A man was coming down the hill. The way he swung his arms as he walked made the wide road seem narrow. I looked closer; it appeared to be Su-gŏn. I realized he would be embarrassed if I called out to him and he saw it was me, so I quickly hid myself in the shade of a tree at the side of the road.

He stared up at the moon, not looking at the road, and kept repeating the same words from the song. Perhaps that first line was the only line he knew. And he was puffing away on a cigarette—something I'd never seen him do before.

To Su-gŏn, too, a moonlit night called forth all sorts of sentiments.

---

1. "Teardrops and sighs"; from a Japanese song popular in Korea at the time.

A Ready-Made Life

CH'AE MAN-SHIK

Ch'ae Man-shik—fiction writer, playwright, essayist, critic—was born in Ŭmnae, a coastal village in North Chŏlla Province, in 1902. Like many of the intellectuals of his generation, he studied for a time in Japan, then returned to Korea to work at a succession of writing and editorial jobs. He died of tuberculosis in 1950.

Ch'ae is one of the great talents of modern Korean literature. His pene-trating mind, command of idiom, utterly realistic dialogue, and keen wit produced a fictional style all his own. The immediacy of some of his narra-tives produces a strong sense of a storyteller speaking to his listeners.

Often pigeonholed as a satirist, Ch'ae was much more. Long before such satirical sketches as "Ch'isuk" (My innocent uncle, 1938), about a political misfit during the Japanese occupation, and "Misŭt'ŏ Pang" (Mr. Pang, 1946), set during the American military occupation, Ch'ae had written "Kwadogi" (Age of transition, 1923), an autobiographical novella about Korean students in Japan testing the currents of modernization that swept urban East Asia early in this century. In other early works, such as "Segillo" (In three direc-tions, 1924) and "Sandungi" (Sandungi, 1930), he dealt with the class differ-ences that are so distinct in Korean society past and present. In these earlier stories Ch'ae is concerned as well with the plight of the unemployed young intellectuals turned out by the modernization movement—young men such as P, H, and M in the story translated here, who perpetually make the rounds of publishing houses, pawnshops, and cheap bars. Ch'ae was also at home depicting the rural underclass, so long suppressed as to be almost incapable of autonomous action, in stories such as "Ch'ajung esŏ" (On a train, 1941). T'aep'yŏng ch'ŏnha (Peace under heaven, 1938), on the other hand, is a pointed treatment of traditional Korean etiquette in the person of one who thrived materially but wasted spiritually during the Japanese occupation. It has been acclaimed one of the great Korean novels.

Ch'ae's later works are somewhat more bitter and introspective. In these stories the author's wit is tempered by the spiritual turmoil of having to come to grips with the role of the artist in a colonized society. "Minjok ŭi choein" (Public offender, 1948–1949), for example, is a semiautobiographical apologia for those branded as collaborators for their failure to actively oppose Japanese colonial rule. "Maeng sunsa" (Constable Maeng, 1946) is a satirical sketch of a member of the Korean police force during the Japanese occupation. "Ch'ŏja" (The wife and children, 1948) portrays a man who finds himself out of political favor after Liberation. The man's exile from his family echoes not only premodern Korean history, in which victims of factional infighting in the capital were frequently banished to the countryside, but contemporary history as well, with its record of house arrests of dissident politicians. In this and other works Ch'ae also offers keen insights into the long-standing oppression of Korean women.

"A Ready-Made Life" (Redimeidŭ insaeng) was first published in 1934 in the journal *Shindonga*.

1

President K of the newspaper stifles a yawn and buries himself deeper in his armchair. "Jobs are hard to come by around here," he says halfheartedly. He extends his arms, looking as if he would like very much to stretch his entire body.

This is K's answer to P, who sits respectfully on the opposite side of the circular table. P, displaying an ingratiating smile and an expression that seems to say, "You are my senior, sir, and I esteem and venerate you to the extreme," has mobilized all the rhetoric at his command and implored K at great length for a position. But in the end he is not overly disappointed by K's nonchalant, cursory refusal, for he is an old hand at being turned down in his job-hunting campaign. As the old saying goes, "A hundred battles, a hundred losses."

K's response has made it clear that there is no point in pressing the issue. But P decides anyway to put in one last word for himself.

"Well, under the circumstances, I guess I can't very well ask more of you at this point. . . . But if something should happen to open up, would you be good enough to . . ."

Until then, P had deferentially averted his gaze, but now he cautiously looked K in the eye. K, though, merely shook his head and answered in the same sleepy tone.

"Don't get your hopes up. . . . Even if we were to have an opening from time to time, there are dozens of well-qualified men waiting in line. . . ."

P lowered his head without a word. The case was closed. All that remained was to bid K farewell and leave. He should therefore say something like "I see" and briskly rise. But in comparison with his polite demeanor thus far, that would seem abrupt. Realizing this, P feigned disappointment and remained seated a bit longer.

Noticing P's apparent dejection, K decided to show as much concern as he could. After all, it wouldn't cost him anything.

"This is a big problem—all you good men trying so hard to find work."

P silently snorted, making no attempt to reply.

Relieved to see that P had given up, K abandoned his halfhearted, yawn-filled expressions in favor of the lecture he always kept in store for young men such as this.

"Like I always say, you men shouldn't be spending all your energy trying to find this kind of work. Instead of a nine-to-five job in the city, you should go down to the farming villages and—"

"What are we supposed to do there?" P interrupted. Now that his hopes of finding a job with K's newspaper had gone awry, he might as well provoke K and get everything out of his system.

"Well," K huffed, "that doesn't show much intelligence. . . . Why, Korea is a farming nation—farmers make up eighty percent of the population. Therefore we can view the Korean problem as a farming problem, pure and simple. There are all sorts of things to be done in the farming villages."

"I'm afraid I don't follow you. It doesn't seem to me that there's much for people like us to do there."

"That's not so. For example . . . uh . . . well . . ."

There's a reason K can't finish. His advice to go work in the countryside (and his next proposition—to drum up some kind of project there) doesn't have any basis in reality. These vague proposals are just his way of dealing with the flood of educated young job seekers. There's nothing specific about his suggestions. They merely give K a chance to show off, and they're a means to discourage job hunters. K uses these words the way that Chinese general Chao Zilong squandered his flimsy lances in battle.

Most of those who heard K's vague sermon listened inattentively and withdrew. But not this man P. It appeared K would have to come up with some concrete explanations for him. Hence his improvising. He voiced the thoughts that came to him in fits and starts.

"For example . . . uh . . . well . . . take the literacy campaign. Did you know that ninety percent of the population can't read Korean, much less Chinese! And the modernization movement—that's something you could devote yourself to."

"*Devote* myself to?"

"Why, certainly. . . . If you're going to do something, you might as well put your heart into it."

"You can't put your heart into work if your stomach is empty. If we could afford to do these good works in the farming villages, do you think we'd be going to all this trouble to find a job here?"

"That's where you're wrong!" K snorted. "Anyone who has the means to make a living, but loafs instead of working on behalf of society—what a degrading thought."

As K grew unreasonable, P smiled inwardly.

"The college graduates who go to the farming villages to root out illiteracy and modernize the life there, they've never soiled their hands," said P. "They're not exactly welcomed with open arms. Far from it, they're a nuisance. The farmers may be ignorant and uncultured, but the root cause of their wretched lives isn't a matter of not knowing how to read and write or how to modernize their lives. Besides, do you think that all the educated young people of Korea are humanitarian enough to devote themselves to these problems?"

"Why not? Is that so farfetched?"

"If it isn't, then I'd have to call that kind of humanitarianism a fantasy."

"So, young P, does that make you a socialist?" K scoffed.

"Almost. I got crushed along the way and I'm just a remnant now. But if I were a diehard socialist, I wouldn't have come here looking for a job, sir."

"It's no good. That's a radical brand of thought you're tilting toward. . . . Well, if you're so set against working in the farming villages, why don't you and the others who feel the same way go in on something together? Our country could always use another newspaper—why not set one up? Or if you're not so ambitious, you could try a new magazine. Or even a commercial venture."

"I've thought of that. But who's going to advance us the capital?"

"Where there's a will there's a way."

By now P was tired of these ridiculous exchanges. This seemed an appropriate time to stop, and so he rose. He felt better having voiced his feelings, but the thought of failing again left a bitter taste.

In the hallway, P ran into C, editor-in-chief of the newspaper. The two of them had long been close.

"Were you seeing the president?" C asked.

P lied and said no. It would have been embarrassing enough to admit having been turned down. But there was another reason as well: P had asked C to put in a good word for him, but just now he had seen the president without C's knowledge. To admit this would have been tantamount to confessing that he didn't trust C.

"Well, I think it's a lost cause, anyway," said C.

This meant C had already interceded on his behalf. P felt his visit that day had been fruitless to begin with—doomed from the start—and he now regretted seeing K without having spoken first with C.

"I saw the president yesterday morning—said you were in a bad way, told him I hoped he'd consider you. I told him all sorts of things I thought would help, and ended up with egg on my face. 'This newspaper's not a charity—are we supposed to help out everyone who's in a fix?' That's what he said. . . . And you know, he's right, even if—"

"Not a charity"—this last comment cut P to the quick.

Sons of bitches! P fumed. He left without saying good-bye to C.

2

P arrived at the Kwanghwa Gate intersection and stopped at the pavilion there. Where next?

The spring sky had cleared, and the lush warmth of the sun's rays enveloped him. The young people had shed their baggy winter overcoats. Radiant as spring sunlight, they promenaded about, smartly tailored in cheery new suits. The more stylishly dressed women wore scarves that fluttered gently like butterflies. Their plump, silky legs reminded P of a chicken cutlet he had once eaten.

The sight of these people of spring, framed in the wide-open windows of the streetcar, made P feel like riding to the outskirts of the city. But then he took inventory of himself: worn-out shoes that hadn't tasted polish for months; wrinkled suit pants; jacket pockets drooping like a bull's testicles in summer; grimy dress shirt; creased necktie; the old hat that had once brought an offer of two coppers' worth of taffy from the taffyman. How could a man dressed like that even think of a stroll in the outskirts? Better simply hurry home and burrow into his quilt.

Just then an automobile pulled up in front of the pavilion, and out stepped a Western couple. As they walked about the pavilion, the man explained something to the woman. She then took a photograph.

The Taewŏngun must be turning in his grave, thought P with a smile.

3

The Taewŏngun was the Don Quixote of the waning years of the Chosŏn kingdom. For protection against lightning he wore a calabash hat. Crack! The calabash never had a chance. History did not leave this tiny plot of land called Chosŏn untouched for long.

A bud had sprouted in the form of the Kapshin Coup of 1884, and liberal public opinion, tempered by the onslaught of the Japanese occupation and the historic changes that followed, took its first definite steps in the March 1919 Independence Movement. Public spirit, hoisting aloft the new banner of liberalism, reigned triumphant:

"*Yangban?*" you could hear them snort. "We have two legs, just like they do."

"We're all equal before the law."

"Money—if you have it you can do anything."

The newly emerging petite bourgeoisie, flying the flag of democracy, pacified the laborers and the farmers, made peace with the economically powerful feudal aristocracy, and at the same time created a demand for a whole class of intellectuals.

"Teaching your child one book is better than leaving him a fortune." This homily from feudal times was baptized with the ideas of liberalism, and thus adorned it inspired the populace with wild enthusiasm.

"Study your lessons! Anybody with learning can become a *yangban* and live well."

These fervent shouts rose with frightening speed along the length and breadth of the country.

Writers for newspapers and magazines wore out their writing brushes arousing enthusiasm for learning. Hot-blooded patriots toured the countryside villages, clamoring for education with all the eloquence at their command.

"Study! Learn! Even a humble man can become a *yangban.*"

"Teach your children—even if you have to sell the paddies and the house! And if you can't do that, then work your way through school."

"Confucius and Mencius have had their day. Cut off your topknots and take up the new learning."

"Establish night schools."

Under the banner of his Cultural Policy, Japanese governor-general Saito established more public schools. Grade school principals donned their leggings and struck out for the hinterlands to enroll pupils.

The students received free textbooks and school supplies, not to mention tuition waivers.

Farsighted citizens put up money for the construction of schools. A private university was planned. Night schools were organized by youth associations. Organizations helping self-supporting students appeared, and the students hawking the pastries supplied by this group became a new sight in Seoul. Self-supporting students enjoyed the respect of the public.

A new expression entered the language—"the woman student"— and a new breed of female emerged.

In these ways, the government and people of Korea acted in harmony, exerting themselves to increase the level of knowledge of the populace. More precisely, the stage of development targeted for the country's culture was rapidly achieved. And thus the efforts to spread learning among the populace bore fruit.

The nation was supplied with low-level government clerks, with policemen, with extension agents fresh from agricultural workshops.

Bank clerks appeared, office clerks as well. There were now schoolteachers, ministers, journalists. As the populace grew better educated, readers of newspapers and magazines proliferated, and doctors and lawyers prospered.

Writers of fiction made a living from their manuscripts, artists from their paintings. Musicians shed the lowly name of *entertainer* and became respectable. Printing shops and bookstores thrived. Tailor shops and shoe stores were lined up in rows. Love marriages increased, providing extra income for the ministers who officiated at church ceremonies. Contractors became rich building homes with modern conveniences. And so the petite bourgeoisie was dealt the best hand, while the intelligentsia among the educated segment of the population was in the middle.

But the workers and the farmers drew the short end of the stick. To them, the nation's development and its cultural advances added to their burden rather than lightening it. It was as if you gave someone an orange and were tossed the peel in return.

And the intellectuals? Among this group were people with no technical know-how, who had only a college diploma and some common-place knowledge, people who couldn't find jobs. Every year they increased by a thousand or so. These were the ones who received a raw deal.

All the petit-bourgeois places of employment became saturated; no more did their numbers increase. It was as if the intellectuals were lured into climbing the ladder of success, only to have it pulled out from under them. There was no demand for these people.

If they hadn't been intellectuals, they could have become laborers. But since they were intellectuals, 99 percent who tried to join the blue-collar ranks couldn't fit in and had to drop out. These rejects were dispirited and jobless, a powerless, cultured reserve force, and they heaved great sighs. They were like dogs who had lost their masters and become unwanted.

In short, they were ready-made human commodities turned shop-worn.

4

"Shit," grumbled P as he left the monument where he had been standing. Everything in the world was irritating and hateful.

As he sauntered along the main avenue near Kwanghwa Gate toward the Japanese Governor-General's headquarters, he noticed his foreshortened shadow ahead of him. He wanted to stomp on that shadow. But every time he extended his foot to do so, the shadow advanced the same distance. He and his shadow—his desire to stomp on it and his inability to catch up to it—these reflected the polar duality of his personality. At the Tongshipcha Pavilion P crossed the street to a tobacco stand.

"A pack of cigarettes," he said to the man inside the booth as he reached into his pocket for money.

"Makko?" the man said, naming the cheapest brand.

P glared at the man, surveyed his own shabby appearance, and became cross. Instead of change he produced a one-wŏn note, but the man had already proffered a pack of Makkos with matches.

"Make it Haet'ae," P barked as he thrust the money toward the man.

But the man was unruffled. "All right." He replaced the Makkos with Haet'aes and gave P eighty-five chŏn in change.

The man's insensitivity made P feel even more hateful. He lit a cigarette, recrossed the streetcar tracks, and stepped onto a sidewalk along a sewer creek.

A few days earlier P had pawned his overcoat for four wŏn. He was two months behind on his room rent and electricity bill. Three wŏn would take care of a month's rent, and a month's electricity would require a good portion of the remaining wŏn. He had wanted to pay off these debts and put what was left toward some beef-and-rice soup or Chinese pancakes. But that would have left him just about enough to sustain him for a day. And so he had let the money sit in his pocket, and the better part of a wŏn had been used up in the last two days. He hadn't meant to buy those Haet'aes, but his display of bravado had cost him the remainder of that wŏn, with the result that he now had three wŏn left.

P reached into his pocket and felt the mixture of coins and bank notes. He began to entertain the notion of doubling the money, counting on the fingers of his left hand.

Six wŏn, 12 wŏn, 24, 48, 96, 192—call it an even 200—400, 800, 1,600, 3,200, 6,400, 12,800—skip the 800 and you've got 24,000, 48,000, 96,000, 192,000, 384,000, 768,000, 1,536,000. . . .

Double 3 wŏn eighteen times and you have 1,536,000 wŏn. With that kind of money. . . . Such thoughts made him feel puffed up.

With that kind of money, or even just a million, he could start up a sixteen-page newspaper, sell it for fifty chŏn a copy, and listen to President K wail in despair.

But why be greedy? He would settle for 150,000 wŏn, or 15,000, 1,500, 150, even 15. With 15 wŏn he could pay off his room rent and electricity bill and live for a month on what was left over.

P sighed. A month? And then what? . . . Actually it was not fifteen wŏn he needed but several hundred wŏn, or rather several thousand, or rather tens of thousands. . . .

It was not unusual for P to engage in such absurd daydreaming. And as this habit had grown more and more prominent recently, the idea of finding employment didn't seem so urgent.

Even if he found a job, it would pay only forty to sixty wŏn a month—barely enough to scrape by on. What kind of enjoyment was a person to derive from such a life? Suppose he economized, started a monthly savings program, bought a house, took a wife; suppose the president or one of the other executives took him under his wing and he was able to advance to department head or a similar position. This kind of stability would mean an end to his present hardships. But to

P, who still possessed the ambition of his youth, such makeshift stability would make for a bland life, and he would much rather avoid it. Better to achieve more prominence in the eyes of others, to live a more colorful and carefree life, a life unfettered by the establishment. . . .

Of course, if someone were to approach at this instant and offer him a job at thirty wŏn a month, he'd jump at it like a starving dog pouncing on meat. That was the reality, but his grand designs made him talk a different story inwardly.

P arrived at Kŏnch'un Gate, on his way to Samch'ŏng-dong. A woman in a smart spring outfit was coming down the opposite side of the street. P occasionally saw her on the street, and assumed she lived in the vicinity of Samch'ŏng-dong, as he did. He would always pretend he wasn't watching, when in fact he was observing her closely and entertaining the notion of having a fling. What appealed to him especially were the smooth outlines of her roundish face, which suggested a disposition as even as her features were regular.

The young woman must have recognized P from a distance, because of her frequent encounters with this man in the shabby suit, and she gave him a wide berth as she approached. She carried herself with a demure bearing befitting a young single woman.

P kept erect and looked straight ahead, but his mind was at work: what would I do if she came up to me and asked for my love in a soft, affectionate voice? And if she threw herself into my arms—then what? These fantasies prompted a sheepish grin from P, but the woman, walking right past him, seemed not to notice at all.

Well, what do you know? P silently snorted. What's the matter with you, bitch? I told you, I don't need the likes of you. I ought to give you a swift kick in the butt.

And with that he threw out his shoulders and swaggered on.

P arrived at his house at the crest of Samch'ŏng-dong—actually a tiny rented room more fit for servants than tenants. Alone in an unfamiliar area, one would do well to live in a boarding house, but P didn't like the idea of being harassed if he fell behind on his board bill, and so he had taken a rented room instead.

As for meals, there was no set routine. Rather, depending on the amount of money in hand, he might have Chinese pancakes, beef-and-rice soup, or even a Western-style lunch in a department store. And he could skip several meals at a time if he had to.

Mildew formed in the sunless room, even in winter. Dust collected on the floor, where P left his bedding unfolded for days at a time. Seeing the wretchedness and clutter of the room, he was in no hurry to sit. As he stood absentmindedly, he heard the door to his land-lady's room slide open and shut. The woman emerged, clearing her throat. P grew apprehensive: it would be the rent again. But instead she handed him a letter from his older brother, who had remained at the family home in the countryside.

P read the letter and heaved a great sigh. Then he tore it up.

5

The letter concerned P's nine-year-old son, Ch'ang-sŏn. When P and his wife had divorced several years earlier, she had implored him for one thing only—custody of the little boy. Raising him would give meaning to her solitary life, she had said. She promised to send him at least through middle school.

P would hear nothing of this idea, though it would have relieved him of one of his burdens.

Generally, when children are raised from an early age by a mother who is abandoned by her husband or out of favor with him, they're exposed to her grievances; they hear her cursing him. And so they don't develop positive feelings about their father. It wasn't that P was dead-set on keeping his son. Rather, he couldn't bear the thought of a grown-up son coming to see him and acting in a disagreeable manner. He wasn't eager to be visited in his old age by a vigorous young man whose mother he had abandoned.

With this in mind, P had refused to hand Ch'ang-sŏn over to his wife. But having snatched his son away, he realized he couldn't sup-port him by himself. The boy wasn't even five at the time. And so P had no choice but to leave Ch'ang-sŏn with his uncle, P's older brother, even though he too was hard up. P had then left for Seoul by himself, saying he would send for the boy when he was ready to enter primary school.

The previous year, P's brother had enrolled Ch'ang-sŏn in school. But the family's extreme poverty had prevented them from paying even the nominal monthly tuition, and they had been forced to pull him out. P had seen no use in educating his son, so when his brother first wrote that Ch'ang-sŏn should be sent to school, P had responded instead by asking that the boy be put to manual labor so he could get used to it while still young. But his brother, out of a sense of duty as

Big Uncle and his concern for the family reputation, couldn't bring himself to do this. And since he couldn't afford to provide the boy with decent clothes and schooling, he much preferred having P take him to Seoul. He had been saying this in his letters since the year before.

Around the beginning of the present school year P's brother had written several more times. The following year the boy would be too old to enroll, he said. It was imperative that P take him to Seoul and put him in school before then.

"I can no longer bear to see the boy envying others who go to school while he himself goes hungry half the time and lets his talents go to waste. It would do my heart good not to have to see him in these miserable circumstances," P's brother had written this time. The end of the letter read thus: "As soon as I can raise money for the ticket, I'll put him on the train and wire you. You can pick him up at the station. If I weren't so hard pressed, I wouldn't be sending a young boy off to his father in an unfamiliar place like this. But chances are he'll die of malnutrition if he stays here, and so after mulling it over I've decided to send him up to you."

P crumpled the shreds of the letter, threw them into the corner, and heaved a deep sigh. He finally had to face up to it: he had to bring the boy to Seoul. But then what? P resented his brother for urging him over and over to put the boy in school, when his real concern was to send Ch'ang-sŏn off to his father. Whether the lad was sent to Seoul or kept in the countryside, he would suffer either way. To P, it would be better in many respects to let him work as a manual laborer in the countryside.

"The family reputation!" P huffed. "Education! Well, I'll never let him turn into an educated man like me."

"Bad news from home?"

P looked up to find his elderly landlady standing outside his room. She was trying to sound sympathetic.

"No," P replied without much conviction.

"Well, something must have happened." Trying to find the right opening, she kept on pretending she was concerned, despite P's denials. "It's all because of poverty. . . . An intelligent young man like you— it's all because of poverty. Still nothing in the way of a job?"

"I'm afraid not."

"What a shame. Something has to turn up soon. . . . I'm in a bad way myself . . . and I'm just an old woman. . . . Haven't you been able to scrounge up any money?"

"Not quite yet. . . ."

"What am I going to do? Today's the day they come around for the water and electric bills!"

"Couldn't you put them off for a few more days? I'll pay you—believe me."

"Oh, I trust you all right. It's just that I'm so hard up myself."

While the woman chattered on, P thought about the room he had rented before from a family he knew. He had fallen two or three months behind on his rent, but out of friendship they didn't bother him about it. This had made P feel all the worse, so he had moved here. But now that he was actually being hounded for what he owed, he longed for the old place.

The woman prattled on, still standing at the threshold to P's room. He was rescued by the arrival of his friends M and H.

"Going somewhere?" M asked, noticing that P was standing up.

M had a broad, flat nose, and his ready smile revealed a gap between his front teeth.

H, heavyset like M but shorter, had been hidden behind his friend, but now he emerged beside him.

"Hello."

P smiled. M and H lived in the same boarding house and often went around together. When P saw them walk along side by side, he was struck by their appearance—the one so tall, the other so squashed.

M had the rough-and-ready look of a politician—he wouldn't have looked out of place in a boxing ring—whereas H had the placid appearance of a clerical type. In everyday speech and behavior, H reflected his background in legal studies, often explaining things by reciting the appropriate article of the national legal code. M, on the other hand, spoke like a member of the leftist camp, befitting his involvement in the student movement in Tokyo and his major in government and economics.

"I see you two are still dressed for winter, just like me," P said, looking down at his own attire.

M removed his shoes, stepped inside, and perched himself on the edge of the dust-covered desk.

"Spring is here in name only," he said, reciting a well-known classical Chinese verse.

H followed M in, sat down on the floor near the wall, and added his two cents' worth.

"Don't worry. There are still a lot of people going around in winter clothes."

"What do you mean, 'Don't worry'? Whenever we go out, I hear cries for mercy from every direction."

"What!"

"It's spring getting mashed beneath our feet."

All three laughed.

"How'd you make out on the exam?" P asked H, referring to the examination for government clerks administered by the Governor-General's Office.

"Don't ask. . . . At this point, my best bet's the bar exam."

Because H lacked worldly experience and connections, all his job hunting had been fruitless, and for this reason P always felt sorry for him.

"All right. You go ahead and pass that exam, and I'll take you on as legal counsel when I set up my big-time corporation," said M.

This was M's perpetual joke. He had spent a year now searching for work, but he didn't let this bother him. He might have landed a position by now if he'd been more active. But because of his innate nonchalance and his temperament, his refusal to flatter others, he had become a straggler, as it were, in the battle for jobs.

There was little in the way of business that compelled these three to see one another. Alone, though, they usually felt depressed, and that was why they often sought out the others. Sitting down over conversation or idle chatter cheered them for the moment. Bands of jobless such as P, H, and M wandered Seoul every day with nothing to do, and whoever happened to have a few coppers would squander them, standing the others to a drink at a cheap bar. Such groups were too many to count.

If anyone were to entrust them with work, they could do it to perfection. But here they were, idling away their time.

There was no position in which they could fit. Moreover, the social situation in colonial Korea had not yet matured enough to warrant their joining the popular front and being effective. The proof of that? A good portion of them had continued their active participation in the class struggle while students in Tokyo, but had dropped out of the movement upon returning to Korea. And when they tried to enter the capitalist establishment, they found there was no demand for them. Since they were ready-made commodities, they were picked up only as needed, a few at a time.

M produced a pack of Makkos and lit up. P didn't dare take out his Haet'aes. His face flushing, he took one of M's.

P then prepared to launch into one of his fanciful ideas, explaining it as if it were a game. If someone had urged P himself to put it into effect, he would have hesitated, but what he was about to outline was nevertheless extremely satisfying as an idea.

"The first thing we do is go to national police headquarters and tell them straight out: Our target isn't the Governor-General's Office; it's the Korean big shots. So keep out of our way."

"So, you're proposing a government-authorized May Day demonstration?"

"Sure. What's wrong with that? . . . And we'll have a banner—let's see—'Down With the Jerks Who Inspired Us to Get an Education.' How does that sound?"

"Not bad."

" 'Jobs for Intellectuals'—we'll compose a song and sing it."

"Yeah, we'll expose those big shots, those 'distinguished' people, for what they are. If we can round up a few dozen people to do this, we'll have ourselves a demonstration."

M burst into laughter, knowing they would never carry out this scheme.

"Come off it," H said to P. "If a bunch of guys in fancy business suits march down Chongno waving a banner, the kids will come up and say, 'Give me a handbill, mister.' They'll think we're advertising something!"

This brought laughter from the other two.

From outside P's window came the sound of a peddler offering wild greens at a cut-rate price.

"Hey! A spring clearance sale," said M in response.

"Listen to him talk," H snorted. "You can smell an economist a mile away. . . . You know, we don't get enough fresh vegetables at our boarding house."

"Maybe they'd feed you better if you paid your board bill on time."

"You've got a point there."

"I'm three months behind."

"Me too, I think."

"You guys ought to live in an 'apartment,' like me," said P with a hollow laugh at the thought of calling his dump an apartment.

"Right! A Korean-style apartment. But if we lived in a real apartment, we would have died paupers a couple of months ago."

"I've forgotten what money looks like," said H. "If I saw some, I'd probably say, 'Hi there. I'm your old friend H. Remember me?' "

"Look here," said M in a solemn tone. "You say it's been a long time since you've seen money?"

"Yeah."

"I have an idea," said M.

"I'm all ears."

"Pawn a few of your books."

"Uh-uh," said H.

"Why not? You can take a good long look at the money you get, and then we'll put it toward a few drinks."

"Now that you mention it, these days I do feel like getting stinko and blowing off some steam."

"All right, then. So let's go hock some books. Five ought to do it."

"Nothing doing," said H.

"I'll get them back for you later."

"Fat chance."

"I'm serious."

"No dice."

6

That night P and M pestered H until he pawned several of his legal reference books in return for six wŏn. The three men then set out on the town. After getting pleasantly drunk at a cheap bar, it was on to a café with hostesses, where they finished two bottles of Western liquor, talking and joking till midnight.

Two wŏn remained when they left the café. How to dispose of it? Before long they had reached the same conclusion: off to the Tong-gwan! And so away they went, weaving and staggering. P was the most intoxicated of the three.

They came to a stretch of dilapidated thatch-roof brothels from which there blared the kinds of songs you would hear at the cheapest bars. As if arriving at a familiar place, the three of them marched right into one of the brothels.

"Come on in."

"Welcome."

Two young women had appeared on the veranda. One wore her hair in a ponytail; the other was pregnant, her stomach tight as a drum.

P inadvertently took out his Haet'aes and lit up.

"Can I have one too?" said Ponytail, putting an arm around P's neck and touching her mouth to his cheek.

P, taken aback that a girl would ask for a cigarette, extended the pack toward her open palm.

"Bravo!" roared M and H, clapping in unison.

As they entered a room and sat down, they heard from the veranda a tray being loaded with liquor and snacks.

The pregnant woman was ignored by the men, but Ponytail went back and forth from M to H, and was fondled by both. Whenever they touched a sensitive spot she produced an exaggerated squeal of pain. P guessed from the way they bantered with the woman that they had been here before.

Compared with the drinking bowls, the kettle of rice wine they were served looked as tiny as an eyedropper. M readily accepted the bowl poured for him by Ponytail, and promptly requested a song from her. But instead of a song, she drained the bowl M had set down and put the empty vessel to his lips.

To P, the liquor tasted flat, like dishwater. Two bowls later, and his stomach was queasy. He lay down to try to settle it. H sat Ponytail down in his lap, became more animated, and began singing. He sang out of tune and off rhythm. No surprise there.

M had his way teasing the pregnant woman, then stole Ponytail from H and whispered something in her ear. The two of them shot P several glances while exchanging meaningful grins.

A short time later Ponytail approached P.

"He says tonight you and I ought to . . . What do you think?" she whispered.

"Sure, why not?" P gruffly responded.

"You're no fun at all!" She pinched P, then scurried back to M.

M whispered something else in her ear, and she returned to P.

"Spend the night, huh?"

"I just said I would."

"Promise?"

"Yeah."

"Shake."

"All right."

Four kettles of wine were served in all, but the three men had no more than a few bowls each. The rest was consumed by the women. Sloppy drunk by now, the two women were blathering.

Seeing H pay the bill, P rose to follow the others out. But M nudged him back inside while Ponytail pulled at his shirttail.

"You said you were going to spend the night."

P sprawled out on the floor.

"Where are you from?" he asked the girl, who had sat down beside him.

The girl named a provincial town.

"How long have you been in Seoul?"

"About a year."

P sat up, wanting to settle his stomach, now churning again, but the girl, thinking he was trying to leave, pushed him back down.

"How old are you?"

"Eighteen."

"Where are your parents?"

"You think I'd be doing this if my parents were still alive?"

"Why? Do you think what you're doing is bad?"

The girl snorted. "Of course. I'm a person too, you know."

"No kidding! I thought you were a fairy goddess, and here you turn out to be a person!"

"Oh, shut up!"

The woman looked askance at P, then smiled and pulled his head close.

"You *are* going to stay, aren't you?"

"If I do, my wife'll be after me with the yardstick."

"Then you can come here and live with me. . . . If you can scrape up eighty wŏn, I can pay off my debt to the madam—"

"Eighty wŏn?"

"Yeah."

"I'm leaving."

P tried to stand up again, but the girl wouldn't release him.

"Don't go. . . . I'm in love with you."

"Cut it out."

"I mean it!"

"Let go."

"No. I want you to stay. . . . Just give me a little money."

"Do I look like a man with money?"

"Well, I can hear it clinking somewhere."

Sure enough, the change in P's pocket had been jingling on and off since he had tried to get up.

"Sleep with me and give me some money. Just a teenie bit will do."

"How much?"

"Whatever you want. . . . Fifty chŏn, or twenty, even."

P shot to his feet as if a fire had been lit under him. He thrust a hand into his pocket, grabbed what was there, and threw it on the floor. The two one-wŏn notes and the nickel coins lay scattered in disarray.

"There you are—money!"

As P ran outside, tears gathered in his eyes.

7

P was no chaste, innocent young man. He had been married at fourteen, though being married at that age was like playing house. Later, during his student days in Tokyo, he had lived with another woman. Upon returning to Korea and finding a job, he had had an affair with an entertaining woman who had carried him to such heights as to make him oblivious to everything else. There had been romances with a couple of other women as well. But in his thirty years he had never spent a night at a high-class bordello, a brothel, or a cheap cathouse. This was a peculiarity of his. He would have nothing to do with any woman who had not captured his affection. On the other hand, once he took a liking to a woman, he would never look back; he would develop a profound passion for her, accept her completely, and give her his all. With P and women, it was all or nothing.

P realized that this was not the best way to get ahead in the world. And he also realized that this was useless stubbornness on his part, but he was powerless to correct it. And on that evening as well, he had no intention whatsoever of taking advantage of the young woman. Drunk, wanting only to settle his aching stomach, he was genuinely upset when she had said, "Whatever you want. . . . Fifty chŏn, or twenty, even."

The girl seemed dead set on degrading herself. P, always a keen observer of things, was not unaware that money made the world go around and that people fought for it like animals. But to offer up one's virtue for the grand sum of twenty chŏn—that was too much. P also knew that such a woman would attach no great importance to selling her virtue. Accordingly, P's interpretation was not based on any notion of immorality or some such thing. His viewpoint was more sophisticated than this.

However, "twenty, even"—that was going too far. The words had called up all sorts of thoughts in P. They were degrading and ugly, but they had caused tears to well up in his eyes. And then he had flung down all the money he had, some three wŏn, in front of her and run off like a man bereft of his senses.

Having left their drunken friend by himself, H and M had decided to wait for a time near an alley. Upon seeing P run toward them, they tried to make light of the situation.

"You owe us a drink."

"For making a man out of you at last."

P shook his head, thinking, an absent expression on his face. P was a man who as a rule abhorred hypocrisy that masqueraded as humanitarianism. And yet consider his behavior that evening. How was he to explain it? This question tormented him. He'd have to go hungry the following day because of the money he had thrown away. But it wasn't the loss of the money in and of itself that bothered him. The girl would have been content with twenty chŏn as the price of her virtue. Why had he declined her, and instead given her all his money? Why had tears gathered in his eyes?

8

P had a splitting headache and a queasy stomach, and he couldn't think straight. He parted abruptly from his two friends, without saying a proper good-bye, and returned to his room in Samch'ŏng-dong. All he wanted was to lie down.

No matter how untidy the room, and whether or not a fire had been lit to heat the floor, there was no place like home—especially when you were under the weather.

P buried himself in his unfolded bedding without removing his threadbare suit. The liquor went to his head once again, and any thoughts of undressing were completely forgotten. And so he fell asleep as he was.

Sometime later P was awakened by the suffering of his body. He had a raging thirst. But there was no water. That realization made him even thirstier.

He had no idea what time it was. The light in his room was still on. He heard no sign of life in the alleys and streets, nor did he hear the streetcar. There was only the occasional sound of an automobile horn, far away as if coming from another world.

If it were earlier, he could have knocked on the gate to the inner quarters and asked his landlady for water. But it would have been improper to do so at this late hour. In addition, because he hadn't been paying his rent on time, he had contrived to avoid facing the old woman. Therefore, he dared not knock on the gate. So he listened next for the creaking of the water peddler's carrying frame, but it was all in vain.

He grew thirstier and thirstier. His lips were parched, his mouth dry, and he almost expected to hear a dry, rustling sound from his throat. Even his innards felt desiccated.

His thirst was maddening. He could almost visualize the blue expanse of the Han River and water gushing from a faucet. P had often experienced hunger, but this was the first time he had suffered from thirst like this. Hunger might sap your strength and subdue your spirits, but extreme thirst would drive you to the verge of insanity.

He could go out and climb to the crest of Samch'ŏng-dong, where he would find rivulets and wells. But how was he to find his way on such a dark night, and in any event he would need a bucket on a rope to lower into a well.

Somehow he endured. In actuality it was less than sixty minutes, but to P it seemed like hours.

Finally he heard the water peddler and he rushed out to the community faucet. With no explanation he stuck his mouth to the faucet and took gulp after gulp of the cold water, while the peddler looked on in amazement. P gave the man a knowing wink and left him tsk-tsking in disapproval.

P had longed for the water more urgently than food, and now that he had drunk his fill, his hangover eased and his head began to clear. At long last, he removed his suit, tossed it aside, and snuggled back into bed. Sleep had deserted him, however, and he remained wide awake, the events of the previous night unfolding in his mind.

Mulling over these vexing recollections was like trying to eat something inedible. Try as he might to remove them, they were stuck fast in a corner of his mind, blemishes that refused to fade away. He wouldn't be able to put his mind at rest until he somehow made sense of those events.

A woman who names a mere twenty chŏn as the price of her virtue. . . .

Even now there were women who killed themselves after being deprived of their virtue. And on the other hand, there were women content to sell it for twenty chŏn.

If a woman's virtue was so precious that to lose it could lead her to suicide, then how was one to account for the reality of living, breathing women who would offer it up for twenty chŏn? And if it was so worthless that women would sell it for a pittance, then how to explain the women who dispose of themselves if robbed of it?

You couldn't credit both types of women with having good sense. But if you were to find fault with one of them, it would have to be the woman who killed herself. You couldn't blame the woman who sold her virtue for twenty chŏn.

Here was a girl who had been kicking around the cathouses for three years, ever since she was sixteen. Probably she had never received a proper perspective on life from anyone, not even a half-baked moral view.

A man drops by for a drink. If she can get him to order one more copper's worth of booze, the madam is that much richer for the night, the girl gets a compliment, and everyone is happy.

And if the man cozies up to her and asks for some you-know-what, that's fine too. She might get some pleasure out of it even if the man ejaculates too soon, and she's certain to come away with twenty chŏn at least.

There are enough people who encourage her to behave as she does, but no one to teach her it's wrong. Streetwalkers in general manage to put on a show of virtue, but at best it's only a front. To them, whoring is justifiable labor. But whether they will benefit from our pity and sympathy is quite doubtful.

Proper sexual mores have yet to be established in our time. The various currents of thought of our age have been crammed together in one generation. And so a woman's virtue is not simply a matter of black and white, of right and wrong.

A woman who is content with twenty chŏn as the price of her body for a night obviously has a different set of sexual mores than others, and so she doesn't lament the fact that she's degrading herself.

There's no compelling reason to blame the woman, nor are there grounds for sympathizing with her. And the woman is by no means pitiable.

Even the love of Jesus (whatever that is), however large or broad, is applicable only to a "pitiable person" and to a "sinner." There is no need for human pity or sympathy for a "nonpitiable," "nonsinning" cathouse girl in a red-light district.

Well, am I being too speculative? P thought. All right, so I am— and you can call me what you want. But all I'm doing is putting into words what this woman is carrying around inside her. And if the reality of it is abnormal, then putting the knife to it is a matter for the body politic to decide, on the basis of their historical consciousness; intellectual self-righteousness and moral indignation have no place in the argument. Even so, by throwing away three whole wŏn on that woman, you give her only a fleeting taste of joy.

"Wow, I hit the jackpot! . . . I knew that dream I had last night meant something, but this time my number really came up. Who would have thought it? . . . What kind of a dope would do that?"

Surely the girl's thoughts had stopped there. And who could possibly blame her?

P forced a bitter smile, then snorted.

"How ridiculous can you get. Me pity her? Does a blind man pity someone with cataracts?"

Tsk-tsking, P rolled over.

9

In the year 1934 there occurred in this world a miracle: P did not starve to death. For the past week, he had had no source of income. He hadn't found a job, had had no occasion to earn money. Nor had he gone door to door begging a spoonful of rice, or turned into a thief.

And yet he hadn't starved. He was thinner, true, but alive and kicking. If people with a life like P's were to disappear from the face of the earth, the laboring people might have an easier time of it.

If P had been a working man and not an intellectual among the petite bourgeoisie, he would have become a beggar or taken some other drastic measure. But P lacked such fortitude. Funny thing, though—he was still alive. Even so, the matter confronting him now —a matter more excruciating than death—gave him not a moment's respite.

The previous day, a letter had arrived saying that Ch'ang-sŏn, his son, was being sent to him. And then that day he had received a wire informing him the boy would arrive at Seoul Station the following morning.

The telegram had arrived around noontime. P suddenly seemed to perk up, and proceeded to scurry about scrounging money. He needed at least twenty wŏn. . . . By evening his going about had netted him barely fifteen.

With this money he went to Chongno and bought a small charcoal stove, a cooking pot, an aluminum bowl, chopsticks, spoons, and other basic household utensils. And on the way back up the hill to his rented room he stopped at a certain printing shop and visited A, the head typesetter, whom he had met while working for a magazine.

There was a young boy he wanted A to take on, P implored the man. It didn't have to be a paying job—just as long as the boy could learn a skill.

A tried this way and that to beg off, assuming P was trying to recommend the son of a close friend.

"Has he finished grade school?"

"Far from it," P frankly replied.

"How old is he?"

"Nine."

A was surprised. "Nine?"

"As long as he's going to learn a trade, I might as well start him out young."

"But good lord—that's too young. Who is he, anyway?"

"He's my boy," P said, feeling a slight flush on his face.

A looked even more surprised. He stared, slack-jawed, at P.

"What's wrong with that?" said P. "Is there a law that says I can't send my own son to work in a print shop?"

"You can't be serious."

"Why not?"

"Come on. You've got to be kidding. You're just saying it's your son so I'll take him in."

"Uh-uh. He's my boy."

"Then why aren't you getting him an education?"

"Learning the printing business is a kind of education."

"I still think you ought to send him to school."

"For one thing, I don't have the means. And even if I did send him to school, where would it get him?"

"I can't figure it out. Here's a guy like me breaking my back so I can put my boy through school, but a gentleman like yourself, who should know how to educate his son, sends him instead into apprenticeship."

"I went to school, and what use did it do me? My boy's going to have a different sort of education."

"Well, if you insist. I'll teach him the printing business inside out, and I'll treat him like my own son. . . . But good lord, he's so young it's pathetic."

"Don't I know it. I *am* his dad. But it'll do him good. . . ."

P thanked A for this favor, then left. He felt as if he had relieved himself of a great burden, and his mind was at ease. On his way home he stopped at a grain store and arranged for delivery of a sack of rice. He also bought several heads of Chinese cabbage. So far he had spent about five wŏn.

Of the remaining ten wŏn, he gave six to his elderly landlady. She broke out in a broad smile. Seizing this opportunity, P handed her the cabbages and asked if she would make kimchi. She gladly agreed. What's more, when P told her he was bringing his boy to live with him, she presented him with generous portions of radish kimchi and condiments such as soy sauce and soybean paste.

10

The next morning, P did something without precedent: he rose at the break of day. After a clumsy job of cooking rice over the charcoal stove, he set out for the railroad station.

In his letter, P's brother had written that he was having Ch'ang-sŏn tag along with S, a friend of P's who was traveling to Seoul. So much time had passed since P had seen his son, it was S whom he decided to watch for at the station. The train steamed in, panting, and began to spit out passengers. Sure enough, S stepped down from the coach, and there was Ch'ang-sŏn in tow.

The boy was wearing a student's black cotton uniform and a hat with a round tin school badge. P had no idea where these had come from. The boy also carried a cloth bundle on his back, and he held something that was wrapped up.

My boy! thought P. His face flushed in embarrassment, but for some reason he also pitied the boy.

S was looking all about, his hands full with baggage, and when he saw P approach he shouted in delight. Ch'ang-sŏn removed his hat and bowed stiffly, the way a student would. P wasn't at all happy to see that his face resembled his mother's people even more than it had when he was four or five—the last time P had seen him.

"How have you been?" S asked.

"Oh, can't complain. . . . I'm afraid we've put you to a lot of trouble with all that baggage."

"Oh, what are you talking about. . . . Your boy's not very old, but he's got a good head on his shoulders." S turned to Ch'ang-sŏn. "You remember your father?"

The boy was too shy to answer.

P led them onto a pedestrian overpass.

"His mom's mother bought him the uniform, rice cakes, everything," said S. "She came all the way to your brother's. . . . And when we left yesterday, she came with us to the station. . . . All sorts of reminders she wants me to pass on to you."

P's long-standing resentment toward his mother-in-law resurfaced as S conveyed the disagreeable messages.

"Who asked her to worry? . . . He's my boy, and I'll take good care of him. If she thinks she's going to keep an eye on me. . . ."

"Well, you know how it is with old folks. . . . She said if it really gets difficult taking care of him all by yourself, away from home, she can always take him in. . . ."

"What's she talking about? They don't have anything to do with him. . . . No way they'll get custody of the boy. I fought like hell to get him back that time, and I did it for a reason."

P grew angrier, suspecting his former wife was behind all of this. He felt like having the boy remove his uniform, then throwing it away, but thought better of it.

11

For the first time in his life, P alone was providing for his son.

It was the night Ch'ang-sŏn arrived. P heard the boy's regular breathing from where he slept on the warm part of the floor. He was probably sinking into a lonely dream, P thought. And then an affection he had never felt before welled up inside him.

Early the next morning he took Ch'ang-sŏn to the print shop and entrusted him to A. With a heavy heart he turned back for home. You might have heard him mutter to himself then:

"Looks like my ready-made life has finally found an owner."

The Photograph and the Letter

Kim Tong-in

Kim Tong-in (1900–1951) was born in Pyongyang. Like many other young Korean intellectuals, he received his higher education in Japan. It was there in 1919 that he and other advocates of an art-for-art's-sake literature founded the influential but short-lived journal *Ch'angjo* (Creation). In so doing, Kim and his colleagues took a stand against the didactic literature of social engagement championed by Yi Kwang-su—a contest that in various incarnations has survived in Korea to this day.

A brilliant, iconoclastic aesthete, Kim was one of the most public figures of the first generation of modern Korean writers. At the same time, he is one of the fathers of modern Korean fiction. He helped make the literary language more colloquial, and, perhaps influenced by the European writers he read in Japanese translation—Zola, Maupassant, and Turgenev, among others—he pioneered the tradition of realism that was to become paramount in twentieth-century Korean fiction. He also wrote historical novels and was a prolific essayist and critic.

"The Photograph and the Letter" (Sajin kwa p'yŏnji), first published in *Wŏlgan maeshin* in 1934, was inspired, according to a postscript by the author, by Hungarian writer Ferenc Molnar's "The Last Afternoon." It is an interesting variation on the battle of the sexes, one that appears to have few parallels in Korean fiction of the 1930s.

H e saw her again that day. She was sitting the same way, in the same place, as if waiting for someone.

A seaside resort—

She had been there the day before, and the day before that, sitting in that familiar way. Her mind seemed to be elsewhere. She must have been in her mid-twenties, and to all appearances she seemed married. At a seaside resort, it's only natural that people should enjoy themselves in the water. But not this woman. Every day she sat in the same place, looking out to sea.

His curiosity aroused, young L often went out of his way to walk past her.

"Nice weather," he finally ventured.

"Yes, isn't it?"

The teeth beneath the scarlet lips seemed to dance. They were so white you might think them transparent.

"Did you come here to swim?"

"Mainly just to relax. . . ."

Thus did L and the woman pave the way for a relationship.

"Would you care to take a walk?"

"All right."

"Why don't we have lunch first?"

"Fine."

The two of them became better acquainted. And then one day L visited the woman—it turned out her name was Hye-gyŏng—in her room at the inn. There on the wall was a man's photograph.

"Who's that?" L asked a bit apprehensively, pointing to the photo.

"My husband."

"Is that so? He's a fine-looking man."

L spent a sleepless night. The photo he had seen in Hye-gyŏng's room kept flickering before his eyes.

Normally there are several ways you could describe such a man—"handsome," "good-looking," "a commanding presence." But never in his life had L seen such a good-looking man as the subject of the photo. He was attractive not in the sense that a young woman is pretty but in a noble, dignified way characteristic of a man. Perhaps such a man could have existed in Greek sculpture, but you couldn't very well picture him in flesh and blood. His handsome looks were matchless.

L himself was acknowledged handsome, both by himself and by others. He was confident he wouldn't appear at a disadvantage wherever he might be presented. But he could only pound his chest in frustration when he compared himself with the man in the photo. For he realized then that he was no better than the men who appeared in pictures in the sample books of tailors or the men who modeled hats in advertisements. His looks lacked a classic, refined elegance. To compare him and the man in the photo would be as fruitless as comparing the ocean and a puddle of water.

Why the warm reception for the likes of me if she has such a fine-looking husband? L wondered.

But this didn't mean he had to give her up. As long as she seemed to receive him favorably, speculation should remain speculation, and his affair with the woman should continue.

Before meeting Hye-gyŏng the following day, L did everything he could to improve his grooming, combing his hair for almost half an hour, shaving three or four times, and knotting his tie a dozen times before he was satisfied with the look. And he immediately wired home and had his entire wardrobe sent to the resort.

He began wearing three different outfits a day, changing at midday and again in the afternoon. In short, L went to great pains to improve his appearance.

There ensued a fierce competition between L and the man in the photo. For L, of course, this involved seizing upon any means to improve his looks even the slightest bit. By virtue of this, L, already known as a handsome man, was able to better his appearance day by day. At the same time, he gradually became more deeply involved with Hye-gyŏng.

The swimming season came to an end, and the people who had flocked to the ocean returned to the cities.

Hye-gyŏng likewise returned to the city, as did L. And their affair continued as before.

"Hye-gyŏng."

"Yes?"

"Where is he now?"

"Traveling in Italy."

"Would you introduce me to him when he returns?"

"Really—now why are you always thinking about him? When he comes back I'll have to return to him. No offense, but you're a temporary companion—someone to talk with while he's away. . . ."

What! L felt intensely rebellious. I'll make myself better-looking than he is, he resolved. I'll make it impossible for her to leave me, even when he returns. And so, day by day, with no letup, L groomed himself ever more fastidiously.

His situation filled him with an indescribable anxiety. At present, he clearly monopolized Hye-gyŏng's affection. But he realized that with the return of her husband, his days would be numbered. He had no way of knowing, though, when she would leave him. Every now and then, when he and Hye-gyŏng were promenading along Chongno or Chungmuro, he would see his reflection in a show window. Although the image made him even more confident that he was handsome enough to be fit company for Hye-gyŏng, his mind was ever unsettled by the photograph he had seen in her room at the seaside.

L would be second to none in any ordinary contest of looks, but when it came to the man in the photo, he couldn't measure up to his heels. When he imagined Hye-gyŏng and that man walking down the street arm in arm, he burned with jealousy and shook his fist over and over. He couldn't let himself lose to that man. He would use any means to win. Thus resolved, L proceeded to devote still more attention to his appearance.

Autumn passed, then winter. Hye-gyŏng's husband still hadn't returned from Italy by the following spring, and her affair with L continued.

One spring day, Hye-gyŏng called on L. L entertained her until the evening, and after she left, L discovered a piece of paper on the floor where she had been sitting. He picked it up and saw it was a letter. Hye-gyŏng must have dropped it by mistake.

L opened the letter. It was to Hye-gyŏng from a friend of hers, and it read in part as follows:

"How happy you must be to have your husband back from Europe. The day after tomorrow we'd like to meet the two of you at the theater. After the play, we can have some refreshments—it's been so long since we've done that. Be sure to come. We'll see you then."

L's heart dropped: so, he's finally returned! And now, of course, Hye-gyŏng would leave L and go back to her husband, as she herself had declared. That explained why she had become a bit cool toward him lately. And now he would be discarded like a pair of old shoes. L trembled in indignation at the thought of Hye-gyŏng sitting beside that classically elegant gentleman in the theater.

Two days later, L also went to the theater. He couldn't have explained why this was necessary, but he felt compelled to do so at any cost.

He spotted Hye-gyŏng immediately. But where was her husband, that classically elegant gentleman he had seen in the photo in Hye-gyŏng's seaside room? L scoured the theater but could find no one who resembled the man in the photograph.

On the contrary, sitting next to Hye-gyŏng watching the play was a man old enough to be her father, a man who appeared to be about fifty. His bearded face was as hairy as a wild animal's; his eyes were almost nonexistent, and his nose was small and squashed. There could have been but few men in all the world as ugly as the man sitting with Hye-gyŏng absorbed in the play.

L was bewildered. This man was too ugly to be the father of a beauty such as Hye-gyŏng. A short time later, L inquired about the man to a mutual acquaintance. The ugly, evil-looking creature was not Hye-gyŏng's father, but her husband.

You can imagine L's consternation. At first he refused to believe it. It was impossible!

Later, though, after the play when the spectators were leaving, L happened to pass by the couple and overhear the ugly creature speak to Hye-gyŏng:

"All I got out of that stupid play was a backache. Let's hurry up and eat with your friends and then go home."

L now had no choice but to accept the truth.

L's love for Hye-gyŏng immediately soured. When he recalled how she had tittered in the embrace of that ugly creature, the very thought of seeing her again became distasteful.

L stopped grooming himself. Rebelling against the knowledge that the man in the photograph was Hye-gyŏng's husband, he had attempted to rival the man by paying minute attention to his grooming. But if that ugly, hairy creature was indeed Hye-gyŏng's husband, then L could have stopped bathing for ten years, could have let his hair grow for three years, could have forsworn shaving for a month, and he would still have been a thousand times better-looking.

L had once said that his face would itch if he didn't shave three times a day, but now he had no qualms about going around town with a dark stubble beneath his nose.

The last afternoon: Hye-gyŏng and L met at a secluded place to conclude their affair and bid farewell to each other.

"L."

"Yes?"

"Here are all the letters you wrote me. I'd like you to take them back."

L silently accepted the bundle of letters.

"All right, then, I wish you well. Why don't you leave in that direction, and I'll go this way. . . ."

As she was about to leave, L seemed to come to his senses.

"Hye-gyŏng."

"Yes?"

"One last question."

"And what is that?"

"Remember the photo you once showed me at the seaside? You said it was your husband. . . ."

Hye-gyŏng smiled.

"Yes, I did, didn't I?"

"Who was he, anyway?"

Hye-gyŏng laughed.

"Why do you ask? I don't know who he is, either. I bought the photo at a studio in Shanghai for a couple of taels, or something like that. He's probably some Chinese actor, or maybe an aristocrat."

"Shanghai? Two taels? But then—why—?"

"Why did I tell you it was my husband?"

"Exactly."

"You still don't know? Well, you must know this much anyway: after I showed you the photo and said it was my husband, you liked me quite a bit more. And as long as I'm having an affair with someone, I prefer a better-looking gentleman. And so the photo was a tactic. Please forgive me. There was no harm intended. To be honest, after you saw the photo, you became three or four times better-looking."

L was astonished. He tried to reply, but nothing came out. Finally he managed to say something.

"In other words, I was like a dog that high-class ladies drag around, give a bath to, and sprinkle with perfume?"

"That's going a bit far, isn't it?" she laughed.

"All right, let's leave it at that. It was an ingenious tactic, all right. But why is the ending so anticlimactic? Why didn't you carry your idea through to the end?

"I don't follow. Could you be more specific?"

"Sure. Remember the time you visited me, and left a letter behind by mistake? Because of that letter, I was able to have a look at your husband. I saw that hairy—no offense—creature. That creature—"

"Watch your language."

"Do you mean to say that creature isn't your husband?"

"He is my husband. And what of it?"

"All right, then. It was because I saw that creature that our relationship cooled. Before, when I saw that cheap photo, I tried and tried to improve my looks. But from the time I saw that hairy—no offense—creature, I gave up. If I didn't shave for a month, I'd still be a thousand times better-looking than that hairy thing. In other words, it appears your efforts have amounted to failure, all because you couldn't safeguard a letter."

Hye-gyŏng looked up at L and smiled.

"L."

"Yes?"

"Listen to me. To hear you talk, a person would think you didn't have much experience with women."

"Why do you say that?"

"Well, do you think a married woman who has the presence of mind to carry out an affair would go around misplacing letters?"

"Are you saying you've never misplaced a letter?"

"No, I'm not."

"Well, then?"

"Obviously, I left a letter behind that time I visited you. But it wasn't a mistake; I did it on purpose. I planted the letter."

"What are you talking about? You left a letter behind, and that caused me to go to the theater, and at the theater I saw that creature—no offense—and you're telling me the whole thing was planned?"

"Of course."

"If that's the case, then when I saw that creature, I stopped grooming myself, and in addition we became estranged—and you planned it all?"

"Now listen to me, and don't get so excited. Yes, it was all a plan."

"But why?"

"Oh, why do you men have to be so slow? To put it simply, that photo I showed you at the ocean, I've already shown to someone else. In other words, even if you stopped grooming yourself entirely, it wouldn't matter to me at all. Now do you understand?"

L remained silent.

"Remember one thing, L. With just a letter and a photo, we can manipulate men as we wish. From now on, if you happen upon a photo of someone, or a misplaced letter, don't take it for what it

seems. . . . Gracious, what a frightening glare. Since this is the final
scene, let's go our separate ways with a smile instead. We can still be
friends. . . . Well, as I said earlier, why don't you go that way and I'll
go this way. It's almost time for me to see this other man I showed
the photo to, and I'm in a bit of a rush. And so, farewell."

A twilit street—
    Humming, the woman walked effortlessly down the street.
    L, bid by the woman to leave in the opposite direction, didn't stir.
Like a man bereft of his senses, he continued to stare after her.

A twilit street.
    A desolate street.

Mama and the Boarder

CHU YO-SŎP

Chu Yo-sŏp was one of modern Korea's most versatile men of letters, a writer of poetry, fiction, and essays, editor of the journal *Shindonga*, and later in life head of the Korean Literary Translators Association. Born in Pyongyang in 1902, he studied briefly in Japan, then returned to Korea after the Japanese suppression of the March 1, 1919, Independence Movement. After making his literary debut in 1921, he spent several years in China, obtaining a university degree in Shanghai in 1927.

Most of Chu's stories from the 1920s depict the lower classes in Shanghai. "Illyŏkkŏgun" (Rickshaw man, 1925) is representative. After a hiatus of almost ten years in which he published only a single story, Chu returned to literary life in 1935 with the story that follows (Sarang sonnim kwa ŏmŏni), published originally in the journal *Chogwang*. His signature story, it marks a profound departure from the gritty stories of the previous decade. Chu published sporadically after Liberation and the Korean War, his last story appearing shortly before his death in 1972.

1

My name is Pak Ok-hŭi, and this year I'll be six years old. There's just two of us in my family—me and my mother, who's the prettiest woman in the whole wide world. Woops—I almost left out my uncle.

He's in middle school, and what with him gallivanting about, he's hardly ever around except for meals. A lot of the time we won't see hide nor hair of him for days on end. So can you blame me if I forgot him for a second?

My mother is so beautiful, there's really no one else like her in the world. She'll be twenty-three this year, and she's a widow. I'm not sure what a widow is, but since the neighbors call me the "widow's girl," I figure she must be a widow. The other kids all have fathers, but not me. Maybe that has something to do with it.

2

According to Grandma, my father passed away a month before I came along. He and my mother had only been married for a year. My father was from somewhere far off, and he came here to teach school. So when they were married my mother stayed here and they bought this house (it's the one next to Grandma's). They weren't here even a year when my father suddenly died. Because he passed away before I came along, I never saw him in person. And I can't picture him no matter how hard I try. A couple of times I've seen what's supposed to be his picture, and he sure was good-looking. If he was still alive, he'd definitely be the most handsome father in the whole world. It's just not fair that I never got a chance to see him. It's been quite a while since I've seen his picture. My mother used to keep it on her desk, but every time Grandma came she'd tell her to put it away. So now it's gone and I don't know where. Once I came home and saw my mother sneaking a look at something from the chest. When she heard me she hid it in the chest real quick like. I guess maybe that was his picture.

My father left us something to live on before he passed away. One day last summer—actually I guess it was almost fall—Mother took me to a little mountain a few miles away to see it. At the bottom of the mountain was a house with a straw roof. We scooped up some chestnuts, then went inside and had some chicken soup. She said this was our land. We get enough rice and such from it, so that we don't have to go hungry. But there's no money for meat and vegetables or goodies. So Mother takes in sewing. That's where she gets the money to buy herring and eggs, and candy for me.

So there was really only my mother and me. But since Father's den was now empty, my mother decided to get some use out of it and at the same time have someone to run errands for her. And that's how Little Uncle got to live with us.

3

One day Mother said she was going to send me to kindergarten in the spring. You should have seen how proud I was with my playmates.

But as soon as I came home from playing, I saw Big Uncle (I mean the big brother of Uncle who lived in my father's room) sitting there talking with someone I'd never seen before.

"Ok-hŭi," Big Uncle called me. "Ok-hŭi, come here and say hello to this man."

I felt bashful and just stayed where I was.

This man I'd never seen before said to Big Uncle, "What a lovely girl—is she your niece?"

"Yes, she's my sister's daughter. . . . She wasn't born yet when Kyŏng-sŏn died. She's his only child."

"Ok-hŭi, come here, hmm?" said the stranger. "Those eyes are just like your father's."

"Ok-hŭi, you're a big girl now—why so shy? Come here and say hi. This man's an old friend of your father. He's moving into your father's room here, so you'd better say hi and get to know each other."

The stranger was moving into my father's room? That made me very happy. So I went up to the man, gave him my best bow, then ran out to the inner courtyard. I could hear Big Uncle and the man laughing.

I went into Mother's room, and right off, I tugged on her sleeve.

"Mother!" I said. I was still all excited. "Big Uncle brought a man here! He's moving into the guest room!"

"That's right."

I guess she already knew about it.

"When's he moving in?"

"Today."

"Yippee!"

I started clapping my hands, but Mother grabbed them.

"Now what's all this fuss?"

"But what about Little Uncle?"

"He'll stay there too."

"You mean the two of them together?"

"Umm-hmm."

"In the same room?"

"Why not? They can close the sliding partition, and then they'll each have a space."

I didn't know who this new uncle was. But he treated me nice, and right away I took a shine to him. Later I heard the grown-ups say he was a friend of my father ever since they were little. He went off somewhere to study, and just came back, and he got assigned to teach at a school here. He's also a friend of Big Uncle, and since the boarding house rooms in our neighborhood aren't too clean, they arranged for him to stay in our guest room. Best of all, the board money he paid us would give us some of the extras we wanted so much.

This new uncle had a whole bunch of picture books. Whenever I went in his room, he sat me in his lap and showed them to me. Every once in a while he gave me a piece of candy. Once I sneaked into his room after my lunch. He was just starting his meal. I sat down without a peep to watch him eat.

"Now what kind of side dish does Ok-hŭi like best?" he asked me.

Boiled eggs, I told him. Well, wouldn't you know it, he had some on his meal tray. He gave me one and told me to help myself. I peeled it and started eating.

"Uncle, which side dish do *you* like most?"

He smiled for a moment.

"Boiled eggs."

I was so happy I clapped my hands.

"Gee, just like me. I'm going to tell Mother."

I got up to go, but the uncle grabbed me.

"Oh, don't do that."

But once I make up my mind there's no stopping me. So I ran out to the inner courtyard.

"Mother! Mother!" I yelled. "The new uncle's favorite side dish is boiled eggs, just like me!"

"Now don't make such a fuss," Mother said. And she gave me her please-don't-do-that look.

But the fact that the new uncle liked eggs turned out quite nice for me. Because Mother started buying eggs in bunches from then on. When the old woman with the eggs came around, Mother bought ten or twenty at a time. She boiled them up and put two of them in the uncle's place at mealtime, and then she almost always gave me one. And that wasn't all. Sometimes when I visited the uncle, he'd get an egg or two from his drawer for me to eat. After that I ate eggs to my heart's content. I really liked the uncle. But Little Uncle grumbled sometimes. I guess he didn't take to the new uncle too well. And he didn't like the way he had to run errands for him—that was probably the real reason. Once I saw Little Uncle arguing with Mother.

"Now look," said Mother, "don't you be running off again. Why can't you wait in his room? You'll have to take him his dinner tray when he comes back."

Little Uncle made a face.

"Aw shit, whenever yours truly has something to do, it seems like he's always late for his meal."

"Well, what can I do? I need *somebody* to take him his meal."

"Can't you do it yourself, Sister? Times have changed. Why do you have to be so old-fashioned when it comes to men?"

Suddenly Mother's face was all red. She didn't say anything, but you should have seen the look she gave Little Uncle.

Little Uncle gave a laugh to lighten the mood, and went out to the guest room.

4

I started kindergarten, and our teacher taught us songs. She also taught us dancing. She was real good at the pedal organ. The organ was a little thing compared with the one at the Protestant church we went to, but it still made a nice sound. Then I remembered seeing something that looked just like our kindergarten organ sitting at the far end of our room. So as soon as I got home that day I pulled Mother over to it and asked:

"Mama, this is an organ, isn't it?"

Mother smiled.

"That's right. How did you know?"

"It's just like the one at kindergarten. Can you play it, too, Mother?"

I had to ask, because I'd never seen her playing it. But she didn't say a word.

"Try it, Mother—please?"

Her face got kind of cloudy.

"Your father bought this organ for me. I haven't even raised the lid since he passed on. . . ."

She looked like she was about to burst into tears at any second, so I changed the subject.

"Can I have a candy, Mommy?"

And then I led her back to the near end of our room.

Before I knew it, a month had passed since the uncle moved in. I stopped by his room almost every day. Once in a while Mother would tell me it was no good pestering him like that. But if you want to know the truth, I didn't pester him one little bit. It was the uncle who pestered *me*.

"Ok-hŭi, those eyes of yours look just like your father's. But maybe that cute little nose came from your mother. And that little mouth, too. Am I right? Is your mother pretty like you?"

"Uncle, you're silly! Haven't you seen her face?"

But when I answered him that way, he didn't say a word.

"Shall we go in and see Mother?" I asked, taking the uncle by the sleeve.

You should have seen how strongly he reacted.

"No, we'd better not—I'm busy now," he said, pulling me back the other way. But he really didn't seem all that busy, because he didn't ask me to leave. Instead he patted my head and gave me a kiss on the cheek—he wouldn't let me go. And he kept asking me such funny questions: "Who made you this pretty jacket? . . . Do you sleep with your Mama at night?" He made me feel like I was something special to him. But when Little Uncle came back, the new uncle's attitude changed all of a sudden. He stopped asking me about these various things, and he wouldn't hug me tight. Instead he got all proper and showed me a picture book. Maybe he was afraid of Little Uncle.

Whatever the reason, Mother scolded me for pestering the uncle. And every once in a while she kept me in our room after dinner. But pretty soon she'd get caught up in her sewing, and I'd try to sneak out. When she heard the door slide open she'd wake up and catch me. But she never got mad at me. "Come here so I can fix your hair," she'd say. And then she'd pull me inside and make my braids nice and pretty again. "We want your hair to look nice. What's the uncle going to think if you go around just the way you are?" Or she'd braid my hair and say, "Now what did you do to your jacket?" and make me change into a new one.

5

One Saturday the new uncle asked me if I wanted to go for a short hike. I was so happy I said yes right away.

"Go inside and ask your mother first," he said.

Gee, he's right, I thought.

Mother said it was okay. But before she let me go she scrubbed my face and did my braids over. Then she hugged me real tight.

"Now don't be too late," she said in a loud voice. I'll bet the uncle heard it too.

We climbed to the top of a hill and looked down for a while at the train station, but no trains were running. I had fun pulling the long blades of grass and pinching the uncle while he was lying on the ground. Later when we were on our way down the hill, the uncle was holding my hand and we ran into some of the kids from my kindergarten.

"Look, Ok-hŭi went somewhere with her dad," one of them said. This girl didn't know my father had passed away. My face got hot, maybe because I was thinking just then how nice it would be if the uncle really was my father. I wanted so much to be able to call him "Papa," even if it was just once. You don't know how much I enjoyed walking home through the alleys with the uncle holding my hand.

We arrived at the front gate.

"Uncle, I wish you were my papa," I blurted out.

The uncle turned red as a tomato and gently prodded me.

"You shouldn't say things like that," he said almost in a whisper. His voice was shaking an awful lot. The only thing I could think of was that he must have gotten angry. So I went inside without saying anything more.

Mother gave me a hug and said, "Where did you go?"

But instead of answering I started to sniffle.

"Ok-hŭi, what happened? What's wrong, honey?"

All I could do was cry.

6

The next day was Sunday, and Mother and I got ready to go to church. While she was changing I poked my head inside the guest room to see if the uncle was still in a bad mood. He was sitting at his desk writing something. I tiptoed in, and when he looked up he had a big grin on his face. That smile made me feel easy again. Now I knew he wasn't mad anymore. The uncle looked me over from head to toe.

"Ok-hŭi, where are you going all prettied up like that?"

"I'm going to church with Mama."

"Is that so?" said the uncle. For a moment he looked like he was thinking about something. "Which church?"

"The one right over there."

"Oh? Over where?"

Just then I heard Mother's soft voice calling me. I hurried back to our room, but on the way I turned around to look at the uncle. His face was red and angry again. I couldn't figure out why he was getting mad so easy these days.

We took our seats in the church and sang a hymn, and then there was a prayer. During the prayer I got to wondering if maybe the uncle was there too. So I sat up and looked over at the men's side of the aisle. And what do you know—there he was. But he wasn't praying with his eyes closed, like the other grown-ups. His eyes were open, just like us kids, and he was looking around every which way. I recognized the uncle right away, but I guess he didn't recognize me. Because even when I gave him a big smile he didn't smile back; instead he had a faraway look in his eyes. So I waved at him. But the uncle ducked his head real quick. Mother finally saw me waving, and pulled me back with both hands. I put my mouth to her ear.

"The uncle's here," I whispered.

When Mother heard this she gave a little jump and put her hand over my mouth. Then she sat me in front of her and pushed my head down. This time, I noticed it was Mother who was red as a tomato.

Well, church that day was a big flop. Mother was mad till the end of the service. All she did was look straight ahead at the pulpit. She didn't look down and give me a smile once in a while like she usually did. When I looked over at the men's side to see the uncle, he didn't once look back at me but just sat there mad. Mother didn't look at me either but just kept grabbing me and pulling me down—it was too much. Why was everyone cross with me? It got to the point where I felt like bawling out loud. But then I noticed our kindergarten teacher not too far away, and I managed to keep from crying, though it wasn't easy.

7

When I started going to kindergarten, Little Uncle walked me there and back. But after a few days I could do it all by myself. When I got back home Mother was always waiting for me at the side gate. (Our house has two gates—the side gate and the gate to the uncle's room, and Mother only used the side gate.) When Mother saw me, she'd run over and hug me and we'd go inside.

But one day, Mother wasn't there, and I didn't know why. I thought she'd probably gone to see Grandmother, but still, here I was back home with no one waiting for me. I thought it was awful of her to leave the house like that. Well, I decided I'd give Mother a hard time. Just then I heard her voice outside the gate.

"Goodness, I wonder if she's home already."

I ran inside, taking my shoes with me so she wouldn't know I was there. Then I hid in the storage loft. I could hear Mother's voice right outside in the yard.

"Ok-hŭi—Ok-hŭi, aren't you home yet? . . . Hmm, I guess not."

And then it sounded like she went out again. I thought this was fun, and started giggling.

But then a little later the whole house suddenly became noisy. First I heard Mother, then Grandmother, then Little Uncle.

"Well, I was home all day, Mother, until I realized I didn't have any cookies for Ok-hŭi, and that's when I visited you. And now something's happened." That was Mother speaking.

"And at the kindergarten they said she'd left a good twenty minutes ago. Gracious, do you suppose on the way home? . . ." That was Grandmother.

"I'll go out and look for her. Little troublemaker must have gone somewhere." That was Little Uncle.

Then Mother started crying, and Grandmother said something I couldn't make out. I told myself it was time to stop the game, but then I thought, "I've got to get even with her for getting mad at me last Sunday at church," and I lay down. The loft was stuffy and hot, and before I knew it I had drifted off to sleep.

I have no idea how long I slept. But when I woke up I'd completely forgotten about going into the loft. What was I doing lying in such a strange place? It was kind of dark, it was cramped, it was hot. . . . Suddenly I was scared, and I started bawling. And just as suddenly I heard Mother scream close by, and the door to the loft was yanked open. Mother rushed inside, took me in her arms, and lifted me down.

"You little devil!"

She spanked me several times, and that made me cry even louder. Mother pulled me close, and then she started crying too.

"Ok-hŭi, Ok-hŭi, it's all right now, Mama's here. Don't cry, Ok-hŭi.

You're all there is, the only thing Mama lives for. I don't need anything else. You're my only hope. Don't cry, Ok-hŭi, don't cry, hmm?"

While she kept telling me this, she couldn't stop crying herself.

"Little brat—the devil must have gotten into her," said Grandmother. "What made her hide in the loft?"

"What a lousy day," said Little Uncle. He got up and went out.

8

On my way home from kindergarten the next day I got to thinking about how I had made Mother cry so much when I hid in the loft. I felt so ashamed. "I want to make her happy today," I thought. "Now what could I bring her?" Then I remembered the vase on our teacher's desk. It had some beautiful red flowers, though I didn't know their name. They weren't forsythias and they weren't azaleas. I could recognize those flowers, and I knew they'd already bloomed and gone by. The ones in the vase must have come from across the ocean. I knew my mother adored flowers. How happy she would be if I brought her some of those red ones.

And so I went back to my classroom. Goodie! No one was there. Teacher must have gone somewhere, because she wasn't around either. I snitched a couple of the flowers and ran out.

Mother was waiting near the gate, and she took me in her arms.

"Where did you get those lovely flowers?" she asked, taking the flowers and smelling them.

I didn't know what to say. I was too ashamed to tell her I'd brought them from kindergarten. What could I tell her? Somehow I thought of a little fib.

"The uncle in the guest room told me to give them to you," I blurted.

Mother was real flustered. It was like my words had startled her. And then all at once her face turned redder than the flowers. Her fingers holding the flowers began to tremble. She looked around like she was thinking of something scary.

"Ok-hŭi, you shouldn't have taken them." Her voice was shaking so much. Mother loved flowers, and so for her to get so mad over these flowers was the last thing I expected. I told myself it was a good thing I'd fibbed about the uncle and not told her I'd brought the flowers myself. I didn't know why she was mad, but as long as she was going to be mad at someone, I was glad it was the uncle and not me. A little while later Mother led me inside.

"Ok-hŭi, I don't want you to tell a soul about these flowers, hmm?"

"All right."

I thought Mother would throw the flowers away, but instead she put them in a vase and kept them on top of the organ. There they slept night after night, and finally they withered. Mother then cut off the stems and saved the flowers between the pages of her hymnbook.

That night I was back in the uncle's lap reading a picture book. Suddenly I could feel the uncle tense up. He was trying to hear something. I tried too.

It was an organ!

For sure the sound was floating out from our room. It must be Mama, I thought. I jumped up and ran to our room.

It was dark there, but it was around the time of the full moon, and silvery light filled half the room, making it light as day. There was Mother, all dressed in white and very calm, playing the organ.

I was six years old, but this was the first time I had seen Mother play the organ. She played better than our kindergarten teacher. I went up beside her, but she didn't budge and kept on playing. I guess she didn't know I was there. A little later Mother began singing to the music. I didn't know she had such a beautiful voice. Her voice was much lovelier than our teacher's, and she sang better too. I stood there quietly listening to Mother sing. It was a beautiful song. I felt it was coming down to me on a silver thread from Starland.

But then Mother's voice got a tiny bit shaky. The sound of the organ got shaky too. The song grew softer and softer, and finally it was gone. And then the organ stopped too. Mother stood up, still real calm, and gave me a pat on the head. The next instant, she took me in her arms and we went out on the veranda. Mother gave me a big hug, not saying anything. In the full moonlight her face was pure white. "She's a real angel," I told myself.

Two streams of tears were running down Mother's white cheeks. The sight of those tears made me want to cry myself.

"Mother, why are you crying?" Now I was sniffling too.

"Ok-hŭi."

"Hmm?"

She didn't say anything for a minute. And then, "Ok-hŭi, having you is enough."

"Yes, Mama."
But that's all she said.

9

The next evening I was playing in the uncle's room when I began to
feel sleepy. As I was about to leave, the uncle took a white envelope
from his drawer and gave it to me.

"Ok-hǔi, would you take this to your Mama? It's last month's
room and board."

I took the envelope to Mother. But when I handed it to her, she
turned pale. She looked even whiter than the night before, when we
were sitting on the veranda in the moonlight. She looked anxious,
like she didn't know what to do with the envelope.

"He said it's for last month's room and board."

"Oh." When Mother heard this she looked startled, as if she had
just woke up. The next instant, her face wasn't white as a sheet of
paper any longer; now it was red. Her trembling fingers reached
inside the envelope and pulled out several paper bills. A tiny little
smile formed on her lips, and she breathed a sigh. But then something else must have surprised her, because she tensed up, and the
next minute her face was white again and her lips were trembling. I
looked at what Mother was holding, and beside the paper money
there was a piece of white paper folded into a square.

Mother looked like she didn't know what to do. But then she
seemed to make up her mind. She bit her lip, unfolded the paper real
carefully, and read it. Of course, I didn't know what was written
there, but I could see Mother's face turn red right away and then
back to pale again. Her hands weren't just trembling, they were posi-
tively shaking, enough to make the paper rustle.

A good while later Mother folded the paper back into a square
and put it in the envelope along with the money. She dropped the
envelope into her sewing basket. And then she sat down and just
stared at the light bulb like someone who had lost her senses. I could
see her chest heaving. I thought maybe she was sick or something, so
I ran over and snuggled into her lap.

"Mama, can we go to sleep?"

Mama kissed me on the cheek. But her lips were so hot. They felt
just like a stone that's been warmed up in a fire.

We went to sleep, and after a while I half woke up and reached out for Mother. I was in the habit of doing this from time to time. I'd reach out half asleep and feel her soft skin. Then I'd go back to sleep. But this time she wasn't there.

Mama wasn't there! Suddenly I was afraid. I opened my eyes wide and looked all around. The light was off, but the moon shone full in the yard, and enough of its light came into the room so I could see things just a little. At the far end of the room was the small chest with Father's clothes. Sometimes Mother took them out and felt them. Now the chest was open, and the white clothing was piled on the floor. Next to it was Mother in her night clothes, half sitting and half leaning against the chest. Her head was up but her eyes were closed. I could see her lips move. She looked like she was praying. I sat up and crawled over and wormed myself into her lap.

"Mama, what are you doing?"

She stopped whispering, opened her eyes, and looked at me for the longest time.

"Ok-hŭi."

"Hmm?"

"Let's go back to bed."

"All right. But you too, Mama."

"Yes. Mama too."

Somehow her voice gave me a chill.

One at a time Mother picked up Father's clothes, gently smoothed them with the palm of her hand, and returned them to the chest. When the last one was in, she shut the chest and locked it. Then she gathered me up and back we went to bed.

"Mama, aren't we going to pray first?"

Mother didn't let a night go by without praying when she put me to bed. The only prayer I knew was the Lord's Prayer. I had no idea what the words meant, but from following along with Mother, I knew it by heart. But then I remembered that for some reason Mother had forgotten to pray the night before. I felt like reminding her then, but she looked so sad that I kept quiet and ended up falling asleep without saying anything.

"All right, let's say our prayer," Mother said in her calm voice.

All of a sudden I wanted to hear the gentle voice Mother used when she prayed.

"Mother, you pray."

" 'Our Father who art in heaven,' " she began, " 'hallowed be thy name. Thy kingdom come, thy will be done, on earth as it is in heaven.

Give us this day our daily bread; and forgive us our trespasses, as we forgive those who trespass against us; and lead us not into temptation . . . and lead us not into temptation . . . lead us not into temptation . . . lead us not . . . lead us not . . .' "

I couldn't believe it—Mother had lost her place! It was so funny. Even I can say the prayer without losing my place.

" '. . . lead us not . . . lead us not . . .' "

Mother kept saying those words over and over, and when I couldn't wait any longer I said, "Mama, I'll do the rest: 'but deliver us from evil. For thine is the kingdom and the power and the glory forever and ever.' "

After a long while Mother finally whispered, "Amen."

10

It was all I could do to figure out Mother. Sometimes she was quite cheerful. In the evening she might play the organ or sing a hymn. I liked that so much that I just sat quietly next to her and listened. But once in a while, what started out as her singing would end up as tears. When that happened, I would be in tears too. Then Mother would give me more kisses than I could count, and say, "Ok-hŭi, you're the only one I need, yes you are." And she kept crying, on and on.

One Sunday Mother got a headache and decided not to go to church. (It was the day after kindergarten closed down for the summer.) The uncle in the guest room was out somewhere, and Little Uncle was out somewhere, so it was just Mother and me at home. Mother was lying down because of her headache. Out of the blue I heard her call my name.

"Ok-hŭi, do you miss having a papa?"

"Yes, Mama, I want to have a papa too." I put on my baby act and whined a bit.

Mother didn't say anything for a while. She just stared at the ceiling.

"Ok-hŭi. You know your father passed away before you were born. So it's not that you don't have a papa; it's just that he passed on early. If you had a new father now, everyone would call you names. You don't know any better, but the whole world would call you names, everyone in the world. 'Ok-hŭi's mother is a loose woman'— that's what they would say. 'Ok-hŭi's father died, but now she has another father; what will they do next!'—that's what everyone would say. Everyone would point their finger at you. And when you grew up, we wouldn't be able to find you a good husband. Even if you studied hard and became successful, other people would say you're just the daughter of a loose woman."

She said this in fits and starts, like she was talking to herself. After a few minutes she talked to me some more.

"Ok-hŭi?"

"Hmm?"

"Ok-hŭi, I don't want you to ever leave my side. Forever and always I want you to live with Mama. I want you to live with Mama even when she's old and shriveled up. After kindergarten, after grade school, after preparatory school, after college, even if you're the finest woman in all the land, I want you to live with Mama. Hmm? Ok-hŭi, tell me how much you love Mama."

"This much." I opened my arms wide.

"How much? That much! Ok-hŭi, I want you to love me always and forever. I want you to study hard and be a fine woman. . . ."

I got scared when I heard Mother's voice trembling, because I thought she was going to cry again. So I opened my arms as wide as I could and said, "This much, Mama, this much."

Mother didn't cry.

"Ok-hŭi, you're everything to Mama. I don't need anything else. I'm happy just with Ok-hŭi. Yes I am."

She pulled me close and held me tight. She kept hugging me until she had squeezed all my breath out.

After dinner that day, Mother called me, sat me down, and combed my hair. She made a new braid for me and then dressed me in new bloomers, jacket, and skirt.

I asked where we were going.

Mother smiled. "We aren't going anywhere." Then she took down a freshly ironed white handkerchief from beside the organ and put it in my hand.

"This handkerchief belongs to the uncle in the guest room. Could you take it to him? Now don't stay long—just give it to him and come right back, hmm?"

I thought I could feel something tucked in between the folds of the handkerchief, but I didn't open it to see.

I stopped at the uncle's door. He was lying down, but he sat right up when he saw the handkerchief. For some reason he didn't give me a smile, like before. Instead his face turned awful white. He started chewing on his lip as he took the handkerchief. He didn't say a word.

Somehow something wasn't right. So instead of going in the uncle's room I turned around and went back. Mother was at the organ. She must have been doing some hard thinking, because she was just sitting there. I sat down beside the organ and didn't say anything. And then Mother started playing, soft as could be. I didn't know the tune, but it was kind of sad and lonely.

Mother played the organ till late that night. Over and over again she played that sad and lonely tune.

11

Several days went by, and then one afternoon I finally paid another visit to the uncle. He was busy packing his things. Ever since the day I gave him the handkerchief, the uncle always looked sad, like someone with worries on his mind, even when he saw me. He wouldn't say anything, but just stared at me. And so I didn't go to his room to play very often.

I was surprised to see him packing all of a sudden.

"Uncle, are you going somewhere?"

"Uh-huh—far, far away."

"When?"

"Today."

"On the train?"

"Uh-huh."

"When are you coming back?"

Instead of answering, the uncle took a cute doll from his drawer and handed it to me.

"You keep this, hmm? Ok-hŭi, you're going to forget Uncle soon after he leaves, aren't you?"

"Uh-uh." Suddenly I felt very sad.

I went back to our room with the doll.

"Mama, look! The uncle gave it to me. He says he's going far away on the train today."

Mother didn't say anything.

"Mama, why is the uncle going away?"

"Because his school is on vacation."

"Where is he going?"

"He's going to his home—where else?"

"Is the uncle going to come back?"

Mother didn't answer.

"I don't want the uncle to leave," I pouted.

But Mother changed the subject: "Ok-hŭi, go to the closet and see how many eggs there are."

I trotted inside the closet. There were six eggs left.

"Six," I called out.

"Bring all of them here."

Mother proceeded to boil the eggs. Next she wrapped them in a handkerchief. Then she put a pinch of salt in a piece of writing paper and tucked it inside the handkerchief.

"Ok-hŭi, take these to the uncle and tell him to have them on the train, hmm?"

12

That afternoon, after the uncle left, I played with the doll he gave me. I carried it around on my back singing it a lullaby. Mother came in from the kitchen.

"Ok-hŭi, how would you like to go up the hill and get some fresh air?"

"Goodie, let's go!" I practically jumped for joy.

Mother told Little Uncle to mind the house while we went out for a while. Then she took my hand.

"Mama, can I take the uncle's doll?"

"Why not?"

I held the doll close, took Mother's hand, and we hiked up the hill behind our house. From the top we could see the train station clear as could be.

"Mama, look, there's the train station. The train isn't here yet."

Mother didn't say anything. The hem of her ramie skirt fluttered in the soft breeze. Standing quietly on top of the hill, Mother looked even prettier than she did other times.

And then I saw the train coming around a faraway hill.

"Mama, here comes the train!" I shouted in delight.

The train stopped at the station, and practically the next minute it gave a whistle and started moving again.

"There it goes!" I clapped my hands.

Mother watched till the train had disappeared around a hill in the other direction. And then she watched till all the smoke from the smokestack had scattered into the sky above.

We went down the hill, and when we were in our room again Mother put the lid back on the organ. It had been left open all these days. Then she locked it and put the sewing basket on top, the way it was before. She picked up the hymnbook like it was something heavy and flipped through the pages until she found the dried-up flowers.

"Ok-hŭi, take these and throw them away." She handed me the flowers, and I remembered they were the ones I had brought her from kindergarten.

Just then the side gate creaked open.

"Get your eggs!"

It was the old woman who came every day carrying her basket of eggs on her head.

"We won't be buying from now on," said Mother. "There's nobody here who eats them." Her voice didn't have an ounce of life to it.

This took me by surprise. I wanted to pester Mother to buy some eggs, but when I saw her face lit up by the setting sun I lost heart. Instead I put my mouth to the ear of the uncle's doll and whispered to her.

"Did you hear that! Mommy's a pretty good fibber too. She knows I like eggs, but she said there's nobody here who eats them. I'd sure like to pester her. But look at Mama's face. Look how white it is! I don't think Mama feels very good."

A Descendant of the Hwarang

KIM TONG-NI

Kim Tong-ni was born near Kyŏngju in 1913 and was educated there and in the city of Taegu. He made his literary debut as a poet, but soon switched to fiction. He died in 1995 after a long and distinguished career, which included a teaching position at Seoul's Chungang University.

Kim is especially concerned with the clash between tradition and modernity in Korea. "Munyŏdo" (Portrait of a shaman, 1936), one of his best-known stories, frames the contest as a struggle between a mother's shamanistic beliefs and her son's faith in Christianity. Kim later developed this story into a novel, *Ŭlhwa* (1978). "Hwangt'ogi" (Loess Valley, 1939) is a study of primordial passions, while "Yŏngma" (The post horse curse, 1948) depicts a young man's wanderlust in the light of native folk beliefs.

The contrast between tradition and modernity is readily apparent in Kim's debut story, "A Descendant of the *Hwarang*" (Hwarang ŭi huye), first published in the *Chosŏn chungang ilbo* in 1935. A penetrating sketch of an old-fashioned, down-at-the-heels Confucian "gentleman," it also portrays the bustle of Seoul in the mid-1930s.

1

It was last autumn when I first met Hwang Chinsa. I had finished breakfast and was about to leave for a walk in the hills when my uncle called me from his room.

"How would you like to tag along with me today?" he asked as he walked out onto the veranda.

"Where to?"

"To see a mystic—he came here all the way from Chiri Mountain. I hear it's quite a sight watching him tell fortunes and read faces."

"I'd rather not, Uncle," I said without mincing words. "But why don't you go anyway?"

"You'd rather not? How come?"

"Well, I thought I'd go for a hike."

"Not a bad idea. . . . But why don't you come along just this once?
. . . I mentioned fortune telling and face reading just now. But what I
really meant is that a person can learn something at a place like that.
. . . And the kinds of people who gather there—you might call them
the symbols of Korea."

"Symbols of Korea?" I said with a trace of a smile.

Uncle also smiled.

"That's right, symbols."

Well, my curiosity was aroused by this expression "symbols of
Korea," and I proceeded to change out of my walking shoes.

If you go through Pagoda Park and find your way out the rear
entrance, you come upon a thoroughfare in the center of Seoul. It's
unusually broad for a downtown street, and there isn't much traffic.
This street eventually splits in two, and there at the junction, facing
southeast, is the Central Inn. And indeed this inn is located right in
the heart of the city. Horse carts clatter by; people shout to one
another, their breath mingling with the dust; machines screech night
and day.

A sign reading "Spiritual Powers" hung from this inn. The mystic
received his customers inside.

We entered the mystic's studio to find a crowd of people coming
and going—men of letters, deep thinkers, the unemployed, journalists, bank tellers, office men, altogether too many to count. Clothes
stained with liquor and dirt, veins bulging from their eyes, cheekbones protruding from fleshless faces, they were a dissatisfied lot, for
the prevailing political winds were not blowing in their direction.
Idling in the corner were speculators and gold prospectors.

I felt as if I had entered an opium den. As we sat down I shot my
uncle a glance, hoping we wouldn't have to stay. My face flushed with
embarrassment. But he ignored my discomfort and began to introduce me all around.

A man of about sixty wearing a dark coat, who had been sitting
in the corner calculating his own fortune, turned his sallow face
toward us.

"Mr. Kim, is this your esteemed nephew?" he stammered. With a
look of delight he approached my uncle and took a seat beside him.

"I'm running low on resourcefulness these days, so I've been fooling around with the trigram sticks."

I noticed the man's forehead was peeling for no apparent reason, and his eyes were bloodshot. I rose intending to bow in greeting.

"Th-that's all right, ha-have a seat," he said with a gesture of his hand. "My name is Hwang Il-jae. I'm an in-intimate friend of your esteemed uncle."

I felt as if all eyes in the room had focused on me. Then I noticed the mystic himself, sitting directly opposite us. He glanced a few times at my face, his tiny, flaming eyes looking just like fingernail marks.

"The face of one who was deprived of his parents at an early age!" he suddenly announced. "And you have few siblings. Your early years have been lonely."

He proceeded to inform me that I would make a name for myself in academia, due to my handsome features and the bright luster of the skin between my eyebrows. The prospects for my prime years were excellent, because of my regular cheekbones and the well-turned tip of my nose. And even if I had lost my parents, he concluded, my equally capable uncle would be of great service to me as I made my way in the world.

By now I was feeling very awkward. Blushing, I rose and left the room. Uncle did likewise, followed by Hwang.

At the rear entrance to Pagoda Park, Hwang doffed his soiled, tattered hat and bowed to us several times, then turned to leave.

"Where are you off to?" my uncle called out to his back.

"I'm meeting a friend here. . . ."

And then he disappeared inside the park.

The sun was approaching its zenith. There wasn't a wisp of cloud in the sky, only Pukhan Mountain towering in the distance. My irritation had enervated me, the way a spring day sometimes did.

2

The trees lost all their leaves; autumn was here to stay. One morning when my uncle was out of town tending to his gold-mining business, I was about to begin breakfast when I heard someone clear his throat outside the gate.

"Anybody home?"

I put down my spoon and went outside, and there was Hwang. The "symbols of Korea" hadn't entered my mind that morning, and perhaps for that reason the distastefulness and depression I had felt at the mystic's were now replaced with delight at Hwang's appearance.

"What brings you here on such a cold morning?"

"N-nothing much. Is your esteemed uncle at home?" His stammer was more pronounced than before.

In the light of day I could see that his coat was made of calico. It was a tawdry, uneven blue, and was smeared with a dark ointment. A dull yellow sweater peeked out over the collar. But he looked terribly cold in spite of this extra layer of clothing.

"No, I'm afraid he went somewhere."

"You don't know where? Is it f-far from here?"

"Yes."

"When was he planning to r-return?"

"Well, probably not for a few days."

He heaved a sigh of disappointment. It sounded just like a ponderous groan escaping from his throat.

"Was there something you wanted to? . . . Why don't you come in out of the cold for a minute?"

He withdrew his hands from his coat and reached for his hat. But then he hesitated, searching my face, and instead wiped his nose with his right hand. At the same time, his left hand plunged back inside his coat and fumbled for something.

"I hope y-y-your esteemed family will take good care of this," he said, handing me an object wrapped in paper.

Inside was something that resembled a ball of mud mixed with bits of chaff.

I looked up with a dubious expression, only to find that Hwang had assumed a haughty air.

"It's cow dung overlaid with dog dung—a wonderful cure-all," he announced in a lofty tone.

I stood there speechless, wondering what he meant.

"Heavens! Don't you realize how valuable this is?"

He glared at me, his moist eyes full of spite.

I regretted my ignorance.

"What do people generally use it for?"

"Why, it's good for everything!" he responded, looking at me askance. "This is precious medicine! . . . You'd be in a pretty fix without it if any of your d-distinguished family was ever in need. I can't believe you don't know. . . ."

He craned his neck toward me in a gesture of considerable chagrin.

Why was he acting so indignant, so resentful? As I pondered this for a moment, he lapsed into a sullen silence, but then erupted once more:

"I just can't believe you don't know these things!"

My aunt must have thought ill of my having left the table just as breakfast was being served. After stealing several glances outside, she finally called to me:

"What are you doing out there?"

She took care to emphasize the words "out there," as if to suggest that perhaps I should invite the visitor in.

Just then Hwang spoke up again.

"Uh, well, would you happen to have any leftovers from breakfast?"

He now wore a fawning smile and nodded obsequiously—a complete about-face from the bluster of a short time before, when he had handed me the mixture of chaff and dung.

I took him inside and had my lunchtime portion of rice served to him.

"I'm truly sorry to have inconvenienced you," he said with a look of utter contentment as he took his place at the table.

He proceeded to attack the rice bowl, finishing it almost in one mouthful. He scraped the bowl clean, and no sooner had he set down his spoon than he was on his feet with hat in hand. He bowed to me several times but said not a word about the medicine. It was as if he had forgotten about it completely.

Three days later, Hwang visited me again. This time a taller man in a white coat accompanied him. I came to think of the companion as "the twitching man" because his eyes, nose, and mouth moved at least as much as Hwang's. This man, whom Hwang introduced as his friend, was toting a small, dust-covered reading desk on his shoulder.

"I'd like you to buy this," he practically ordered me.

"Well, I wouldn't have much use—"

"Oh, don't worry, I'm giving it to you cheap. Come on."

"But I probably wouldn't have any use for it."

"Well, that's why I'm offering it for a bargain price."

I didn't know what to say.

"Only fifty chŏn."

Hwang extended a sallow, dirty palm in front of me.

"But I don't have the slightest use—"

"All right, dammit, just give me twenty chŏn and you can keep the desk until I pay you back."

I kept silent.

"Now what's the matter with that?"

When I still didn't answer, he suddenly began pleading with me, his nostrils quivering.

"Then just give me ten chŏn, and I'll pay you back."

He had become quite animated, and kept wiping his nose with his hand as he spoke.

"The other day when you fed me was the last time I had a decent meal. I'm starving. I looked up my friend here, and he's hard up too. This desk we're offering is the one he uses for his work."

The friend averted his face, but I could see his mouth continually twitching.

It took a few minutes, but I managed to scrape up twenty chŏn inside. When I gave them the money, the two men bowed countless times and left, taking the desk back with them.

3

The roads were frozen, and the more distant mountains were sprinkled with snow. It had been bitterly cold since early in the winter.

My uncle left home several times on business, and he seemed also to have paid an occasional visit to the mystic's studio. Hwang, though, didn't show his face at our house.

Through Uncle I was able to learn something about Hwang—his hometown, somewhere in Ch'ungch'ŏng Province; his lineage, a distinguished *yangban* family; his forebears, which included the likes of prime ministers and other high officials; and the considerable pride he took in his own status as a *chinsa* and in his pedigree, which he kept forever in his mind.

But there was one laughable aspect to all this, and that was Hwang's very notion of himself as a *chinsa*, or one who had passed the first of the government examinations for public office. Hwang had once encountered a playful fellow outside the mystic's. This man had Hwang recite a few lines from *The Book of History* and *The Spring and Autumn Annals*, gave him a passing grade, and jokingly conferred upon him the title of *chinsa*. From then on, everyone Hwang met would refer to him, half in derision, as Hwang Chinsa. But Hwang himself wasn't the least bit fazed. He considered it quite plausible that he was a *chinsa*, and he began to act like one. Indeed, he became quite taken with himself.

One terribly cold day, I had stoked the firebox that heated the floors of our living quarters, then lit the brazier in the corner of my room. Next I had set to work at my desk, and there I stayed well into the afternoon.

"Anybody home?"

The voice rode in on the wind, sounding just like a cry for help. I went outside to find Hwang wiping his nose with his hand, over and over. I had been wondering if he could possibly have survived this bitter cold, and so I was genuinely glad to see him.

I led him straightaway to my room.

"What have you been doing with yourself these days?" I asked.

"I've been staying with a friend," he said with a chuckle. He seemed to be in a good mood. "Well, now, has your esteemed uncle been away from home all this time?"

"He comes and goes."

"That explains it. I feel badly that I haven't paid him my respects."

His voice trailed off in another chuckle as he sat down to warm himself in front of the brazier.

I bought some frozen rice cakes, began toasting them over the brazier, and offered them to my guest. Then I took a moment to finish the work I had been doing at my desk. In the meantime, Hwang busied himself with the long, white cakes, consuming toasted and frozen alike. At the same time, he became more animated, and finally he put his voice to work:

> Chirping lovebirds play and mate at the waterside;
> A virtuous maiden makes a gentleman's bride.

I remained at my desk, pretending not to have heard him intone this first couplet from *The Book of Songs*.

"Well, nobody's perfect!" he shouted while looking at me. And then, with all the bombast at his command: "Master Confucius allowed some indecent lines to slip into *The Book of Songs!*" He looked askance in my direction as if he had discovered some great problem.

But when I continued to pretend I hadn't heard him, he stood up, relinquishing the brazier. He then turned up the tail of his coat, lifted the gusset of his jacket, and reached inside. Was he picking some lice from his underwear to throw into the brazier?

After giving me another glance, he produced a stained money belt. From inside the belt came an ancient tome, a handful of pine needles wrapped in a piece of white mulberry paper neatly secured with a cord, and a few scraps of paper. The book had been written with ink and brush. Its drab pages had lost their corners.

"What book is that?" I asked.

"Good heavens, it's *The Book of Changes!*" he barked.

This was no doubt the case, I concluded after seeing the hexagrams spread out on the dog-eared pages.

But why on earth would anyone want to go around with a copy of *The Book of Changes* in a money belt? I asked him.

"For heaven's sake, Master Confucius himself is said to have given this very book three thousand readings." He then softened his tone: "*The Book of Changes* is said to be the fountainhead of resourcefulness and the wellspring of creation."

I recalled what Hwang had said that first day at the mystic's studio: "I'm running low on resourcefulness, so I've been fooling around with the trigram sticks." I had a hunch he was the type who in his daily life took great stock in this "resourcefulness," this "creation." These two concepts were symbolized by what he carried on his person—the pine needles and the tattered copy of *The Book of Changes,* a volume permeated with the theories of yin and yang and the Five Elements. But how could resourcefulness and creation possibly translate into a reading desk carried around by a friend, into a ball of chaff and mud—"cow dung overlaid with dog dung"? I could only sigh in bewilderment.

Evening arrived, and Hwang fastened his money belt about his waist and left. I asked him to drop by now and then, and he replied with a series of bows that he was sorry he had proved such a bother every time he visited.

That winter Hwang came to see me, or rather my uncle, often enough that his visits did in fact become rather annoying. Whenever he saw me, he expressed his regret at not having paid due respects to my uncle for so long.

On several occasions he brought some Chinese rhyming characters and asked me to compose Chinese poems for him. What was the occasion? I asked. It turned out he was preparing verses for some friends' sixtieth-birthday celebrations. I asked who the friends were, and he said Bureaucrat Yi, Secretary Yun, Vice-Minister So-and-So, and Baron Somebody, naming all the wealthy, illustrious families who led secluded lives in Seoul. But the types I saw with Hwang on the street, and the "friends" he occasionally brought over, were completely at odds with this description. In truth, this bunch didn't seem much better off than Hwang himself.

At the same time, Hwang was pressing me about the subject of marriage. He had some fine young women in mind—wouldn't I like to take one of them for my wife? I inquired about these "fine young women," and he replied at once that they were the daughters of friends. When I asked about the friends, he readily offered the usual array of decorous, well-to-do families—Secretary So-and-so, Viscount Somebody, and so on. And when I asked him about the young ladies' looks, he would point to his own sallow, puffy face and say that their faces, like his own, were blessed in every respect.

"I was hoping they'd be a bit more interesting," I said with a smile.

Hwang flared up at this.

"I tell you, they're first-class women!"

"Well, I hope they're not as heavyset as you are."

"Why, that's a sure sign they've been well fed from birth!" he blustered. "I keep telling you they're first-rate, and still you don't believe me!"

4

Hwang Chinsa was always weeping—that is, if you considered the moisture that gathered in his eyes to be tears. Every now and then he would arrive from a sixtieth-birthday celebration for a "friend," where he could depend on a bowl of rice-cake soup or something else to fill his stomach, along with enough liquor to make him half tipsy. In this condition, he would bemoan his lack of children:

"Divine Providence has turned his back on me! I'm a man from a reputable family, with no flesh and blood of my own!"

And there was a variation on this theme:

"Everywhere I go, I receive proposals for marriage. But a man has to have the proper means of subsistence."

One day my aunt asked Hwang about the young women who appealed to him the most. There were two—a nineteen-year-old named O and a woman just turned twenty named Yun.

"Nineteen?" my aunt asked in surprise.

"She has to be young enough to produce children."

"Women a little older would do just as well," my aunt responded.

"True," said Hwang, "but they'll never be better than younger women."

He gave every appearance of leaning in favor of these two women, come what may.

Several days after this conversation, it came about that my aunt served as a matchmaker for Hwang. At the time, he was dropping by almost every day, and my aunt had become privately concerned about his straitened circumstances. Uncle happened to be home then, and he and my aunt put their heads together and decided to propose as a marriage candidate the young widow who lived across the street.

Naturally, I hoped the plan would work out.

"Granted, she's a widow, but do you think she'll take an old man with no money?" Uncle asked us with a smile.

"She doesn't have much choice—there aren't many handsome young widowers around. But he does have one advantage—no children," my aunt said confidently.

Hearing this, I felt somewhat easier about the proposed match.

Hwang came by that evening, and Uncle wasted no time.

"Il-jae, we've found a young woman with some money—would you consider her?" he ventured.

"Would I!" Hwang looked overjoyed. "But as you know, sir, one needs a means of subsistence for these matters."

Seeing Hwang's face brighten, my aunt informed him that a man didn't have to be wealthy to marry. And once he was married, he could wear clean clothes and eat decent meals.

"Yes, of course, that would be splendid! And as for the woman's age . . . and her family's reputation?"

Saliva streamed from his open mouth, and his eyes took on an unaccustomed twinkle. He leaned toward my aunt in rapt attention.

"She's a widow—no getting around that—but a widow in name only. She's not even thirty yet," my aunt said enthusiastically. There was a note of triumph in her voice.

As soon as she said this, however, Hwang's face dropped.

"What? The y-young woman—did you say she was a w-widow?"

"What's the matter with that?"

Hwang's mouth clamped shut and began twitching ever so faintly. His hands, resting limply on his knees, were trembling. Apart from the ticking of the wall clock, there was dead silence. Hwang shook his head.

"This is most improper. . . . Hmph! A w-widow? How could you propose such a thing?"

His puffy yellow cheeks filled as if he were about to snap out a command—or something worse—and he kept glaring indignantly at us.

"I'm a sixth-generation direct descendant of Hwang Hu-am," he said gravely. "A sixth-generation descendant. And you think I would take as a wife a woman who had married into another family? How could you say such a thing? . . . And you, sir, your remarks have exceeded all bounds."

His voice quivered with emotion as he tried to suppress his chagrin. His face twitched in grievous anguish.

"Well, why not marry one of those young women?" my aunt asked. "You could have them tomorrow if you really wanted to."

Disconcerted, she rose.

Uncle, too, tried to remedy the situation.

"Il-jae, Il-jae, forget it. I was just joking. You didn't think I was serious about that woman, did you? A man of your lineage could hardly be expected to accept a woman who was previously married. And don't you think I know about Hwang Hu-am and Hwang Ik-dang, and how illustrious they were?"

Finally Hwang's face flushed.

"Indeed!" he thundered. "A thoughtless suggestion—it's beyond my comprehension. And we all know who Hwang Hu-am and Hwang Ik-dang were!"

5

The year came to an end.

My uncle had returned to his mining operation, and so my aunt and I were left by ourselves to welcome in the new year. Hwang had kept out of sight the latter half of December, but the very first morning of the new year brought the familiar call of "Anybody home?" from outside our gate. The voice had a heartier ring to it than before. I noticed that Hwang's ointment-stained coat had been laundered. More surprising was the pair of dark glasses he wore. He had come, he said, to offer my uncle his compliments for the new year. Upon learning that Uncle wasn't home, he said he would greet my aunt before leaving.

It so happened that my aunt had prepared some edibles for the holiday, and she gladly offered our guest a small tray containing liquor along with rice cakes and other snacks. After repeated expressions of regret at not being able to pay his respects to my "esteemed uncle," Hwang gulped several drinks.

"One glass, another glass, and yet another—that's how we men of breeding should celebrate the new year."

He drummed on his knees, as if keeping time with music. He appeared to be in exceptionally high spirits.

"Will the new year bring you a . . . ?" My aunt hesitated to finish the question.

"A bride? Certainly, as long as I come up with a means of subsistence. After all, I have a good fortune this year: 'The blue dragon is at play.' "

Hwang returned the following day—and two days after that. The rest of the month continued in like fashion, with Hwang dropping by intending to wish my uncle a happy new year. But it turned out that he was unable to convey these greetings to him directly.

The remainder of the winter passed without Hwang setting foot in our house even once. Spring came, the willow twigs filled with moisture, and new buds sprouted on the dark tree trunks. As the new season passed, I often wondered about Hwang.

Summer arrived. Birds grew to maturity in the green shade, and streams echoed in the mountain valleys.

It was then that Uncle was unexpectedly taken into custody by the Japanese police, due to some incident or other. I had looked forward to staying at a rural temple to escape the summer heat, but now I had to abandon this plan. So began a trying summer for me in Seoul. At the time, of course, I didn't know in detail about this "incident" concerning Uncle. However, it was the talk of the town that he had been arrested for complicity in a matter involving a sect, originating among Koreans in Manchuria, that worshiped Tangun, the mythical progenitor of our people. In rapid succession Uncle was arrested, his mines shut down, and his house searched.

One day my aunt and I were returning home after visiting Uncle at the prison outside the old West Gate. We had passed through Kwanghwa Gate when we heard a shout:

"Well, fancy meeting you people on the street!"

I looked up to see Hwang in a light green imitation silk vest. His coat, freshly laundered, was draped over his left arm. He was wearing his dark glasses, and an old yellow panama hat was perched on the back of his head. His uncovered forehead glistened in the sunlight. He approached us from the direction of the Japanese Governor-General's office.

"Master Il-jae, it's been a long time since we've seen you," I greeted him.

"How have you all been? I've often had word about your esteemed uncle. . . . Goodness gracious! Fancy meeting you people like this!"

He then beckoned me off to the side, saying he had discovered some crucial information.

There had been new developments regarding my uncle, and so I thought Hwang might now provide some particulars. My face tensed as I studied him. I tried to suppress the pounding of my heart.

"The things I don't know about my own ancestors! These days I've been finding out about the old, old Hwangs—even my grandfathers weren't able to trace back that far."

I was flabbergasted. This was the last thing I had expected to hear from him, and my face showed it.

"What's the matter? Not feeling well?"

I assured him I was all right, and even managed to urge him to continue.

"Well, it's the damnedest thing. . . . Would you believe that most of the old Hwangs were *hwarang?* They were the warrior elite of Shilla times!"

He seemed overcome with emotion.

I asked how he had discovered this.

He had been looking through various history books, he said, and had stumbled across the information.

It was two months later that I next saw Hwang. I had accompanied my aunt to the hospital, and we were on our way home. We had taken the streetcar as far as the Governor-General's office, and from there we entered P'irun-dong. Hwang was sitting near the treatment center for morphine addicts, but at first we didn't see him.

A small crowd of disheveled beggar children, opium addicts, paralytics, cripples, and quadriplegics had gathered around an upside-down cookie box about a foot and a half long. Displayed on top of the box was a desiccated toad alongside a round metal bucket containing an earthen-colored ointment. A man was explaining the uses of this medicine.

"Toad oil, toad oil!" the man called out, clearing his throat. "Toad oil! Good for poison ivy, scabies, tumor on the back, abscess of the buttocks, burns, chilblains, loose teeth, tooth decay! Cures children's ear infections, prevents baldness! Works for male and female, young and old, adults and children, men and women—makes no difference! Good for Seoulites, good for country folk! Rids sores of their poison, heals putrefied flesh—no matter who you are! Wrap it up nice and tight, stash it away, and someday you'll be very glad you bought it! Toad oil! Extracted from the nose of a toad! So remarkably efficacious it's frightening! And I'm going to show it to you right before your eyes. Your attention, please!"

The man dipped some of the ointment in a bowl of liquid, then stirred.

"And now, look closely, please! If your blood is bad, then one drop of this ointment from the toad's nose and the problem disappears without a trace, just like spring snow melting away!"

He displayed the dish with a flourish before the onlookers, then cleared his throat again.

"Ladies and gentlemen, at this time I would like to introduce to you one of the renowned figures of our nation. For two months, he was confined to his bed with a case of dental caries. But yesterday, thanks to this medicine, the decay vanished, and today he is able to grace us with his presence."

He gestured to the side, and there, wearing the familiar sunglasses and gazing in dignified silence toward the distant mountains, sat our Hwang Chinsa.

"Now this gentleman has performed extensive research in the field of medicine. And not only that, he has prepared a wonder drug, using bear gallbladders, duck tongues, earthworm urine, rat dung, and cat livers. With this drug, he can root out the curse of countless diseases. He is, if you will, a wizard!"

It was about then that the policeman appeared. The circle of beggars, opium addicts, and quadriplegics scattered to their dens.

My aunt signaled me with her eyes and turned to leave. I looked back a few times as I followed her. The man who had been delivering the spiel had picked up the cookie box along with the dried-up toad and the bucket of ointment. He and Hwang, walking in solemn dignity with his hands thrust in the sides of his coat, followed the officer across the street toward the police station.

Wife

KIM YU-JŎNG

Kim Yu-jŏng was born in 1908 in the village of Chŭngni in Kangwŏn Province and studied at what is now Yonsei University in Seoul. He has left us with some thirty stories, most of them published in 1935 and 1936. The playfulness of some of these works masks a profound sorrow: at an early age Kim lost his parents and then contracted tuberculosis. He died in 1937.

Many of Kim's works have rural settings and are characterized by wit and irony. In stories such as "Tongbaek kkot" (Camellias, 1936) Kim writes with affection of Korean farming villages and the foibles of their denizens. Other works are more serious. The budding sexuality implicit in "Tongbaek kkot" becomes more overt in "Sonakpi" (Rain shower, 1935). Still other works, such as "Ttaengbyŏt" (Scorching heat, 1937), are downright gloomy. Whatever the tone, the writing is rich and earthy, for Kim had an excellent command of native Korean vocabulary.

"Wife" (Anhae) first appeared in Sahae kongnon in 1935. It is an inspired, uninhibited monologue, rife with scenes of domestic violence, narrated by an unlettered, sexist woodcutter who is not afraid to poke fun at himself. In bringing alive the character of his wife as well as himself, and in evoking familiar Korean ballads, this man gives us a taste of the *kwangdae*, the narrator of the traditional oral narrative *p'ansori*. Kim was a true original, and there is little else like this story in modern Korean fiction.

M y wife ain't the type you look at and say, "Hey, she's pretty!" That is, unless you're plumb skirt crazy. I mean, I live with her, and I could look at her through the rosiest-colored glasses and she's still not the least bit pretty. But you know, there's more to a skirt than just a cute mug. Hell, I wouldn't bitch if the woman would just turn out a string of boys as strong as oxes. To be honest, a dumb fuck like myself, I get old, no kids, what's going to happen to me? I'll starve, for god's sake. I got no land, physically I'll be shot to hell, I won't be able to work—who'd want to do even a half-assed job of feeding me? So, while we're still young, I want a passel of kids. Turn 'em out, one after another. Get the idea?

Thank god, there's no law that says kids have to be ugly just 'cause their mom is. You'll see when you look at that little Smarty of ours. His mom's mug looks like a rice cake somebody stepped on by mistake, but he's a smart little fellow and a good-looking boy—even when he's pestering you for more food. In fact, the little guy is just plain indescribably precious to me—more than my own father or grandfather. Problem is—and this ain't easy to put up with—the bitch is putting on airs, and it's all because she had this boy. The same woman, mind you, who wouldn't produce a squeak out of that puss of hers *before* the boy came along. Like they say, when it comes to a woman's face, it's all in the eye of the beholder. But with her face, it doesn't help even if your eyesight's rotten.

She has a wide forehead and her eyes are pretty far apart—and don't they say that makes you broad-minded? That's all well and good, but there's really nothing soft and cute about her face. Her jaw's as round and broad as the bottom of a cabbage, and she ain't about to gain no admirers the way her mouth pokes out of it. That thick upper lip of hers is practically inside out, and those crooked upper teeth are all out in the open saying, "Hey, look at me!" Okay, I'm willing to put up with that. But is it asking too much for her nose to be a little more attractive? I mean, it's stuck right in the middle of her face—it's the first thing that draws your attention. But if I keep carrying on like this, people might think I'm carping at the bitch's faults. I try my best to give her the benefit of the doubt, but that nose just plain reminds me of a pig gaping at some mountain way off yonder.

Things being as they are, is it any wonder that at night she keeps her distance trying to read the old man's mood? "Is he going to let me have it again tonight?"—I'm always making her worry. But she's such a pitiful mess to look at, I got to say *something* to her. Like, "What you been up to all day?" "Did you fix the brushwood gate like I asked?" "How come your nose looks so cute tonight?" That kind of thing. It's an effort, believe me, 'cause I'm dog tired. But it works like magic: her face lights up, she cozies up beside me, she rubs up against me with her shoulder and then she rubs some more.

When I say her nose looks nice, she gets all hot and bothered: "Really? You mean it?" You see, it does her heart good to hear it one more time, 'cause she can't quite believe it herself. I know, I ought to be ashamed of myself, but when I tell her her nose don't look squashed no more, the bitch is beside herself with joy: "Whenever I go to the outhouse I pull on it, so maybe it's coming out!"

There are times, though, when half a day between the furrows does me in. It's all I can do just to sprawl out on the floor back home —I sure don't have no energy to chitchat with her. Well, the bitch thinks it's all because of her face and she goes and sulks in the corner. Then she turns her face to the side and sticks up her chin like she wants me to admire the scenery. Damn you, I think. If you got a notion that your profile's any improvement over your front view, you're dead wrong!

This same bitch started acting so high and mighty as soon as she turned out our little Smarty. I get home from the fields and no hello, no glance, zip. Who the hell are you?—that's the impression I get. Keeps her head down and just gives the boy her tit. And if I so much as pat him on the head and say something like "Hey, sleepyhead," she punches my hand away and says, "Cut it out—you want to wake him up?" First time she did this I couldn't believe it—just gaped up at the ceiling. All I want to do is touch my own flesh and blood, and she punches me—what gives? But now that I think about, I got no cause to complain. 'Cause I learned, little by little, that the bitch deserves the right to act like she's something.

And so from that point on it was like we had an agreement—every time I'd say "Hey, woman!" she'd bark back at me. The neighbors started calling us Mr. and Mrs. Pester. Well, they don't know the half of it. I mean, she and I is always ready to go at it. These days we're hard put to have a single day of peace and quiet. Just seeing each other gets us going—"Bastard!" "Bitch!"—and both of us want to start up first.

With other people it's like this:

"Hello, my loving wife—did you eat yet?"

"No, my dear, I was waiting for you." And she jumps up with joy.

But not us. You're not going to find us crawling up to each other and talking sweet. When *I* get home I give her fat ass a swift kick.

"Bitch—get up and fix me some supper!"

"Bastard—what's the big idea! I'm going to break your leg!" And then she favors me with a look and says, "What did you do with the money you got for the firewood, guzzle more booze?"

See? Now that's high and mighty for you. Truth is, it's our way of being affectionate with each other. And it's my idea of having fun with my woman. Baby-faced greenhorn husbands acting chummy with their wives make me want to puke. What's a wife for if you can't cuss her up and down and use her for a punching bag now and then? From the way I talk, though, maybe you think I'm a poverty-stricken guy with a gut full of hate. Well, I got news for you—we're not all that different from other folks. We all have times when we can't do what we want, and we get churned up inside. In farming you got nothing to show for your labor, you got a pile of debt, you get home and your little guy is whining, your woman is shivering 'cause she ain't got no clothes to wear—times like that you don't want to put up with no shit. And so we're at each other's throats, me grabbing her by the bun of her hair and thrashing her. After I get over this fit, the sweat runs down my backbone, I'm panting, and that's when I sort of cool down. Then I push her away, and if I can have me a cigarette then all's well with the world.

That's me with my woman, and I guess I ought to be thankful for her. Which is why I feel like something's missing when she ain't around. Else, why would I pat her on the back, or tell her once in a while that godforsaken nose of hers looks nice? Boosts her spirits, see? And on the other hand, it's not much fun when the bitch is huddled up sniveling and crying. You see, it don't matter who picks the fight, it's always her that catches hell, 'cause whether she comes at me with fists or with jabbering, she's no match for me.

"Lay yourself down here—time to go to sleep," I'll say at last.

"Forget it. Lay your own self down." She sounds like poison, won't look at me, just sits there. But after I ask her a few more times she eventually comes around, and crawls right up to me without me asking. And then what do you know—she lifts up her weepy face and glares at me out of the corner of her eye. So maybe from the bitch's point of view, she gets knocked around, she sulks, and that's the way she likes her marriage.

But don't think 'cause we always fight like cats and dogs that we're lacking in affection. Speaking of which, you're not about to find folks as close as us—why, we're like sticky rice. The more ugly we get with each other, the more we scrap, the more our affection glues us together—it's hard for us to be apart for a second. Now I'll admit I don't know if this is what people mean by "conjugal affection," but we're like leeches in our affection, and I can't explain why. After she's gotten the usual working over and we're finally in bed together the bitch'll say:

"I'm not really that ugly, am I?"

And she cozies right up to me, as if she really is good-looking! Well, what am I supposed to say? About all I can do is shake my head in amazement and stare up at the ceiling.

"You call that a face, woman?"

"Then what is it?"

"Listen, woman, if it wasn't for me, who else would have you for a wife? Who'd put up with that mug of yours?"

"What about you and your chestnut-burr face! If it wasn't for me, who else would have you for a husband? Good grief!"

Times like that I don't got much choice 'cept to get up, let her have it till I work up a sweat, and then flop down again. "Chestnut-burr"! Some nerve! Why, my mother who brought me into the world likes this face so much she says, "Now that's the face of a fellow who's going to get hisself some land one day." But instead of going to the bother of getting up and giving the bitch a slap or a kick, I usually just let it go.

"All right, I'll tell you what—I promise to think you're good-looking, and you just keep turning out babies."

"What's the use of turning out babies when you can't even feed us? You want us to starve?"

"Look, bitch! You can borrow food, you know." There I go, yelling again, but it's all bluster. She's right—what the hell's the use of having a lapful of kids if you can't feed 'em? I ought to know by now the bitch's got a much better angle on things than me. I mean, she can see that kids aren't something you abandon—they'd all end up dead. Well, everyone knows that the farther apart your eyebrows are, the more broad-minded and sensible you are. And hers are a damn sight farther apart than mine.

What we eat these days comes from what I make selling firewood. Summers and such I can hire out for day labor, but when snow piles up, what am I supposed to do, eat the ice? What else can a guy do who lives way out in the woods, 'cept spend one day cutting wood and the next day going to town and peddling it. You got to understand it takes some muscle to pack a couple of backracks that're stacked full up. The idea is to tote them one at a time—you pack the first guy a ways, take a break, go back for the second guy, take a break, bring the second guy up, and before you know it you've covered a good seven or eight miles in half a day. Sure, you could pack just one backrack, but then how the hell are you supposed to eat?

You get your pay—eighty chŏn for two loads if you're lucky, sixty or sixty-five if your luck is shitty—and off you go for millet, beans, laver, and whatnot. You can stretch your meals out if you eat gruel, but we're not that hard up. For us it's got to be real food, even if that means we got to pinch in the gut waiting for the next meal, whenever that is. Little Smarty's four years old, so he's got hisself a pint-sized bowl. I'm his father, so I get a regular bowl and then half a bowl more, but the bitch is in a class by herself—she shovels down a couple of bowls. And she has this way of gobbling up hers before I finish and then digging into mine, too.

I used to think it was nice to have a woman around, but then it occurred to me that maybe the bitch was just a useless mouth—now that kind of gave me the chills. People who don't have nothing can't afford to eat like there's no tomorrow. So when the bitch shovels down her food and I ask her how in the dickens she can eat so much, she says her belly's still big from when she had the baby, and I'd know what it's like if I had a baby, and she screws up her face and sulks. Well, well, says I, then go ahead and gobble. As long as we're going to spend money on food, it might as well end up in your belly.

Sometimes I don't eat so much in order to give her what's left over. Damnable woman! I says to myself. But the fact remains, she gobbles too much.

The bitch didn't get to be as old as she is for nothing. She's got more worldy wisdom than me, and when it comes to scheming she does me one up. "What good's this two-bit farming?" she asks. "We ought to be peddling booze by the drink instead." Well, that's a damn good idea, something resourceful old me ain't never dreamed of. With the proceeds we could eat honest-to-goodness rice, we could have meat, we could wear decent clothes—luxury! But when I examined the bitch's face, all the starch went out of me. You see, the reason men buy drinks from a booze peddler is to get a look at the woman's face. Well, it'd take a pretty stupid bastard to get worked up by that mug of hers. It made me hopping mad—if only the bitch was born with a better-looking face, we'd have a way. I must of been wearing a hangdog look to go with the bitter taste in my mouth, 'cause she could guess what I was thinking.

"You know, booze peddlers need more than a pretty face; the face can be ugly as long as they have a way—"

"So, you got yourself a way, do you?"

"What's wrong with trying?"

That's some gumption she's got. With this bitch, there's noooo problem. I knew her scheme—peddling booze, she could eat her fill. I kept after her about it, and she was sure she could do it, so what the hell, I says to myself, we might as well give it a try. We wouldn't need much start-up money—all I'd have to do is teach her a few songs, and once they sunk in we could hit the road. And so I reckoned at the end of the day after I come home I'd sit the bitch down in front of me and teach her to sing.

Well, the first number I sang was *"Arirang"* and I beat out the time on my knee:

> *Arirang, arirang, arariyo,*
> So long to Ch'unch'ŏn and the mountains of spring,
> Board the Shinyŏn River ferry and farewell.

Every woman who comes from the hills has at least got to do a decent job of Kangwŏn *"Arirang."* But the bitch couldn't learn it. So I went to the easiest version—what else could I do? The bitch sat with her legs crossed, imitating me and beating out the time on her butt. The noise that came out of her throat was like a clay bowl cracking. Well, with a little training, that voice might not be half bad for the old songs. I just wished she could carry a tune, but there was no way on God's green earth.

And so I taught her, but the worthless bitch sang like she's reading a story. What the hell was I supposed to do? I just kept working her, often till the rooster crowed, sometimes till daybreak. The bitch was simply awful, so I tried to show her how it's done, and I tried some more. I'm supposed to be teaching her how to be a booze peddler, but I wound up learning more myself.

Damnable woman—she'd cover her mouth and yawn and then yawn again. I knew she was dying to go to sleep.

But she'd never own up to being sleepy unless she heard me say it was time for bed.

Who brought up this idea of booze peddling to begin with? I says to myself. The anger would build up inside me and sometimes I'd go after her with my fists.

"Wake up, bitch! I'm not going to stay up all night and sing by myself!"

"Bastard—I'll break your arm!"

"Listen, bitch, you're the one who benefits if you can get this song down. Not me. Don't act so big."

And this time I jabbed her right in the forehead and knocked her
backward. Normally, the bitch would give me a look full of poison,
then run off to the corner. But not this time. She knew she was the
guilty party, and she bucked up and waited for me to teach her some
more.

Well, we dug ourselves into a hole. I had my doubts whether this
scheme of ours would work out, we was constantly yawning in each
other's face, but since we was already into it we couldn't not follow
through. Shit! I says to myself, you and me had better change our
luck, and fast. And so I give it my best effort, once and for all. I
hollered out the songs loud enough to roust the mountains and
streams, then had the bitch sing *"Hŭng t'aryŏng"* along with me.

I'll give the bitch credit—once she gets going on something she
takes it serious. That's her saving grace. Otherwise, forget about her
as a weed picker, not to mention a booze peddler. As a matter of fact,
whenever she could squeeze out some time during the day she'd practice singing by herself. If she was doing the wash, she'd sing "Youthful Sixteen" and beat out the time with her laundry sticks. Or she'd
hunker down in the corner and sing a tune while she sewed herself
some quilted socks. For every beat she'd sew a stitch, moving her
shoulders in time. At that rate, we're talking ten days for one sock.
We ain't going to make a living from socks, I says to myself. Just con-
centrate on those songs, woman. Well, the bitch was just aching, as
much as me, for a taste of honest-to-goodness rice and meat, and
sometimes I'd hear her humming merrily along in the outhouse while
I was out in the fields nearby.

It took her till now, and she just barely learned *"Hŭng t'aryŏng"*
to go with *"Norae karak."* How long would the next ballad take her?
Damn woman—really! What's more, the bitch's got so forward she's
asking people to teach her these modern songs. A booze peddler has
got to know the old standards, she says, but the way you get popular
is to know the tunes that are popular now. Well, that's easy for her to
say, but how the hell am I supposed to know what's popular now?
"I'm a guy who digs dirt in a field—I don't know stuff like that!" I
says to her. Well, a few days later the bitch comes home singing one
of the latest songs. She sits herself down around the brazier and beats
time on the edge, proud as a peacock.

> She bloomed, she bloomed, the lotus blossom bloomed,
> But while I was watching she shrunk.

I was amazed. Where in hell did you learn that? I says to myself.
Woman, you got me beat!

Next thing I know, the bitch is finding time to go to night school.
They call it night school, but what it amounts to is a little hut at the
foot of yonder mountain where they teach the farm kids to read and
write in winter. The bitch goes over there for music hour and she
don't mind the cold. I seen her standing outside the door with our
boy on her back, listening to the teacher sing and following along.
You ought to see her carry on when she gets home. These modern
songs, she practices 'em for a few more days and she'll get 'em down.

But no matter how I look at it, I'm still worried about that mug of
hers. She's developing a pretty good set of vocal cords, but with that
damn face there's no hope. If the damnable woman had just been
turned out halfway decent-looking, this scheme of ours would be her
big chance. Once in a while when I think about this, my temper gets
the best of me and instead of saying something I belt her in the gut a
couple of times—I can't help it. The bitch has no idea what's got into
me, and just looks stupid at me. Damn punching bag of a woman,
you got some nerve marrying me with that mug of yours, I says to
myself. I know the bitch sometimes gets exercised on account of her
face, though she won't admit it. And I know she takes out that
chipped hand mirror of hers and gawks at her face from this angle
and that angle, but what's she supposed to see that I can't see? And
then she heaves these spooky sighs that sound like someone who's
had rat poison, and gets all discouraged. But if I happen to be there,
she turns my way and says:

"Look at me! Don't you think my face is getting any better these
days?"

"Yeah, it looks that way."

"Be serious, or else—"

And then the bitch is pinching my arm and coming at me from
every direction. She's a sly woman in her own way and she's sharp
enough to know she can count on me to tell her what she wants to
hear. If she thinks I'll tell her straight out how she looks, she won't
ask me in the first place. So I says her face really did get better, trying
to be a bit sly myself, and this pleased the bitch so much she said it
was probably 'cause she's been prettying it up with face powder
lately, and she said booze peddlers don't have to be that pretty, etcetera, etcetera, etcetera. Damnable woman! You'd think women are
more scared of being told they're ugly than they are of getting knifed.

I mean, I can call her every name in the book, beat her like a dog, and in a few minutes the woman's back in my arms again with an idiotic grin on her face. But if I so much as find fault with her face she'll avoid me like the plague for three or four days, and I find my-self in one sticky situation. If the damn woman's going to get so aggra-vated when I tell her she's ugly, she might as well go around with her wedding veil on. Like I say, the bitch's sly, and if she was the least bit pretty, she'd give me my marching orders and run off with any son of a bitch that has money. If your woman is pretty, you'd better be pre-pared to pay the price. Yeah, I got to admit it—it's my bad luck she's got an ugly mug, but things could be a hell of a lot worse.

I'll bet broads have the time of their life when they two-time their husbands. The bitch swore she had what it takes to make it as a booze peddler, and maybe she thought she could do a little of that herself. One morning I'm up early, taking a crap, and I hear her some-where singing a tune. From the outhouse I look through the straw mat into the kitchen, and sure enough she's practicing while the chow's cooking. A snowstorm's howling outside, and she's hunched up in front of the stove beating out a rhythm with the poker on the lid of the ricepot. She sure looks pitiful singing those modern songs. When the food's boiling full tilt she takes it off the stove and starts right in again:

> Pasqueflower, granny-flower, young or old,
> Don't you look funny, all bends and folds.

Damnable woman! She's crazy about these modern songs, but when I tell her to apply herself to something more folksy, like "The Miller's Tune," nothing doing. Well, just as long as she learns a lot of 'em, I don't care which ones. But now get this: she's fumbling with the front collar of her jacket, and lo and behold, out comes a pipe. She peeks front and back, left and right, looks once more for good measure. No sign of yours truly. She sticks her face into the firebox, lights up, and takes a puff. Then all of a sudden it's *ahchoo, ahchoo, ahchoo,* and she blows her nose—quite a fit! Day before yesterday I caught her pinching my tobacco again, and lit into her. Scolded the hell out of her. I tell the damnable woman it don't cost nothing to learn songs, and what does she do—she steals *my* tobacco. I was about to run out, but nature called. These days our little Smarty has the dickens of a cold. But oh, no, the bitch has places to go, things to do, she carries him on her back to night school, and now look at the shape he's in.

Damn woman ought to be hogtied. She don't know how precious my
boy is to me. Just goes to show you, start peddling booze and your
behavior is bound to turn rotten. You should hear the damnable
woman: it's not enough to know how to sing, she says—you also got
to know how to smoke, you got to know how to drink, you got to
know how to give a man a squeeze, blah, blah, blah. All of it nonsense she heard from a booze peddler who came through the village a
while back. So she can't wait to practice all these things, one at a
time. The bitch has got a notion that she's quite the singer, and she
still can't do a decent "Miller's Tune"!

That damned Mung-t'ae, who lives down below us, knows all
about this, and he's been fooling with my woman. He's as much of a
dirty no-good as she is. What else can you say about a guy who'd get
hot on my wife with that mug of hers? Why does he have to get
chummy with her—is she the only broad on the face of the earth?
The damned son of a bitch, I bet I know what he's up to! He comes
over and finagles the bitch out, telling her they can booze it up for
free 'cause everybody's celebrating the end of the year. "Nothing
doing," she says, "the old man's due home in a little while." "Just till
sunset," he says, pulling her by the wrist. "If you're going to go out
peddling booze the first thing you need to do is see how it's done."
See, he's got this line, and the bitch's hooked—she's only too happy
to tag along. That's about the size of what happened, I reckon. The
bitch is going to be the ruin of our family. Husband's out selling firewood and comes home late, don't he have the right to expect his
woman to be fixing his supper while she waits for him? Here I am
staggering home seven or eight miles and it's nighttime. Snow's piling
up, ankles are about to go out on me, I'm getting numb. By the time I
get back to our village I'm so starved I could drop, believe me. Got to
get home, gobble down a bowl of chow, sit myself down, and start
working her with the songs again. As I'm thinking this I pass by the
tavern and get the surprise of my life—the bitch is laughing her head
off in one of the rooms near the street. I make tracks inside, peep
through a crack in the door, and there she is, the damnable woman,
drinking with Mung-t'ae.

Up to that time, the whole affair seemed so ridiculous that I sort of
left 'em alone, but now I can't hold back. I throw off the backrack,
fling open the door, and the first thing I do is slam the son of a bitch
on the floor. Of course the table gets kicked over and smashes against
the wall. Then I grab the bitch by the bun of her hair and drag her

outside. Got to sober up the drunken bitch with a good scolding, so I plant her face in the snow. I sit down on her and give the damnable woman a royal tattoo on the back. The more I hit her the more she sinks into the snow—she's too drunk to fight back. Well, this is kind of boring—half the fun of beating the bitch is seeing her put up a fight. I leave her be and go back inside for Mung-t'ae, but the asshole has snuck off like the mouse he is. I tell you, it's because of sons of bitches like him that the village is going to hell. You play around with someone else's woman, it's only proper you show up in front of her husband and take your licks. But this guy scuttles off. Huh! Too damn many of them plug-ugly assholes in this world. Nothing left to do now but plop the bitch on my back and totter on up to the house—feel like I'm fixing to die.

The night air is godawful cold, my empty stomach's killing me, I want to get more mad but ain't got the strength. And if that's not bad enough, on the way up the hill to the house I fall down and scrape the hell out of my knee. And when we get home there's little Smarty all by hisself crying his head off for Mama. Damnable whore, I says to myself, what the hell do you think you're doing raising my boy that way? Look at her—she'll never be a straight woman. I can see myself now, going out booze peddling with her, and she'll have me asleep by her side and off she'll run to another man. The proper thing for you, woman, is to forget about booze peddling and keep yourself at home. Live within your means, take care of your health, and turn out more kids for me. I ain't asking much—maybe fifteen tall, broad-shouldered boys. Let me figure this out—in a year one guy can grow himself about ten sacks of rice, so fifteen could come up with a hundred and fifty sacks. And if a sack can fetch you at least ten wŏn, then you're looking at fifteen hundred wŏn all told. Holy shit, fifteen hundred wŏn! That's a lot of money! I didn't realize that! I can grouse all I want, but she's carrying around the makings of fifteen hundred wŏn right in her belly. That's more than you can say about me.

When the Buckwheat Blooms

Yɪ Hʏᴏ-sŏᴋ

Yi Hyo-sŏk (1907–1942) is one of the talented group of young Korean writers whose flame burned brightly in the 1920s and 1930s only to be extinguished by the time of the Pacific War. Much of his early fiction concerns the urban poor and the destructiveness of city life. But by the mid-1930s he was taking inspiration from the Korean countryside where he was born.

"When the Buckwheat Blooms" (Memil kkot p'il muryŏp), first published in 1936 in the literary journal *Chogwang*, is his best-known story. Set in the Kangwŏn-Ch'ungch'ŏng border area that the author knew so well, it depicts the lives of rural peddlers and the colorful sights and sounds of market day— still a feature of Korean villages and towns. Its rich language, vivid descriptions of rural Korea, and masterful plot development have made it a favorite of readers and critics alike.

E very peddler who made the rounds of the countryside markets knew that business was never any good in the summer. And on this particular day, the marketplace in Pongp'yŏng was already deserted, though the sun was still high in the sky; its heat, seeping under the awnings of the peddlers' stalls, was enough to sear your spine. Most of the villagers had gone home, and you couldn't stay open forever just to do business with the farmhands who would have been happy to swap a bundle of firewood for a bottle of kerosene or some fish. The swarms of flies had become a nuisance, and the local boys were as pesky as gnats.

"Shall we call it a day?" ventured Hŏ Saengwŏn, a left-handed man with a pockmarked face, to his fellow dry-goods peddler Cho Sŏndal.

"Sounds good to me. We've never done well here in Pongp'yŏng. We'll have to make a bundle tomorrow in Taehwa."

"And we'll have to walk all night to get there," said Hŏ.

"I don't mind—we'll have the moon to light the way."

Cho counted the day's proceeds, letting the coins clink together. Hŏ watched for a moment, then began to roll up their awning and put away the goods he had displayed. The bolts of cotton cloth and the bundles of silk fabrics filled his two wicker hampers to the brim. Bits of cloth littered the straw mat on the ground.

The stalls of other peddlers were almost down, and some groups had gotten a jump on the rest and left town. The fishmongers, tinkers, taffymen, and ginger vendors—all were gone. Tomorrow would be market day in Chinbu and Taehwa, and whichever way you went, you would have to trudge fifteen to twenty miles through the night to get there. But here in Pongp'yŏng the marketplace had the untidy sprawl of a courtyard after a family gathering, and you could hear quarrels breaking out in the drinking houses. Drunken curses together with the shrill voices of women rent the air. The evening of a market day invariably began with the screeching of women.

A woman's shout seemed to remind Cho of something.

"Now don't play innocent, Saengwŏn—I know all about you and the Ch'ungju woman," he said with a wry grin.

"Fat chance I have with her. I'm no match for those kids."

"Don't be so sure," said Cho. "It's true that the young fellows all lose their heads over her. But you know, something tells me that Tongi, on the other hand, has her right around his finger."

"That greenhorn? He must be bribing her with his goods. And I thought he was a model youngster."

"When it comes to women, you can never be sure. . . . Come on now, stop your moping and let's go have a drink. It's on me."

Hŏ didn't think much of this idea, but he followed Cho nonetheless. Hŏ was a hapless sort when it came to women. With his pock-marked mug, he hesitated to look a woman in the eye, and women for their part wouldn't warm up to him. Midway through life by now, he had led a forlorn, warped existence. Just thinking of the Ch'ungju woman would bring to his face a blush unbefitting a man of his age. His legs would turn to rubber, and he would lose his composure.

The two men entered the Ch'ungju woman's tavern, and sure enough, there was Tongi. For some reason Hŏ himself couldn't have explained, his temper flared. The sight of Tongi flirting with the woman, his face red with drink, was something Hŏ could not bear. Quite the ladies' man, isn't he, thought Hŏ. What a disgraceful spectacle!

"Still wet behind the ears, and here you are swilling booze and flirting with women in broad daylight," he said, walking right up in front of Tongi. "You go around giving us vendors a bad name, but still you want a share of our trade, it seems."

Tongi looked Hŏ straight in the eye. Mind your own business, he seemed to be saying.

When the young man's animated eyes met his, Hŏ lashed Tongi across the cheek on impulse. Flaring up in anger, Tongi shot to his feet. But Hŏ, not about to compromise, let fly with all he had to say.

"I don't know what kind of family you come from, you young pup, but if your mom and dad could see this disgraceful behavior, how pleased they would be! Being a vendor is a full-time job—there's no time for women. Now get lost, right this minute!"

But when Tongi disappeared without a word of rejoinder, Hŏ suddenly felt compassion for him. He had overreacted, he told himself uneasily; that wasn't how you treated a man who was still but a nodding acquaintance.

"You've gone too far," said the Ch'ungju woman. "Where do you get the right to slap him and dress him down like that? To me you're both customers. And besides, you may think he's young, but he's old enough to produce children." Her lips were pinched together, and she poured their drinks more roughly now.

"Young people need a dose of that now and then," said Cho in an attempt to smooth over the situation.

"You've fallen for the young fellow, haven't you?" Hŏ asked the woman. "Don't you know it's a sin to take advantage of a boy?"

The fuss died down. Hŏ, already emboldened, now felt like getting good and drunk. Every bowl of liquor he was given he tossed off almost at a gulp. As he began to mellow, his thoughts of the Ch'ungju woman were overshadowed by concern for Tongi. What was a guy in my position going to do after coming between them? he asked himself. What a foolish spectacle he had presented!

And for this reason, when Tongi rushed back a short time later, calling Hŏ frantically, Hŏ put down his bowl and ran outside in a flurry without thinking twice about it.

"Saengwŏn, your donkey's running wild—it broke its tether."

"Those little bastards must be teasing it," muttered Hŏ.

Hŏ was of course concerned about his donkey, but he was moved

even more by Tongi's thoughtfulness. As he ran after Tongi across the
marketplace, his eyes became hot and moist.

"The little devils—there was nothing we could do," said Tongi.

"Tormenting a donkey—they're going to catch hell from me."

Hŏ had spent half his life with that animal, sleeping at the same
country inns and walking from one market town to the next along
roads awash with moonlight. And those twenty years had aged man
and beast together. The animal's cropped mane bristled like his
master's hair, and discharge ran from his sleepy eyes, just as it did
from Hŏ's. He would try as best he could to swish the flies away with
his stumpy tail, now too short to reach even his legs. Time and again
Hŏ had filed down the donkey's worn hooves and fitted him with
new shoes. Eventually the hooves had stopped growing back, and it
became useless trying to file them down. Blood now oozed between
the hooves and the worn shoes. The donkey recognized his master's
smell, and would greet Hŏ's arrival with a bray of delight and suppli-
cation.

Hŏ stroked the donkey's neck as if he were soothing a child. The
animal's nostrils twitched, and then he whickered, sending spray
from his nose in every direction. How Hŏ had suffered on account of
this creature. It wouldn't be easy calming the sweaty, trembling
donkey; those boys must have teased it without mercy. The animal's
bridle had come loose, and his saddle had fallen off.

"Good-for-nothing little rascals!" Hŏ yelled. But most of the boys
had run away. The remaining few had slunk off to a distance at Hŏ's
shouting.

"We weren't teasing him," cried one of them, a boy with a runny
nose. "He got an eyeful of Kim Ch'ŏmji's mare and went crazy!"

"Will you listen to the way that little guy talks," said Hŏ.

"When Kim Ch'ŏmji took his mare away, this one went wild—
kicking up dirt, foam all around his mouth, bucking like a crazy bull.
He looked so funny—all we did was watch. Look at him down there
and see for yourself," shouted the boy, pointing to the underside of
Hŏ's donkey and breaking into laughter.

Before Hŏ knew it, he was blushing. Feeling compelled to screen
the donkey from view, he stepped in front of the animal's belly.

"Confounded animal! Still rutting at his age," he muttered.

The derisive laughter flustered Hŏ for a moment, but then he gave
chase to the boys, brandishing his whip.

"Catch us if you can! Hey, everybody, Lefty's gonna whip us!"

But when it came to running, Hŏ was no match for the young troublemakers. That's right, old Lefty can't even catch a boy, thought Hŏ as he tossed the whip aside. Besides, the liquor was working on him again, and he felt unusually hot inside.

"Let's get out of here," said Cho. "Once you start squabbling with these market pests there's no end to it. They're worse than some of the grown-ups."

Cho and Tongi each saddled and began loading his animal. The sun had angled far toward the horizon.

In the two decades that Hŏ had been peddling dry goods at the rural markets, he had rarely skipped Pongp'yŏng in his rounds. He sometimes went to Ch'ungju, Chech'ŏn, and neighboring counties, and occasionally roamed farther afield to the Kyŏngsang region. Otherwise, unless he went to a place such as Kangnŭng to stock up on his goods, he confined his rounds to P'yŏngch'ang County. More regular than the moon, he tramped from one town to the next. He took pride in telling others that Ch'ŏngju was his hometown, but he never seemed to go there. To Hŏ, home sweet home was the beautiful landscape along the roads that led him from one market town to the next. When he finally approached one of these towns after trudging half a day, the restive donkey would let out a resounding hee-haw. In particular, when they arrived around dusk, the flickering lights in the town—though a familiar scene by now—never failed to make Hŏ's heart quicken.

Hŏ had been a thrifty youth and had put away a bit of money. But then one year during the All Souls' Festival he had squandered and gambled, and in three days he had blown all of his savings. Only his extreme fondness for the donkey had restrained him from selling the animal as well. In the end, he had had no choice but to return to square one and begin making the rounds of the market towns all over again. "It's a good thing I didn't sell you," he had said with tears in his eyes, stroking the donkey's back as they fled the town. He had gone into debt, and saving money was now out of the question. And thus began a hand-to-mouth existence as he journeyed from one market to the next.

In the course of all his squandering, Hŏ had never managed to conquer a woman. The cold, heartless creatures—they have no use for me, he would think dejectedly. His only constant friend was the donkey.

Be that as it may, there was one affair, and he would never forget it. His first and last affair—it was a most mysterious liaison. It had happened when he was young, when he had begun stopping at the Pongp'yŏng market, and whenever he recalled it he felt that his life had been worth living.

"For the life of me, I still can't figure it out," Hŏ said to no one in particular. "It was a moonlit night. . . ."

This was the signal that Hŏ would begin yarning again that night. Being Hŏ's friend, Cho had long since had an earful of what was to come. But he couldn't very well tell Hŏ he was sick of the story, and so Hŏ innocently started in anew and rambled on as he pleased.

"A story like this goes well with a moonlit night," said Hŏ with a glance toward Cho. It wasn't that he felt apologetic toward his friend; rather, the moonlight had made him feel expansive.

The moon was a day or two past full, and its light was soft and pleasant. Twenty miles of moonlit walking lay before them to Taehwa —two mountain passes, a stream crossing, hilly paths along endless fields. They were traversing a hillside. It was probably after midnight by now, and it was so deathly still the moon seemed to come alive right there in front of you, its breath almost palpable. Awash in moonlight, the bean plants and the drooping corn stalks were a shade greener. The hillside was covered with buckwheat coming into flower, and the sprinkling of white in the gentle moonlight was almost enough to take your breath away. The red stalks seemed delicate as a fragrance, and the donkeys appeared to have more life in their step.

The road narrowed, forcing the men to mount their animals and ride single file. The refreshing tinkle of the bells hanging from the donkeys' necks flowed toward the buckwheat. Hŏ's voice, coming from the front, wasn't clearly audible to Tongi at the tail end, but Tongi had some pleasant memories of his own to keep him company.

"It was market day in Pongp'yŏng, and the moon was out, just like tonight. I'd taken this tiny little room with a dirt floor, and it was so muggy I couldn't get to sleep. So I decided to go down and cool off in the stream. Pongp'yŏng then was just like it is now—buckwheat everywhere you looked, and the white flowers coming right down to the stream. I could have stripped right there on the gravel, but the moon was so bright, I decided to use the watermill shed instead. Well, I want to tell you, strange things happen in this world. Suddenly, there I was in the shed, face to face with old man Song's daughter—the town beauty. Was it fate that brought us together? You bet it was."

Hŏ puffed on a cigarette, as if savoring his own words. The rich aroma of the purple smoke suffused the night air.

"Of course she wasn't waiting for me, but for that matter she didn't have a boyfriend waiting for her, either. Actually she was crying. And I had a hunch why. Old man Song was having a terrible time making ends meet, and the family was on the verge of selling out. Being a family matter, it was cause enough for her to worry, too. They wanted to find a good husband for her, but she told me she would have died first. Now you tell me—is there anything that can get to a fellow more than the sight of a girl in tears? I sensed she was startled at first. But you know, girls tend to warm up to you more easily when they're worried, and it wasn't long until—well, you know the rest. Thinking back now, it scares me how incredible that night was."

"And the next day she took off for Chech'ŏn or thereabouts—right?" Cho prompted him.

"By the next market day, the whole family had vanished. You should have heard the gossip in the market. The rumors were flying: the family's best bet was to sell the girl off to a tavern, they were saying. God knows how many times I searched the Chech'ŏn marketplace for her. But there was no more sign of her than a chicken after dinner. My first night with her was my last. And that's why I have a soft spot in my heart for Pongp'yŏng, and why I've spent half my life visiting the place. I'll never forget it."

"You were a lucky man, Saengwŏn. Something like that doesn't happen every day. You know, a lot of fellows get stuck with an ugly wife, they have kids, and the worries begin to pile up—you get sick of that after a while. On the other hand, being an itinerant peddler to the end of your days isn't my idea of an easy life. So I'm going to call it quits after autumn. Thought I'd open up a little shop in a place like Taehwa and then have the family join me. Being on the road all the time wears a man out."

"Not me—unless I meet her again. I'll be walking this here road, watching that moon, till the day I croak."

The mountain path opened onto a wide road. Tongi came up from the rear, and the three donkeys walked abreast.

"But look at you, Tongi," said Hŏ. "You're still young—you're in the prime of life. It was stupid of me to act that way at the Ch'ungju woman's place. Don't hold it against me."

"Don't mention it. I'm the one who feels silly. At this stage of my life, I shouldn't be worrying about girls. Night and day, it's my mother I think about."

Downhearted because of Hŏ's story, Tongi spoke in a tone that was a shade subdued.

"When you mentioned my parents at the tavern, it made my heart ache. You see, I don't have a father. My mother's my only blood relation."

"Did your father die?"

"I never had one."

"Well, that's a new one."

Hŏ and Cho burst into laughter.

"I'm ashamed to say it," said Tongi with a serious expression, forced to explain himself, "but it's the truth. My mother gave birth to me prematurely when they were in a village near Chech'ŏn, and then her family kicked her out. I know it sounds strange, but that's why I've never seen my father's face, and I have no idea where he is."

The men dismounted as they approached a pass, and fell silent while climbing the rough road. The donkeys frequently slipped. Hŏ was soon short of breath, and had to pause time and again to rest his legs. He felt his age every time he had to cross a pass. How he envied the young fellows like Tongi. Sweat began to stream down his back.

Just on the other side of the pass, the road crossed a stream. The plank bridge had been washed out during the monsoon rains, so they would have to wade across. The men removed their loose summer trousers and tied them around their backs with their belts. Half naked, they presented a comical sight as they stepped briskly into the stream. They had been sweating a moment ago, but it was nighttime and the water chilled them to the bone.

"Who the devil brought you up, then?" Hŏ asked Tongi.

"My mother did. She had no choice but to remarry, and she opened up a drinking house. But my stepfather was a hopeless drunk—a complete good-for-nothing. Ever since I was old enough to know what's what, he beat me. We didn't have a day's peace. And if Mother tried to stop him, she'd get kicked, hit, threatened with a knife. Our family was one big mess. And so I left home at eighteen, and I've been peddling ever since."

"I always thought you were quite a boy for your age, but to hear all this, it sounds like you've *really* had a hard time."

The water had risen to their waists. The current was quite strong, the pebbles underfoot slippery. The men felt as if they would be swept from their feet at any moment. Cho and the donkeys had made quick progress and were almost across. Tongi and Hŏ, the younger man supporting the older, were far behind.

"Was your mother's family originally from Chech'ŏn?" asked Hŏ.

"I don't think so. I never could get a straight answer out of her, but I've heard say they lived in Pongp'yŏng."

"Pongp'yŏng. . . . What was your dad's name, anyway?"

"Beats me. I never heard it mentioned."

"I suppose not," mumbled Hŏ as he blinked his bleary eyes. And then, distracted, he lost his footing. His body pitched forward, plunging him deep into the stream. He flailed about, unable to right himself, and by the time Tongi had called out to Cho and caught up to Hŏ, the older man had been washed some distance away. With the sodden clothes on his back, Hŏ looked more miserable than a wet dog. Tongi lifted him easily from the water and carried him piggyback. Soaked though he was, Hŏ was a slender man, and he rested lightly on Tongi's sturdy back.

"Sorry to put you to this trouble," said Hŏ. "I guess my mind's been wandering today."

"It's nothing to worry about."

"So, didn't it ever seem to you that your mother was looking for your dad?"

"Well, she's always saying she'd like to see him."

"And where is she now?"

"In Chech'ŏn—she went there after she split up with my stepfather. I'm thinking of moving her up to Pongp'yŏng this fall. If I put my mind to it, we'll make out somehow."

"Sure, why not? That's a swell idea. Did you say this fall?"

Tongi's broad, agreeable back spread its warmth into Hŏ's bones. And then they were across. Hŏ plaintively wished Tongi might have carried him a bit farther.

Cho could no longer suppress a laugh.

"Saengwŏn, this just isn't your day."

"It was that donkey colt—I got to thinking about it and lost my balance. Didn't I tell you? You wouldn't think this old fellow had it in him, but by God if he didn't sire a colt with the Kangnŭng woman's mare in Pongp'yŏng. The way it pricks up its ears and prances about —is there anything as cute as a donkey colt? There are times I've stopped at Pongp'yŏng just to see it."

"Must be some colt to make a man take a spill like that."

Hŏ wrung a fair amount of water out of his sodden clothes. His teeth chattered, he shivered, he was cold all over. But for some unaccountable reason he felt buoyant.

"Let's hurry to the inn, fellows," said Hŏ. "We'll build a fire in the yard and get nice and cozy. I'll heat up some water for the donkey, and tomorrow I'll stop at Taehwa, and then head on to Chech'ŏn."

"You're going to Chech'ŏn, too?" asked Tongi, his voice trailing off in surprise.

"Thought I'd pay a visit—haven't been there in a while. How about it, Tongi—you and me?"

As the donkeys set off again, Tongi was holding his whip in his left hand. This time Hŏ, whose eyes had long been weak and dim, couldn't fail to notice Tongi was left-handed.

As Hŏ ambled along, the tinkle of the donkeys' bells, more lucid now, carried over the dusky expanse. The moon had arched far across the heavens.

Mystery Woman

Yɪ Kᴡᴀɴɢ-sᴜ

Yi Kwang-su (1892–1950) casts a giant shadow over twentieth-century Korean intellectual history. Born in the Chŏngju area of present-day North P'yŏngan Province in North Korea, Yi was orphaned at ten and went to Japan at thirteen to study, graduating with a degree in philosophy from Waseda University in 1918. A prolific author (one edition of his works runs to twenty-four volumes), Yi was also a prominent journalist.

Yi's contribution to the evolution of modern Korean culture and society cannot be overemphasized. In a variety of literary forums, he attacked the repressive Korean political tradition and Confucian social structure, championed the rights of women, and pressed for a vernacular literature that would address contemporary themes. His major works of fiction include the pathbreaking novel *Mujŏng* (The heartless, 1917), *Hŭk* (Soil, 1932), and the novella "Mumyŏng" (The unenlightened, 1938). Yi was abducted to North Korea after the outbreak of the civil war in 1950; sometime thereafter he died in custody.

Yi is often thought of, with some justification, as a didactic writer. In any case, like most of the first generation of twentieth-century Korean writers, he is underrepresented in translation. This is unfortunate, since several of his shorter pieces of fiction, such as "Halmŏm" (Granny, 1940) and "Taramjwi" (Squirrels), are gems of human insight written in a fresh, unmannered style.

"Mystery Woman" (Morŭnŭn yŏin) was first published in 1936 in *Sahae kongnon*.

M‌y grandfather was approaching eighty and my sister was only seven when I left home. After six months in Seoul I returned to visit them. The previous year, the Russo-Japanese War had erupted and the first battle had taken place near my hometown. Grandfather had been teaching me Mencius, and that summer I had asked him, "What's the use of studying this if the government isn't giving the state examination anymore?" With those words I had dismissed thoughts of Mencius and set out for Seoul. Grandfather's aged concubine had been with him then, but while I was in Seoul, this stoop-backed old woman had passed away. Grandfather had been unable to maintain the house after the old woman's death, and so he had sold it and moved with my sister to a little house far across the hill from the village where his mother's family lived. This out-of-the-way place was where I would visit him and my sister.

It was a thatched house with a gate made of sorghum stalks. There were only two rooms, a kitchen, and a storeroom, but Grandfather had seen fit to wallpaper the room nearer the firebox. Although the walls were warped and uneven, his handiwork was evident in the white paper he pasted over them. A cushion lay on the warmest part of the heated floor, and Grandfather's stationery chest and inkstone case were placed beside it. These were surrounded by a half-height folding screen embroidered in the Anju style. In that room, at least, nothing seemed to have changed in the six months since I had left the other house. Later I heard from my sister that the screen and the stationery chest had already been sold, and that when winter passed they would be taken away by the new owners.

To a fourteen-year-old boy like myself, nothing in life could have been more wretched than the sad plight of my grandfather. He had been preceded in death by his two sons and by the woman he had shared his twilight years with, and his possessions were gone. His only grandson had fled to Seoul under the pretext of study, and now he lived on with only his young granddaughter. The vestiges of his better days had been sold—such things as his folding screens, books, and clothing cabinets—and now he was barely scraping by. An elderly cousin on his mother's side occasionally supplied him with firewood. I had learned all of this before leaving Seoul.

The day I arrived seemed more like late winter than early spring, judging from the mantle of snow on the hills. It was dusk, but the lamp in Grandfather's room hadn't been lit, and I could barely see him as he sat silently in the gloom. I prostrated myself before him.

"Well, so it's In-dŭk. I heard you were coming, and I waited on the hill. But I began to feel the chill just now, so I came inside. I trust you're well?"

His voice sounded just as it had the previous year. He didn't seem to have declined all that much.

"Did Kyŏng-ae go out somewhere?"

"Maybe so. She made dinner, and ever since, she's been fussing around waiting for you. Goodness, I wonder if she went for water—sweetie! Oh, sweetie!"

Presently I heard the clatter of a gourd dipper in a water jar. I opened the door and raced outside.

"Brother!" she cried, straightening in surprise. The water jar she carried on her head looked about to fall off.

My little sister—she was eight years old now. It had been two years since we had lost our parents, one of them before the August full-moon holiday, the other one shortly after. My youngest sister had been given up to another family as an infant and had died of dysentery, leaving Kyŏng-ae as my only sibling.

The sight of her in the twilight brought back these memories, and I felt warm tears flood from my eyes. She stood there in the cold with the water jug on her head, the string of the carrying cushion between her teeth, one hand steadying the jar and the other pressing against her chest, just like the adults did. Her cotton clothing was soiled, but at least it was thickly padded.

"How far do you have to go for water?"

"Pretty far. There's a well closer by, but it's frozen over. Brother, are you going away again?" She wiped away her tears with the back of her hand.

I couldn't bear to tell her that I had decided to go abroad to study. I reached out to take the water jar from her head.

"Uh-uh, I know how to do it."

She was so small she didn't need to stoop to go through the kitchen door, but she did so anyway, entering the kitchen ever so carefully and setting down the jar. Then she wiped her hands on her apron and looked up at me from the door. "Go on in. I'll bring dinner." I heard a clatter as she busied herself in the dark interior of the kitchen.

That little girl fetched water just to make my dinner! I thought as I wiped away my tears with my fist. I sighed, then went inside.

Dinner arrived. First came a tray with Grandfather's rice and soup, then a tray with mine. Kyŏng-ae brought her meal in last, carrying the bowls in her hands, just as a mother would do.

Grandfather had lit the oil lamp, and the light of the tiny flame shone on the three of us as we sat down to eat. Dinner, such as it was, consisted of rice, kimchi, soup made from the outer leaves of cabbage, and, perhaps in my honor, a bowl of egg stew.

"Where did the eggs come from?" asked Grandfather.

"From Sam-sun's mother. I told her Brother was coming, and she gave me two eggs to cook for him," my sister said proudly.

"Did you see Po-bu's mama?" Grandfather asked Kyŏng-ae while mashing the rice with his toothless gums. In Grandfather's prime his appearance had been the talk of the county, but now his face had darkened with liver spots.

"No, she didn't come today, either."

"Must not be feeling well."

"Who's she?" I asked. It was the first time I had heard of this woman.

"We call her Po-bu's mother. She's from over there a ways," explained Kyŏng-ae. "After Grandmother died she spent all summer, fall, and winter helping us with meals, laundry, sewing—stuff like that. Po-bu's her daughter. She's bigger than me—she's fifteen. Gee, is she pretty! So we call the woman Po-bu's mother. Grandfather, you're right—she might be sick—she hasn't come here for three days—or maybe little Turtle's sick."

Grandfather turned to me. "Why don't you go over and look her up tomorrow?"

"All right."

Why had such a helpful woman arrived on the scene? I wondered. Gratitude toward this woman, whoever she was, welled up in my heart at the thought that she had been helping Grandfather all winter long when our own kin pretended not to be aware of his predicament.

"Why would someone spend all that time helping out here?" I asked Kyŏng-ae.

"I don't know. She's a total stranger to us. All I know is she used to work at a tavern. They say her husband's a gambler, but they seem to live well enough. And they say he's not drinking these days. I've been to their house several times, but I only saw him once. He's really scary-looking. But his daughter's so pretty. And little Turtle's a handsome boy, too."

There was a terrible snowstorm the next day, but in the morning I left for the woman's house, as Grandfather had asked. Everyone knew where Po-bu's family lived, so I had no trouble finding them.

I hesitated outside their door, wondering how to announce my arrival, and then I remembered the name of the daughter.

"Po-bu!"

A very pretty girl in a pink skirt and a yellow jacket trimmed in maroon stuck her head out, looked at me, and flinched. Then there appeared a stout woman with a fair complexion who looked to be in her thirties, a very handsome woman the likes of which you don't often see in the countryside there.

"Well, it's the young master from Seoul!" she said, probably recognizing me by my cropped hair and black school uniform, or by my resemblance to Grandfather and Kyŏng-ae. She quickly emerged from the doorway, took my hand, and then led me inside.

"To think you came in such cold weather! Our little Turtle's been sick, and so I haven't been able to visit your family—now you come sit here," she said as she led me to the warm part of the heated floor, where the baby they called little Turtle was lying. Though she said he had been sick, he looked well enough to me.

The woman observed my face with delight, squeezing my hand over and over. "This is our daughter, Po-bu. She's been wanting so much to meet you. Po-bu, why don't you come over here. . . . Now what's there to be shy about? My, my, isn't the young master handsome. And this is our son—good-looking boy, isn't he? He caught a cold, the poor thing! But he's better now." The woman didn't try to hide her look of utter delight.

I managed to thank the woman for looking after Grandfather and Kyŏng-ae. Grandfather had been worrying about her, I said, and had asked me to stop by.

"Oh, I haven't done all that much. Besides, it's not right that older people should have no one to look after them, so I just stopped by now and then—that's all. Goodness, I forgot to ask you about breakfast. I'll bet you haven't eaten yet."

I shook my head as she was about to get up. "Thank you anyway, but I ate before I left."

"Now you don't think I'm going to send away an honored guest without feeding him, do you? The least I can do is make you some rice and soup. Po-bu, sweetie, how about having a chat with the young master. You're always talking about how you'd like to meet him. I'll be right back."

After the woman left, Po-bu approached, as if to sit next to little Turtle, but she ended up sitting beside me and staring at my cropped hair and my unfamiliar uniform, which had been tailored in Seoul. Dyed cloth wasn't something you saw very often in the countryside back then.

"Where did your father go?" I asked.

"Why should he be here? He's always going from one gambling

den to another. And when he does come home he gets in a fight with Mother—grabs her by the hair, hits her, kicks her—and he hits me, too." She spoke disparagingly of her father, emphasizing the words, but not so much that her mother could hear from the kitchen.

"Why do your mother and father fight?" I felt comfortable with Po-bu already, and as my inhibitions vanished I opened up with her.

"No special reason—maybe it's because he's drunk all the time." She fixed her eyes on little Turtle, and then on my face. Then she placed a hand on my shoulder and pulled me toward her, putting her lips so close to my ear that I could feel their warmth. "Who do you think our little Turtle looks like?" she whispered. Again she looked into my eyes, her arm still curled around my shoulder.

"I don't know," I said, gaping at her in surprise.

"From what I can see he takes after . . ." She didn't know how to address me, so instead of calling my name she brushed my cheek once with her fingertips, then put her mouth to my cheek. Again she brought her lips to my ears.

"That's why Father beat her up this time until she was black and blue. She hasn't left the house in three days," she said in a barely audible tone. "Everyone in the village could see that the baby resembled Mr. Kim, your grandfather." Quick as a flash of lightning she touched her lips to mine. Then she covered her face with her hands and looked away.

I gazed in astonishment at little Turtle, asking myself over and over if it was me I saw in his face.

All this was some forty years ago. Already it's been over thirty years since Grandfather passed away. I've had no chance to see the woman, Po-bu, and little Turtle. I don't know their whereabouts, and I've long forgotten the names of the woman and the little one. The woman must be over seventy if she's still alive, Po-bu in her fifties, and little Turtle forty—enough time for them all to have white hair by now.

Could little Turtle really have resembled me?

Most likely not. He couldn't have. I say this for the reputation of Grandfather and that generous woman. But even if I'm wrong, there's one thing I can say for sure: the three faces I saw that day have become an intimate presence in my memory, never to be forgotten.

The Haunted House

CH'OE CHŎNG-HŬI

Ch'oe Chŏng-hŭi was born in 1912 in Tanch'ŏn, South Hamgyŏng Province, and was educated in Seoul. After a brief sojourn in Japan, and while still in her teens, she went to work for the journal *Samch'ŏlli*, where she made her literary debut in 1931. In a career that spanned fifty years she published essays, criticism, and twelve volumes of fiction. She died in 1990. Her daughters, Kim Chi-wŏn and Kim Ch'ae-wŏn, are award-winning fiction writers.

Ch'oe, along with Pak Hwa-sŏng, was probably the most successful of the early modern women writers. Her story "Sanje" (The memorial service on the mountain, 1938), like Hyŏn Chin-gŏn's "Pul," can be read as a rebellion against sexual tyranny. "Chŏmnye" (1947) is an engaging sketch of a country girl of that name.

"The Haunted House" (Hyungga) was first published in *Chogwang* in 1937. It is an unusual story for its time in that the narrator is a single mother (her son apparently born out of wedlock) who supports an extended family on her job as a newspaper writer. Looming in the background, like the mask in her room that proves so unnerving, is the strain created by her various familial and professional responsibilities and the recent discovery that she has tuberculosis.

The house was supposed to be haunted.

But at the time I had no idea. Clad in my simple traditional jacket and sheltered by an umbrella, I clutched the hand of an elderly realtor as he strode along in front of me, crossed a creek that had swollen after an early-morning downpour, then looked around the outside of the house.

The front gate was locked. But I learned to my delight that since the house was empty, we could move in as soon as we signed the papers. The realtor then disappeared around the hillside to fetch the owner, leaving me alone at the gate beneath my umbrella to sweep my eyes back and forth at what lay beyond the fence. Cherry, apricot, and persimmon trees surrounded the house, and there were some nicely shaped rocks where the hills came down right in back.

Buds had sprouted from the cherries, and sap ran from the apricots and the crab apple trees. Only the persimmon trees looked dark, famished, lifeless, but it wouldn't be long before they were thick with leaves. This sight made the house even more to my liking. You can imagine how anxious I was for the realtor to hurry back around the hill with the owner.

Our family desperately needed a house, and I was determined, if we could only come to terms with the owner, to have this one, especially since it had a crab apple tree in the garden—and even if it didn't have the detached kitchen Mother had been wanting ever since she came up from the countryside two years before. At least that was my plan. . . .

It all seemed to have turned out so well. The owner appeared with the realtor some thirty minutes later. It would be fine, he said, if we moved in on the spot, no strings attached, just so long as we paid him thirty wŏn for three months' rent. And that was it. According to my experience from the past six or seven years, even a single room that rented for three or four wŏn a month involved a good forty or fifty wŏn up front, what with the deposit and several months' advance rent. But here we had a house with three rooms, a kitchen, a veranda, a spacious yard, and good scenery on top of it all. And yet there was no deposit, nothing was said about paying several months' rent in advance, there were no questions about job or family—he simply handed us the place. I wondered about the reason for this, but I was more worried about the owner changing his tune, to our disadvantage. So I made a firm promise to return at six that evening with thirty wŏn, and home I went.

It was a good thing, because our family, together with the hundred-odd other people who occupied a house in Chŏng-dong, had finally been evicted by the process server, the lawyer, and the constable. We had loaded up all our possessions, which had been tossed into the courtyard, filling it so you could scarcely make your way about, and moved into a room at the house of a friend's friend who lived just outside Chaha Gate. This was supposed to be temporary, but we ended up staying there well over a month.

No matter how solid the relationship between friends, a friend's friend is a friend's friend. Besides, I had never met the latter, and the fact that his wife and I, it turned out, went to the same girls' high school made things much more awkward. I had known nothing about the identity of the wife, and when my mother, my son, my younger siblings, and I, a ridiculous sight with all our shabby possessions, finally arrived there late in the evening after plodding over the Chaha Gate ridge, and I learned who the lady of the house was, I felt so ashamed I wanted to cry.

What was even more embarrassing, Sŏgi, the errand boy who lived there, was forced to vacate his room for us the following day and move in with relatives who lived two or three miles downtown. From there, he would make the climb back to the house every morning, rubbing the sleep from his eyes as he arrived.

But instead of a day or two there, we ended up staying well over a month. It must have been quite hard on Sŏgi; he asked, every time my son ventured outside, when we were going to move.

In the midst of all this the door didn't remain shut for an instant what with the comings and goings of my boy. He would make a mess and fuss, or write or draw pictures on the nicely papered door and walls, or go into the vegetable garden where he didn't belong, or pick flowers and break branches off the flowering trees and the fruit trees. If we told him not to do these things, he'd make an even bigger fuss.

One Sunday, my day off from the newspaper, he was making trouble and finally I lost my temper. I clamped my hands over his mouth, pinched his cheeks as hard as I could, and shook his head back and forth. He screamed his lungs out at me, then quivered silently in outrage. Mother, sitting flustered in the corner, arms crossed, observed this spectacle and ended up taking the boy into her arms and crying along with him.

Then, in a trembling undertone, she took me to task: "You're overdoing it—what does he know at his age?"

I felt like wailing myself, but it would have looked even more miserable for me to be bawling in front of Mother and the boy, and what would the landlord and his family think? And so instead I sought out the big pine tree on the other side of the hill in front of the house. I wished I could sob my heart out. Sighing as I thought of Mother weeping with the boy, I gazed up at the hills and the ruins of the fortress and the thick white clouds floating above them.

The rays of the April sun warmed me. Those rays made me long for human warmth and affection.

The very next morning, a Sunday, having paid thirty wŏn in rent, we moved into the house. It was very close to the house where we had been staying, but even with my brother and sister and Sŏgi lending a hand (Sŏgi was overjoyed to get his room back), the moving still took well over half the day. In the course of a year we'd moved several times, but although I'd always complained that we ought to get rid of what we could do without, our belongings never became any lighter, because we felt that we might get some use out of them and that it would be wasteful to actually dispose of them. So when they were all gathered together, the whole inventory, they seemed so numerous. Our new residence had been vacant for the longest time, and you wouldn't have believed all the weeds and blight in the yard, and the spider webs and mildew inside. We did a rough cleanup, then set the ricepot in the cooking range and cleaned the mildew and grime from the veranda and the floors of the rooms. Hanging new paper in the rooms would have to wait. I selected for myself the room across the veranda from our family room, and there I arranged my desk, chair, and books along with the gourd mask that a friend had brought me from the South Seas. Then my mother and siblings roughly arranged their prize possessions in the rooms they would be using. By that time it was well past nine at night, and finally we lit the candles above the sliding window in the family room, gathered all together, starving, and had our evening meal.

After she had finished and felt more rested Mother voiced some worries: "It's a nice place, but where are we going to get ten wŏn a month for rent?"

But after all this time, my immediate reaction was one of relief. This was the first time in six or seven years that I had a quiet room of my own. I was simply delighted.

"We've already put out thirty wŏn this month; there won't be much left of your salary," Mother continued. "How are we going to get by?"

"Oh, we'll make do. We can put a couple of students in the room beside the gate and use their board money for rice and firewood, and my salary will cover the rent plus our spending money, so don't worry."

Thus mollified, Mother responded, "Now that we have an entire house to ourselves, we won't have to feel embarrassed if our meal table isn't fancy or the kids make a fuss. The veranda is big enough so we can fold and iron all our laundry. And we can have visitors from back home without feeling ashamed."

Each day felt more like spring. The green of the vegetables in our kitchen garden turned almost to blue, and the neighborhood children made music on willow-leaf flutes. White blossoms appeared on the crab apple and apricot trees in front and back of the house, and the shade of the cherry trees grew lush. The cuckoos produced hearty calls in the hills out back. All of us liked the house. My brother, who had never held a broom before, now swept the courtyard every morning; Mother reported that the house appealed to her more and more; my son proudly pointed out to anyone who visited that we had a kitchen and three rooms; and for the first time in three years my sister brought friends home from school to play. And as for me, I was so happy to be in a house I liked that whenever I had a spare moment I would stroll among the crab apples and imagine the smell of the fresh white blossoms yet to come. It was marvelous the way all of us took such delight in spring at this house.

And then about three weeks after we'd moved in I went to the hospital for a checkup. X-rays were taken, and they showed spots on my lungs. On my way home, as I passed in front of the Shaman Shrine, always a source of cheer on my daily passage through the Chaha Gate, I thought of the story told to me by the old handyman as he helped set up our kitchen the day we moved in, and of the dream I had that same night in which a woman, supposedly the madwoman who owned our house, appeared and grabbed me by the hair and beat me. And finally I came to the conclusion that the house was indeed haunted, and that there lay the origin of this recent misfortune of mine.

The old man had related the story with a perfectly dour expression. It was quite a lengthy account.

"This is actually the second time I've worked on setting up this kitchen. The first time was when the former woman of the house got married and moved here. Proper arrangement of the firebox and the family kettle has a lot to do with a family's luck in a new house, you know. As far as money goes, the woman's husband had a pile of it. Everyone around here called him Moneybags until . . ."

"Until what?" I had to ask.

"You mean to tell me you rented this house without knowing? Oh well, even though the site is ill favored, everything depends on the power you bring to the house, they say. You see, the husband wasn't even forty when he up and died. And then the woman of the house went crazy. After a while people began saying the house was evil and haunted, and not a soul came around. The place was left empty for two years, and so—"

"Where does the lady live?"

"Ah yes, the lady. She's with her husband's older brother, and she has no one to turn to. She has a five-year-old daughter, but what can *she* do? The brother-in-law was only too happy to take over the woman's household belongings and assets, and she had a lot of them. That no-good—can you imagine treating your own brother's family like that? His brother had barely stopped breathing, and there he was arguing with the widow about the assets—who had what claims to which property, and so on—can you believe it? I would have been surprised if she *hadn't* gone crazy! That was what she had to put up with—and damned if she didn't start these laughing fits, right in the room where her husband was stretched out, and finally she went crazy. It was pitiful. Even now the brother-in-law and his family have nothing to do with the woman and the girl; they avoid them when they can, give 'em dirty looks when they can't. If he didn't have to worry about what others think, he'd have gotten rid of them a long time ago. He has the time of his life spending what he makes from those fruit trees—cherries and apricots in spring, crab apples in summer, persimmons in fall, something every season. You'd think with all those crab apples the guy might offer one to the neighbors, or at least to the village elders. Nope. All he's concerned about is filling his own belly. In the meantime, he's picked out all the expensive furniture and other possessions and sold off whatever he couldn't use himself. All that's left is cheap rubbish, soy sauce and bean-paste crocks, and such."

"Do you mean that the shed over there still holds all that stuff from the old days?"

"Yes indeed. All the rubbish and dirty sauce crocks that he didn't take for himself, he locked up in that shed yonder. In summer the crocks are swarming with maggots and they stink to high heaven."

"So that's why. I noticed the shed smelled funny. Anyway, the realtor told us we weren't supposed to use it."

"With all the stuff in there, there was no way they could let you. But you should have insisted on the use of it anyway.

"Folks whisper about how the owner of this house died, but the fact is, he simply overworked himself. You see, he planted a lot of fruit trees in that big orchard, and he spent so much time tending 'em he practically forgot to eat and sleep. He moves into this house, and seven years later he's dead. All that time he was out working the orchard, day and night. And when his orchard finally begins to pay off, he ends up dead. He must have thought the whole thing was darn unfair.

"So the crazy woman used to stop anyone on the street and ask what that person had done with the seven thousand bushels of her precious apples, or with her money, all five thousand *nyang* of it, or by what right had that person redone her bedcloth into skirts, and then she'd start that crazy laughing of hers. Just two days ago she was right out there rattling the locked gate and screaming, 'Who's living in my house?' When the weather's foul she wanders out of her brother-in-law's house and comes here to rattle the gate like I just told you, or walk round and round the fence muttering something or other. The neighbors aren't exactly pleased about it, but I'm telling you all of this, ma'am, because I figure 'modern' people like you won't mind hearing these spooky things concerning the house you rented. The most important job at the moment, though, is to get your stove and cooking kettles squared away so your family will get rich while you live here."

All of this came out without a break, and without my asking, either, and then the old man bent over to peer into the fuel hole in the fire-box, his rump thrust up toward the sky. At first this story seemed so awful I didn't want the others in my family to hear it, and so I had to keep reminding the old man to keep his voice down. And then he said two or three times that the fortunes of the household depended on how well he set up the firebox and kettle. I sensed he was being a bit too pushy about the merits of his work, and to stop him from talking further I urged him to get on with the job. But if what he had said was true, how wretched it must have been for the woman who owned the house—losing her husband while she was still young, seeing her precious belongings and all her assets being enjoyed by others, unable to live in the house she wanted, treated like an outcast

by her brother-in-law and the neighbors. Not only did my heart
go out to her, but even if the house was in fact haunted, as the
old man had said, then what could I do in my position? On the
other hand, I thought it was fine that the house carried a curse. That
meant we wouldn't be hard pressed or evicted if we were late with
the rent.

Perhaps because of this old man's story, I had a very funny and
weird dream my first night in the house. At the time, I didn't give a
second thought to either the dream or the old man's story.

Be that as it may, on our third day there, I raised a fever that didn't
go away. Then came the chills, and after three weeks of this I was
growing discouraged. It was the flu, Mother said, and it would surely
go away. I too thought I'd been strained to the limit, mentally and
physically, because of the series of events leading up to moving into
the new house. And so we had let it go.

The doctor's diagnosis of tuberculosis frightened me so much I
went home early that day, and there I suddenly thought back to the
story the old man had told me. And I could argue that the bad dream
I had that very night was the result of that fright. But in fact, my
immediate reaction was not to worry about my lungs. Instead I was
concerned about how my family would get along. It's true, though,
that I dreamed the crazy woman who owned the house grabbed my
long, long hair and beat me at her pleasure, and after the dream I
ended up losing all my energy.

I had no doubt that the woman who took me by the hair and beat
me in my dream was the woman who owned the house. And the
questions she asked me—"Why did you take my quilt casing and
make skirts out of it? Why did you move into my house?"—weren't
they just as the old man had said?

I had never actually seen this woman, but I convinced myself she
looked like the woman in the dream, who had four eyes, a big head,
and short, stumpy legs.

Those four eyeballs had scared me the way they rolled around,
and I shuddered at the thought of how she had grabbed my long hair
with her left hand while she beat the living daylights out of me with
her right hand.

I cried out in my sleep, then half-awakened to find that the candle
at the head of my bed had burned out. The room was utterly still.
Moonlight filled the west-facing window, darkly etching the shadow
of a persimmon tree upon it. While I tried to control my leaping

heart, I looked around, but saw nothing to lessen my fear. All I could make out were the desk, chairs, books, and gourd mask dimly lit by the moon. My eyes enlarged like a pair of big lanterns and I gazed at the shadow of the persimmon cast on the window. It flickered with every gust of wind, frightening me into a cold sweat. It seemed just as if the woman beating me in the dream were outside the window playing a devilish trick on me. I resented the moonlight, and wanted other light instead. I groped clumsily about the head of my bed, hoping just a tiny stump of candle might be left, but it was all gone. My eyes wouldn't leave the window. I felt that if I looked away, then the woman of my dream, whom I imagined standing outside, would open the window in a flash and be inside. If only the shadow of the persimmon would go away! How elegant that tree had seemed as it stood right against the window when I had looked about the grounds that first day.

Sweat streamed from me like water and the fever made my forehead hot as a fireball. I couldn't budge and simply felt as if I would die.

I wanted to call Mother but couldn't. Not so much because I didn't want to wake her but because I was too frightened. We wanted electric lights, and had constantly called the electric company during the twenty days we'd been here, but since we were outside the city, several other houses besides ours would have to request service before they would hook us up. This thought made me feel all the more hateful.

What time is it? Should I call Mother?

But the sliding door between the family room, where she slept, and my room across the veranda was probably too thick for her to hear me.

As I wondered what to do, trembling, perspiring, my eyes still glued to the window, I heard a rooster from one of the houses across the way. I strained to listen, hoping to hear it again. For the crowing would mean a new day had drawn near—and the ghosts would leave, wouldn't they? And the woman I imagined outside the window would leave too. Overjoyed, I called out to Mother.

But there was no answer. I called out to her again, this time louder. Again there was no answer, only the quavering echo of my voice clamoring throughout the stillness of the room.

Perhaps it wasn't dawn after all. But surely I had heard the rooster? And it was Mother's habit to rise at dawn. Well, maybe it was still early at night, and when a rooster crowed then, didn't it mean something bad was going to happen?

Back when we lived in the countryside, when Mother was young and Grandmother was still alive, a rooster had once crowed and flapped its wings early at night. According to Grandmother, this meant a terrible disaster was approaching, and on the spot she wrung the rooster's neck and dumped it in a pot of boiling water, and we ended up eating it.

When its neck was wrung the rooster stuck out its beak and spewed blood. Its eyes bulged and it moved its legs. It struggled for a time and then stretched out its wings before Grandmother was able to put it in the boiling water and pluck its feathers. The plucking produced a strange sound.

The next morning at breakfast, while they added boiled rice to the chicken soup, Mother and Grandmother said not a word about this ominous incident involving the rooster, and so I didn't comment about it either.

And now the rooster across the way was crowing once more. The sound made my flesh crawl, and I snuggled into my quilt. For this certainly sounded like a rooster crowing at dusk, not at dawn. Wrapped up as I was in my quilt, I still thought I could see the shadow of the persimmon cast by the dazzling moonlight on the west window, and I still thought I could hear the rooster crowing. It was so frightening. By now I couldn't even muster the energy to call out to Mother.

"We can have visitors from back home without feeling ashamed." I had remembered these words of Mother's, as well as what my son had asked with a tearful face the day we moved, as the sun crested the Chaha Gate ridge—"Mama, why do we always have to move? . . . Is our new house at the end of the sky?" Even so, my only thought now was to get our money back from the owner of the house as soon as it was dawn and move out.

After suffering this fright I seemed to have fallen asleep beneath my quilt for a brief time. When I removed the quilt and opened my eyes the moonlight and the shadow of the persimmon had vanished from the window, which was already bright with a light that was not moonlight. Nor did I hear the rooster crowing. Not in keeping with my recent habit of getting up in the morning and going directly to the west window to open it, my hair in disarray and my nightclothes disheveled, I opened instead the sliding door that faced the family room. Everyone had risen, and the sliding doors of the family room that I presumed were shut, the doors that seemed as thick and stout as a fortress gate, were wide open. And so I pushed open the front window, then returned to the west window and forced myself to push it open with my fist. No moonlight, no persimmon tree shadow. Even so, with the previous night fresh in my mind, and the window making a queer sound as it knocked against the wall, I looked around outside. Nothing to be frightened of. Only the sight that always brought gladness to me—the hills and the crab apples, the flowering apricots and the persimmon tree, the cherry orchard and the rocks.

For the longest time I sat resting my chin on the windowsill and gazed at hills and trees, flowers and rocks, thinking of something or other—I can't remember what—as shimmering heat waves enveloped the ridgeline and rose to the summits of the hills. My vision grew hazy, my head spun, my chest pounded—all of it making me uneasy, as if I had been beaten up by someone.

I lay down again. Blue sky was visible through the open front window. Frightened by that blue, I rose and closed the door. But once I had laid down again the open west window and the sliding door to the family room made me uneasy—they seemed like carved-out hollows—and I closed both of them. Now, though, my room was terribly gloomy, and once again I was frightened. I thought of my dream and of what the old handyman had told me as he worked on our kitchen—"Even though the site is ill favored, everything depends on the power you bring to the house."

Was the house site indeed ill favored? Had I fallen ill and dreamed that frightening dream all because the house site was cursed? Would not the madwoman who owned the house rush out of her brother-in-law's before nightfall and come this way?

Once again I broke out in a cold sweat, and I had a racking headache.

What to do? We would have to move. And if so, we would have to get back our rent for the next two months. But it wouldn't amount to much more than twenty wŏn. With that amount of money we'd be lucky to rent a single tiny room. Did that mean we were stuck here in this haunted house? Would I have to be sick and frightened, and end up dying here?

As I was thinking these thoughts, the eyes in the gourd mask on the opposite wall seemed to bug out at me and the lips seemed to twitch.

I opened my eyes wide, but the more I looked at the mask the more frightening its expression seemed. I jumped up, took down the mask, and put it under the desk. Too frightened to stay longer in my room, I went to the family room. As I lay down there on the heated part of the floor I thought back to the day we had moved in and to the pleasure I had taken in selecting my room and arranging the desk, chair, and books and hanging the mask on the wall.

After breakfast my sister went to school, my brother left, my son went out with his chums, and Mother, sure I had the flu, bought some Chinese medicine for me and began boiling it. As I lay in the still of the family room I thought about my illness and the medicine, my dream and this house, our money and the family livelihood while gazing at my old mother's wrinkled face.

The medicine in its earthenware pot was boiling before I knew it, and the paper cover had turned yellowish and risen. The steam drifted softly to the ceiling and though the rich smell seemed quite all right to me, what use could this flu medicine be? Mother was ignorant of the true nature of my illness, and I couldn't bring myself to tell her, knowing as I did how discouraged she would be. Tears welled up in my eyes, and to conceal them I quickly turned toward the wall.

From the hills in back of the house came the call of the cuckoos.

The Barbershop Boy

Pak T'ae-wŏn

Pak T'ae-wŏn was born in Seoul in 1909 and graduated from high school there, then spent two years at Hosei University in Tokyo. In 1933 he and such literary luminaries as Yi T'ae-jun, Yi Hyo-sŏk (both included in this anthology), Kim Ki-rim, and Yi Mu-yŏng formed the Kuinhoe (Circle of Nine). Later Pak was active in the Chosŏn Writers Federation, and in 1948 he migrated to North Korea.

Pak's first published works were poems, but by 1930 and the publication of his story "Suyŏm" (Beard) he had established himself as a prose writer. His two best-known works are the novella *Sosŏlga Kubo sshi ŭi iril* (A day in the life of Kubo the writer, 1934) and the novel *Ch'ŏnbyŏn p'unggyŏng* (Streamside sketches, 1936–1937), from which "The Barbershop Boy," which follows, is taken. The first describes poverty in Seoul in the early 1930s by focusing on bar girls and out-of-work intellectuals. The latter is a collection of vignettes set alongside Ch'ŏnggyech'ŏn, a stream (since paved over and today a broad avenue) coursing through downtown Seoul. After Liberation in 1945 Pak began publishing historical novels such as *Yi Sun-shin changgun* (Admiral Yi Sun-shin, 1948), in which he drew on earlier biographies as well as contemporary newspaper accounts. Pak published at least two such novels in the 1960s in North Korea.

Like other members of the Kuinhoe, Pak experimented with form and technique. The sentences of stories such as "Owŏl ŭi hunp'ung" (The warm breezes of May, 1933) are economical in the extreme, while those in "Chint'ong" (Labor pains, 1936) approach two pages in length. And in stories such as "P'iro" (Exhaustion, 1933) and "Ttakhan saram tŭl" (The wretched, 1934) we find numerals, symbols, and even newspaper ads. Apart from these ongoing attempts to refine his craft, Pak will be remembered for his camera-eye accounts of everyday life in Seoul during the occupation period, of which "The Barbershop Boy" (Ibalso ŭi sonyŏn) is a delightful example.

M in Chusa was not pleased with the face that greeted him in the mirror. The gray that was less noticeable when his hair was shaggy (the irony of this had not escaped him) seemed for some reason to stand out as the barber's expert trimming proceeded in time with the snip-snip of the shears. This was no revelation, of course. In recent years Min had always felt this way in the barber's chair, but still the grizzled hair reminded him of his years, however reluctant he might be to acknowledge them; and the inescapable realization of the great age difference between himself and the woman from Ansŏng, with whom he had begun living the previous year, caused him plenty of suffering. For during the current year Min Chusa had turned fifty—the age, according to Confucius, at which one comes to know Heaven's dictates—and this young concubine whom he'd established in Kwanch'ŏl-dong was precisely half that old.

The narrow cast of Min's face was accentuated by his hollow cheeks, and as he looked morosely at the creases and the wrinkles he so disliked and recalled that of late he'd been playing mah-jongg to the wee hours practically every other night, he told himself that dissipation was harming his health and that the first sure sign of this was his bad complexion. "I'm going to have to limit myself with these games," he muttered.

On second thought, though, even if mah-jongg meant staying up all night, there were times when he couldn't find a game for lack of players, and then he had a bigger headache—trying to satisfy that young bitch of his. This thought depressed him even more.

As the shears played above his scalp, Min kept looking with a kind of envy at the face of the barber, who couldn't have been older than twenty-five or so, a face so full of vitality, and he found himself scoffing at the notion that modern medicine was much advanced—the mere idea made him angry, though he didn't show it. He had religiously taken the yohimbine urged upon him by the young pharmacist in whom he had placed so much trust, and although the drug temporarily boosted his vigor, he feared more than anything the characteristic unpleasant aftereffects—the exhaustion and the more pronounced physical and psychological enervation. He came to believe that instead of this temporary aphrodisiac, if only there were a drug, or a technique, for enhancing the essence of one's spirit and energy, he would gladly spend a thousand wŏn for it. And Min Chusa had the wherewithal to do so.

But he felt all the more keenly that finding such a drug was no simple matter, and before long he had given up the notion, thinking, "Oh, what the heck, I have money, though. . . .

But in truth such rationalizations offered little comfort, because

Min was not all that wealthy to begin with, and besides, there were
the expenses connected with the upcoming City Council election: if
he didn't set aside some two thousand wŏn toward that end, it would
be a disaster for someone like himself who had taken such pains to
declare the candidacy he had had his heart set on. At this abrupt realization, wealth and fame grew even more dear to him, for it seemed
that the prospect of attaining these, unlike youth, held out an inkling
of possibility.

Heck, it's money and status that come first.

Startled at how close he had come to mumbling this thought, Min
searched the other faces in the mirror to see if anyone had sensed
what he was thinking, and his eyes met those of the barbershop errand
boy sitting at the window that looked out onto the main street. Fear-
ing his expression had betrayed his thoughts to the rascal, Min
grew embarrassed in spite of himself and instantly adopted a solemn
expression.

But the boy didn't show much interest in Min. His gaze returned
to the people visible through the window as they sauntered along the
stream in the waning sunlight.

The boy never tired of watching what went on outside. Apart from
neatly arranging the customers' shoes and offering them slippers, and
running little errands such as buying cigarettes and obtaining small
change, his only real duty at the barbershop was to wash the customers' hair. Now who would stay on at a job like that, that offered
only room and board, if you couldn't look outside from time to time
as he did? Of course that might be overstating the case, but in any
event he enjoyed being a witness to the outside world.

He found it the most fantastic thing that his daily spectating
revealed so much about the people who always passed by on both
sides of the stream; things simply became evident to him. And so
when he heard a customer speak up from behind him, as frequently
happened, "Say, boy, what are you gawking at?" he would answer,
"Look at that," and as if he'd been awaiting the opportunity he
would point outside the window and say, "That man there, coming
this way along the stream, where do you think he's headed?"

"Where? Who are you talking about?"

The hand knotting the tie would come to a stop and when its
owner looked to where the boy had gestured, sure enough, there was
a rough-hewn fellow in worn overalls and a dirty cap with no brim
clumping up the ladder from the streamside laundry area.

"That's the snake dealer, isn't it?"

"Snake dealer?"

"The beggar boss, boy."

"He's actually the second in charge. But where do you suppose he's going?"

"You little imp—how should I know?"

And then, proud as could be, the boy would say, "Now watch—he'll go to that shop stall near the bridge."

"Where? . . . Well I'll be damned. That's exactly where he's going. Is he buying cigarettes?"

"Nope. He'll just come right back out. Watch him. See him coming this way?"

"Okay, so where's he going now?"

"He'll go into that cheap drinking place near the stream. Watch."

"Where? . . . Well I'll be damned. That's right where he's going. But the guy must have gone into that shop to buy *something*. Why would he come out with nothing to show for it?"

"I can explain, if you'd like. Every once in a while that man there goes down under the bridge and collects ten or twenty chŏn each from a couple of beggars. He uses that money to buy liquor and food. But since it comes from begging, it's all in coppers, the whole twenty or thirty chŏn. But that man would never go into the drinking place with coppers, no sir. Instead he goes into the shop and gets 'em changed into ten-chŏn coins. . . ."

But every time the boy carried on like this, obviously enjoying himself, something was bound to come up, and then young Mr. Kim, the barber, who had not worked there very long, would speak up in that hectoring tone of his: "Boy, stop your blabbering and make sure there's enough change." This would annoy the boy considerably.

Next the boy spotted Fathead, the shoe shop owner's brother-in-law, leaving the streamside with two large canfuls of water loaded on a backrack, as he always did after spending half the day baby-sitting.

"Looking after his nephew, packing water—I wonder if he'll do that till the day he dies. . . ."

Young as he was, the boy felt sympathy for the man, but this feeling soon passed, and when he caught sight of a dignified middle-aged gentleman strolling past the shop a cheerful smile crossed his face.

The first thing to notice about this gentleman was that he was a corpulent sort, belly spilling out in front of him. His face was correspondingly large and, to be sure, fleshy, and the eyes, nose, ears, and

lips of that face were likewise correspondingly large. The most spec-
tacular of those features was the nose, especially the large, rounded
bridge characteristic of a pug nose, and though the man had recently
forsworn alcohol, there remained that memento of the days he had
been fond of drink, so bright and red like a strawberry that it almost
made your mouth water. Atop that face sat his beloved derby hat,
and when he sauntered along in his slippers, all who encountered
him were secretly delighted, and why not? The more dignified his
manner and gait, the more the boy laughed to himself. For he had
learned from the barbershop gossip that although the watch the man
enjoyed looking at in public was genuine gold, eighteen carat, the
watch chain that he wanted others to believe to be also genuine was
actually no more than five carat.

But of course there was nothing spiteful about the boy's smile. If
anything it conveyed goodwill. The boy had no grounds for despising
or scorning this man who believed that his brother-in-law's being a
city councilman was an unparalleled honor, and who from time to
time liked to have lunch with his family, including his sixty-year-old
mother, at a department store restaurant.

This gentleman lived in the central part of Tabanggol, once the site
of many *kisaeng* houses, and he operated a dry goods shop on a main
street near the Kwanggyo intersection, within hailing distance of his
home. He appeared at the shop in the morning and returned home in
the evening, and the route he took to the shop never varied: he would
emerge from an alley and cross the makeshift pontoon bridge to the
north side of the stream and from there proceed to Kwanggyo. The
barbershop being on the north side of the stream, between the bridge
and Kwanggyo, the boy was able to observe the man morning and
evening through the window. And whenever the boy saw the gentleman he felt a secret delight. And along with it a certain expectation.
If it be known, this expectation that the boy harbored toward the
respectable-looking owner of the dry goods shop concerned the position of the derby atop his head.

It was obvious to the boy that the man's hat was a good fit. But
the man never placed it firmly enough on his head so that it looked
secure to others. He just let it perch lightly there as he moved along.
Clearly if at some point the wind suddenly picked up, the hat in its
present position was vulnerable. It was this possibility that the boy
anticipated so cheerfully. But like most expectations, this one was not
soon realized. . . .

Once again the boy watched in vain as the gentleman crossed the pontoon bridge and disappeared down the alley. The boy's gaze then shifted to the bar named Peace on the far side of the stream.

Like most bars, this one looked unsavory, even unclean, in the light of day. The windows, painted in red and blue, seemed all the more tawdry when the lights were off inside, and the couple of token conifers that had been squeezed into the tiny patch of ground outside bore a lazy coat of dust and dirt.

These particulars, though, didn't draw much of a reaction from the boy. He was more curious about the small, fiftyish woman who for some time had been lingering outside the bar, peeking first through the open window and then through the hole in the rice-paper panel that served as a clumsy replacement for the broken glass pane in the door to the kitchen. This woman was the mother of the bar girl who went by the name of Hanako.

I just saw Hanako leave for the bathhouse, the boy told himself. He felt sorry for the woman, who had a temporary servant's job near the East Gate or some such place. She must have gone to some trouble to make this visit, but sadly enough her trip was in vain.

The woman, needless to say, had no way of knowing this. She paced back and forth anxiously in front of the door. By now everyone in the bar knew who she was, and especially around this time of day, when not a single customer had appeared and the barmaids hadn't yet put on their makeup, no one would have minded had she slipped into the kitchen and asked about her daughter. But she never did so. Such was the diffidence she felt about seeing her daughter.

For the fourth time the woman stood on tiptoe and peeked in through the half-open window. Just then the kitchen door opened and out stepped a barmaid who must have been in her thirties. She wore a soiled apron and no socks inside her white rubber shoes, and was not at all attractive in either looks or figure. This was the woman called Kimiko. Instead of descending to the streamside, she remained above, looking down at the stream and spitting into it in a masculine way. And then she noticed her sister barmaid's mother.

"She just left for the bathhouse," she said curtly with no change in expression. Her voice was so rough and loud, the boy could hear it from the other side of the stream.

Those who didn't know better might ask what this woman was doing working as a barmaid. After all, she was plain-spoken, plain to look at, and just plain too old. But such a question would only betray their ignorance. In fact, it was rare to find a girl who could sell as many drinks for her proprietor as she did. For one thing, Kimiko herself was a good drinker. Oh yes, the customers assigned to her table would have to pay nearly double the amount that their own drinks cost. A few customers disliked her, and that was the main reason. You would think that in the absence of beauty and (most of all) youth she might be an amiable talker and quite the charmer. Well, that wasn't the case either. Not once, even by accident, had she offered a pleasant word of greeting, or favored another person with a friendly smile. That Kimiko, who seemed to have every sort of characteristic that would estrange her from those who frequented places like bars, enjoyed more loyalty and affection than the other women, was quite a strange thing; or perhaps these times being what they are, her qualities were somehow considered attractive.

She did, though, have a strong point that others, understandably enough, would have difficulty emulating, and this was her tendency to look out for others. Here was a woman who by her own testimony had no kin to speak of on the face of the earth, and yet, or perhaps because of this, she went out of her way to be attentive to those in genuinely difficult circumstances; it really was remarkable. . . .

The boy watched as the woman looked off in the direction of Kwanggyo with a pained expression, seemingly lost in thought. Presently she said a few words to Kimiko.

"All right, why don't you do that?" said Kimiko in the same loud voice.

The woman took her leave with a slight nod and set off toward the main street.

Looks like she's off to the bathhouse. Suppose she'll ask Hanako for money?

With this thought he transferred his gaze to the home of the herb doctor across the stream, where he saw a young couple emerging.

Always together, those two, he said to himself, and a broad smile broke out on his face.

The barbershop boy wasn't the only one to point out these two as lovebirds. The man was the eldest son of the herb doctor and a graduate in English literature from a private college in Tokyo. He and the woman had been married going on three years now, and their habit of strolling about, shoulder to shoulder, dated back a year earlier still, when they had first met. That the herb doctor's son, having just returned from Tokyo, was courting a "New Woman" Ewha girl had

been big news at the streamside laundry site, and the neighborhood
gossips awaited the outcome with a good deal of curiosity, wondering what the stiff-necked herb doctor would think about the match
between the two young people. Well, the old-fashioned doctor proceeded to confound everyone's expectations by hearing out his son,
arranging a formal marriage interview with the girl, and with no
further ado consenting to the marriage. For this the doctor was
acclaimed enlightened by the neighbors, but the young couple were
for some time the subject of many neighborhood opinions as to
whether they were indeed happy: "People in a love marriage have a
worse relationship," and the like. Despite the occasional person who
made such remarks, the couple's love seemed truly sincere, and the
old-fashioned neighborhood crones who were frequently tempted to
poke fun at the "New Woman" ended up changing their tack: the
young couple were up to par after all. One couldn't help regarding
this emerging consensus as a blessing.

Through the barbershop door's glass panes, which the boy had
polished so well, he watched as the herb doctor received a visitor in
his guest quarters. The house was not that large and the family's
standard of living not so opulent, but if you were to believe what
others said, the doctor earned a thousand bags of rice a year. When
the boy considered that the doctor had amassed all of it single-handedly, risking all himself, he secretly looked up to this man with the
unprepossessing appearance as he would have a great man.

The herb doctor finished what he had to say, and his rustic visitor
emerged. He wore a yellowish brown felt hat that should have been
sent to the cleaners long before, a silk topcoat the color of dark
copper that had probably been ironed especially for this trip to Seoul,
and a pair of white rubber shoes. A quick glance revealed him, unfor-
tunately enough, to be missing an eye. It had been a really long time
since anyone had seen a one-eyed man at the streamside, and the boy
meant to keep him in sight as he walked toward Kwanggyo. But then
he spotted Mr. Hong the clerk, who had emerged right on the heels
of the visitor and entered the herb storage shed beside the front gate,
and was now hauling out some large bags of herbs. His gaze turned
toward Mr. Hong and almost without realizing it he swallowed
heavily.

Boy, it's been a long time since I've had some cinnamon bark, he
thought.

It was close to ten days since Tol-sŏk had left the herb doctor's.

The barbershop boy had made friends with the last three errand boys at the herb doctor's, but Tol-sŏk was the only one of them who regularly brought him presents of cinnamon bark, only a tiny piece of which would set your mouth on fire. This thought made him wonder what kind of fellow Tol-sŏk's replacement would be.

Dammit, he shoulda stayed on. . . .

He knew Tol-sŏk had left the herb doctor's because the work was hard and the pay low.

Well, what about me, dammit all? I don't get a single copper. . . .

Granted, other pharmacies supposedly paid better, but at the herb doctor's you got your meals plus five wŏn—that Tol-sŏk didn't realize how fortunate he was!

This thought momentarily put the boy out of sorts, but then he saw Kwi-dol's mother emerge from the herb doctor's gate with a basket, on her way to market for dinner fixings.

That's right, they don't have a new scrubwoman, so she has to do the laundry and go out for groceries, too. . . . She's probably up in arms, having to do it all by herself. . . .

In any event, servants weren't known to be treated that harshly or badly at the herb doctor's. It was just that it was truly difficult to establish a cordial servant-master relationship—which might help explain why the previous servant there had lasted only a year or so.

She's one of a kind, thought the boy as he watched Kwi-dol's mother. She'd been heard to say she'd stay at the herb doctor's till the day she died.

Her husband had begun to abuse her after taking a mistress, and finally she had lost her little boy—her only child. With no reliable means of support, she had become the housekeeper at the herb doctor's in the fall five years ago—the same time that the doctor's youngest daughter, Ki-sun, now a kindergartner, had come into the world. As the boy reflected briefly on how the neighbor women all praised Kwi-dol's mama as a good woman, and watched her walk toward the grocer's near the pontoon bridge, her head tilted slightly toward the left in that way of hers, three girls in their late teens, their hair in braids, caught his eye as they walked in step down to the south side of the stream, chattering and laughing. They had fixed themselves up to look like schoolgirls, but you could tell from their *bento* lunchboxes in cloth wrappers that they worked at the Monopoly Bureau cigarette factory on Ŭiju Boulevard, which had just closed for the day at five o'clock. They were not at all plain, these three who radiated such youth, and one of them in particular, the one with the ready laugh, you could justifiably call a belle. First of all, her complexion was truly appealing, not like that of most factory girls. Her jacket of blended fabric, her dark crepe skirt, and her flats complemented her appearance. She was the sister of the plaster worker who lived near Sup'yo Bridge, and the barbershop boy had heard that she played fast and loose, showing off her good looks.

But when it came to playing fast and loose, her older sister was one up on her. Widowed, this sister now lived with their brother, but even when her husband was alive it seemed she had taken several lovers. The gossip that went on behind her back presented her in quite a light: her husband had an illness, all right, but he was troubled in addition by her misconduct, and he had died at thirty-eight, right in the prime of life. The woman, approaching her mid-thirties, had lost all trace of her youthful attractiveness, and whether or not she should remarry shouldn't have been an issue. But her nature being what it was, keeping her at her brother's would eventually lead to an outbreak of scandalous rumors. Here was a real headache for the brother, who before long would have to marry off the other, second sister, and as you might expect, he seemed willing to hand over the widow to anyone who might come along and offer to take her in. . . .

Fathead finished unloading the water he had brought and once more took his nephew piggyback, and as he emerged from the gate of the shoe shop owner's house the sound of an organ could be heard from the room of that man's second son, whose window faced the stream. The barbershop boy, of course, didn't know the name of the tune, "The Chieftain of Baghdad," but just to hear this marching music, which the second son so delighted in, conjured up images of a young hero chasing a rogue, and the boy was easily enthused. But there was something about the mood of the organ player that made you wonder if listeners would be as enthused at the tune as they normally were. This second son, who would become a doctor if he finished school that spring, had been fond of music since grade school and had learned to play songs first on the harmonica and *taejŏnggŭm* and then on the organ, mandolin, saxophone, and violin. He had had these and other instruments and could play them after a fashion.

Chŏm-nyong's mother praised him to the skies: "He has more talent than anybody."

But they were no longer readily at hand, those instruments. Consistent with the decline of the family fortunes, such things had disappeared to the pawnshop and the secondhand dealer's. The old organ, worth only a few coppers, was all that remained to offer the young man solace from time to time.

The boy moved his gaze to the shoe shop, two houses away. Though it was February, and of course not the season for summer flies, people referred to a slack business period by saying, "Only the flies are moving." And in this lonesome shop, with nary a customer in sight, the owner's eldest son, the one with the crewcut, was leafing through a newspaper. Probably yesterday's, obtained from the herb doctor's. The shoe shop owner had stopped taking the paper months ago.

Those around the barbershop boy couldn't be expected to know about his admirable trait of recognizing the difficult circumstances of others, and they didn't hesitate to startle him from his reveries. As Mr. Kim did now.

"Hey, you! Stop your daydreaming and wash the gentleman's hair!"

The shout came from right behind him, and before the boy knew it he was angry with Mr. Kim. The man hadn't been working that long at the barbershop, but there he was again riding his high horse and lording it over the boy.

"My name isn't 'Hey,'" the boy said grouchily. "It's Chae-bong, and it's a perfectly good name." And with that he followed Min Chusa to the washstand.

Phantom Illusion

YI SANG

Yi Sang was born Kim Hae-gyŏng in Seoul in 1910 and was trained as an architect. During his short literary career he showed an interest first in poetry, turning out some highly idiosyncratic and experimental pieces, and then short fiction. In the fall of 1936 he journeyed to Tokyo, where he soon ran afoul of the authorities and was imprisoned. He died of tuberculosis in a Tokyo hospital in 1937.

His "Nalgae" (Wings, 1936) is one of the best-known modern Korean stories. Whether it's read as an allegory of colonial oppression, an existential withdrawal from the absurdities of contemporary life, an extended suicide note, or simply the degradation of a kept man, it is strikingly imaginative.

Yi Sang was a writer ahead of his time. While his debt to French modernism is evident, scholars have also investigated the influence of traditional Korean literature on his work. Since the 1970s his critical reputation has soared. (For a provocative portfolio on this gifted artist, including translations of his poetry and fiction, see the 1995 issue of *Muae*.)

"Phantom Illusion" (Hwanshigi), one of several of his stories published posthumously, first appeared in *Ch'ŏngsaekchi* in 1938. Readers of "Nalgae" will recognize the antic, self-deprecating narrator, the interior monologues, and the staccato narration.

In the beginning there was an idiot who couldn't tell right from left,
And now, a hundred generations later,
Invalids cursed by heaven proliferate among his hapless
    descendants.

"Whichever way you look at her, the little woman's face seems a bit lopsided toward the left, you know?"

That's what Song said about a month after their marriage.

She wasn't a virgin, but she had a treasure even more precious—a set of Gorky's complete works, which she had read through, every last volume. That's what attracted Song, and I'm sure it's his secret pride and joy.

It was only natural that the newlyweds, Song and Miss Sun-yŏng, should combine their books, and I saw Song's recently purchased Gorky set together with Miss Sun-yŏng's time-worn set. (The sad fact of my having to add "Miss" to her name now that she's married is the motive, such as it is, for this story.)

Ultimately, about a month after their marriage, Song took his newly printed Gorky set and sold it.

"Let's spend half of it," he tells me.

"What about the other half?"

"I have to give it to the little woman. I blew last month's pay on booze, and I've had to go through hell this entire month."

"I thought you were going to spend the other half on cosmetics for her—"

"Cosmetics? You know, don't you get the feeling there's something a tiny bit lopsided about her face, whichever way you look at her? I understand you chased her for four years before we got married. Did you know about her face then? Or were you oblivious to the very end?"

I remember the first time I met her. It was early summer, four years past, a clear night with the stars sparkling. Sun-yŏng was leaning against the old, crumbling rampart wall along the street leading over the hill to the radio station, waiting expectantly, her face as beautiful as if it were bathed in moonlight. From my rather limited perspective I was deeply troubled by the sensuousness of the wheat-colored breaths passing through the coarse texture of her linen summer jacket. Hmm . . . what would be the most skillful and yet most natural way to violate those lips? I wondered.

In a matter of minutes I had drawn up a plan. First of all, I would have to approach Sun-yŏng and look at her head on.

When I did so, something struck me as very strange. Her face, as beautiful as if bathed in moonlight, looked for some reason slightly lopsided toward the left.

Like someone who had committed a crime, I promptly removed myself to her right. For I had to adjust my angle of sight, which was capable of such effrontery.

And then, owing to my disadvantageous position, I could no longer violate Sun-yŏng's lips. (It really was starry, that early-summer night four years ago.) A policeman approached, I had no idea why. When I told Sun-yŏng I was from way down south in Samch'ŏnp'o, she said she was from Hoeryŏng, up on the northern border. Suddenly, with lightning speed, Sun-yŏng and I were hundreds of miles apart on my mental map. In a moment the moonlight had vanished from her face.

My wife wrote me a letter from Samch'ŏnp'o. She said on the one hand she might return to me immediately, but on the other hand there might be a delay—she simply couldn't tell at a time like this.

My wife was AWOL. I had a good mind to call the junk dealer and sell off everything she owned, including the dirty socks she had left behind.

It seemed there was a fifty-fifty chance my wife would return, but in fact, even if I were to tell her to leave again, there was no place she was welcome. Oh well—I lay myself down and figured I'd wait and see if she came back.

Anyway, that was the general idea. In the evening, using young Yun as my cover, I'd hang out at the Morocco Bar, where Sun-yŏng worked.

To a drinking man, one of the best excuses to drink is when your wife flies the coop—after all, it's a pretty sad situation. But you don't let on, no sir, not one iota, that there's a fifty-fifty chance she'll return. To the best of my ability I exaggerated my sorrow—which was anything but—in an attempt to tug at Sun-yŏng's heartstrings. But in the end this sordid job of fakery had no effect on her.

Before long, Sun-yŏng had gone south to Kwangju. The day she left, she had me in a drinking way. I felt like grabbing the hem of her skirt and ripping it. I cried. I told her that life is hollow and empty, blah, blah, blah. But Sun-yŏng apparently took this as a sign that I needed more booze, because she ordered me another beer.

For the next six months I couldn't forget Sun-yŏng. But in the meantime the fifty-fifty chance of my wife returning paid off. What could I do but take her back? I was able to make love to my unwanted wife with ten times my previous ardor, dumping onto her my festering love for the absent Sun-yŏng.

My wife began to despise me.

Six months later Sun-yŏng walked back into my life and spit in my face. The face of a man who had meekly taken back his wife after she'd been on the loose for half a year.

Four useless, wasted years passed. My wife left again, and the chances of her returning were fifty-fifty. I traded in my loneliness for a job that paid one wŏn, forty chŏn a day. In a dismal-looking print shop I stamped out identical todays, tomorrows, and day-afters as if I were a piece of movable type. And when Sun-yŏng moved to a different place to work, I tagged along and made it my hangout. I had sold my life for a daily wage of one wŏn, forty chŏn, and if there were some halfway joyful hours to that life at all, they were the times I sat across from her fingering a drink. But ever since Sun-yŏng had undergone a change of heart toward me—or perhaps I had never occupied a place in her heart—there was an icy distance between us, hundreds of miles apart, and she was on the far side. On the near side were me and Song, who was just as lonely as I, perpetually huddled together and shivering.

Appealing to Sun-yŏng out of my own loneliness no longer worked. Instead, using Song's loneliness as a pretext, I sobbed and blubbered in front of her. This was after Song's job had vaporized his scruples. Song suffered mightily on that account. His complexion turned white as a sheet of paper. To prove my own sorrow by taking advantage of Song's plight, I wasted literally thousands of words. Sun-yŏng seemed to warm up to me, judging from the glow that began to light up her face. But in the process I lost any influence I had. And just when I thought I had barely regained it through all sorts of desperate efforts, phone calls like this one began to arrive:

"Is this Mr. Song? Why don't you come over to the bar this evening—with Mr. Yi Sang?"

Well, as you can guess, I was just extra baggage.

One day the phone call came and Song offered to buy the drinks with his midyear bonus.

We drank.

We got drunk.

In my stupor I thought of leaving the country: I'm going far, far away to Tokyo, I'm going, I'm going—going for good, off to Tokyo.

"Come on, stay a little longer—you're not going to bed this early, are you, Mr. Song?"

Mr. Song must have consulted a fortune-teller. And the prognostication seemed to be: treat Yi Sang to some meat. And so Song got up first, suggesting we take a taxi. I did my best to talk him out of it. After considering his financial situation, I took him to his boarding house, ready to call it a night. When we got to his second-floor room, he puked all over. The only thing that came up was beer, clear beer. I had a hell of a time, but after an hour I had him cleaned up. After putting him to bed I went outside. On that June night a breeze redolent of acacias tickled my languid skin. Over a cup of coffee at the Mexico Tearoom I thought about Song throwing up and crying, throwing up and crying, then falling asleep.

Maybe I should give Sun-yŏng a call.

"Sun-yŏng? It's me, Sang. Song is safe at home now—just wanted to let you know. I don't know why, but I feel so gloomy I can't deal with it. I thought I'd go home and go to bed early, but maybe the Mexico—"

"Yes, come over. Besides, I've got something to talk with you about."

On Sun-yŏng's face, looking calmly at mine, I could plainly see the traces of four years of fatigue. She appealed to me in a low voice, told me she hated her job.

"Well, then," I said in earnest, "why don't you marry Song? Fact is, he's at the end of his rope. He's persecuted by mundane reality. It runs counter to his conscience, and he's all mixed up. It irks him so much he wants to kill himself, and no one realizes how he's suffered."

"I want to see Mr. Song—I can't wait," she said.

Ten minutes later Sun-yŏng and I slid open the door to Song's room, and there with our own eyes we saw that his suicidal agony had materialized.

Next to an empty container of three dozen sleeping pills were two pieces of paper with my name and address and Sun-yŏng's jotted on them. They had an icy feel, colder than that of a knife blade, as if demanding something of us.

I ran around the late-night streets almost until my legs gave out. But the doctors at the hospitals held a human life cheaper than a mah-jongg piece or a glass of beer. After an hour's vain search I returned to the boarding house. Sun-yŏng, lips tinged with blue, had prostrated herself upon the comatose Song, who was snoring loud enough to raise the roof.

In the event, I set the snoring corpse on my back and loaded it into a taxi. We made a beeline for the medical school annex hospital. There I found a watchdog along with two nurses and a doctor to receive us three "patients."

The drugs in the sleeping pills hadn't spread far beyond the stomach. Song's life was not in danger, but he needed an injection of a heart stimulant on the hour. At this time of night he might as well stay at the hospital, and so he was admitted.

The doctor instructed me to stay at Song's side all night, watch in hand, holding the patient's troubled wrist and taking his pulse. The reading fluctuated around 130, but sometimes took a nosedive. Sun-yŏng volunteered to stay up with me, but I insisted she go home.

"Go get some sleep and come back early in the morning. Then I'll rest. It's no good if we both get worn out."

The eastern sky grew light. The footsteps of patients in the hallway sounded eerie. Rushing faucets, hacking coughs, mewling babies —this place was an absolute living hell that reeked of disinfectant.

Song's pulse had gone down almost to a hundred.

As soon as the hospital gate opened, Sun-yŏng came in. She had a small bundle with a fresh set of underwear for Song. My mouth tasted like bitters. I rinsed it at the faucet.

I had a meal and returned to find Song still comatose. At midmorning I left the sickroom to call his office and complete the hospitalization formalities, then called the print shop where I worked. It was two in the afternoon by the time I returned to the hospital. There they were, the two of them, holding hands in plain sight and talking intimately.

I was outraged. What a slap in the face! What was my role supposed to be in this farce? My hatred knew no bounds. How I wanted to kick myself, spit on myself, mock myself.

"Are you some crazy son of a bitch?" I roared at Song. "An idiot? A wicked, heartless fraud? Or maybe you're the essence of Buddhahood!"

Apart from my outcries, was there anything I could do to salvage the situation? I felt like bursting into tears. My legs were still shaky from running around the previous night, and now they were trembling out of control.

I had thought the mountains would collapse when Song took those pills, and I felt I had aged ten years since. And what did I get in return? What had I done to deserve this?

Sun-yŏng's pale face was lowered from view. Song looked up at me with a weepy expression.

"I'm sorry."

I no longer felt obliged to remain there. Behind the sickroom, along the way to the building that had housed the Chongch'in Bureau back in the old days, was a luxuriant garden. I shuffled there in my slippers. Various exotic flowers whose names I didn't know bloomed in profusion beneath the June sun. All without scent, nothing but color. A few patients and some honeybees drifted fretfully about the garden, as if driven by a thirst spurred by the passion of those tropical flowers.

Why was it that everything I touched turned to dirt? But then again it seemed that the curtain was about to fall on this gut-splitting comedy.

I sat down on the grass and took in the sun. All at once, exhaustion flooded into me. My eyelids softly closed as fatigue entered my limbs.

This time I'm going away to Tokyo for sure, I told myself as I stretched out my legs.

Scraps of gauze and bandages littered the grass. A sudden feeling of extreme revulsion attacked my senses, like the feeling you get when you're about to puke. At the same time, the voluptuous petals of those flaming tropical flowers changed before my eyes into something frightening, wicked, sensual. A mere touch, and my fingers would putrefy, decompose, fall away in bits and chunks.

"If your wife's face looks lopsided toward the left, then why not sneak in a look from her right?" I suggested.

Song merely snorted.

"Do you think she's telling the truth when she says she was born in Hoeryǒng?"

"These days it's Vladivostok—I can't figure out what kind of nonsense she's up to—so I told her I was born in Tokyo. Think I should have named a place farther off?"

"It's a hell of a long way from Vladivostok to Tokyo. Must be well over two thousand miles."

"I keep telling her she looks lopsided, but these days she flies off the handle so easily."

"You know, I wasn't serious when I said to sneak in a look from her right. Before you do that you've got to adjust your own angle of sight. So that even if everything else looks completely lopsided to the right, as long as your loving wife's face appears in balance, then your angle of sight has functioned properly. And if that's the case, then it's no longer a matter of Vladivostok to Tokyo—you'll be just one little smooch away from her."

The Mule

HWANG SUN-WŎN

Hwang Sun-wŏn was born in 1915 near Pyongyang and educated there and at Waseda University in Tokyo. He was barely in his twenties when he published two volumes of poetry, and in 1940 his first volume of stories was published. Since then he has concentrated on fiction, producing seven novels and more than one hundred stories.

In 1946 Hwang and his family moved from the Soviet-occupied northern sector of Korea to the American-occupied South. He began teaching at Seoul High School in September of that year. Like millions of other Koreans, the Hwang family was displaced by the civil war of 1950–1953. From 1957 to 1993 Hwang taught Korean literature at Kyung Hee University in Seoul.

Hwang is the author of some of the best-known stories of modern Korea: "Pyŏl" (Stars, 1940), "Hwang noin" (Old Man Hwang, 1942), "Tok chinnŭn nŭlgŭni" (The old potter, 1944), "Hak" (Cranes, 1953), and "Sonagi" (Shower, 1959), among others. In a creative burst in the mid-1950s Hwang produced the story collection Irŏbŏrin saram tŭl (Lost souls). This volume, a series of variations on the theme of the outcast in a highly structured society, is unique among Hwang's story collections for its thematic unity.

Hwang began publishing novels in the 1950s. During the next two decades he produced his most important work in this genre. Namu tŭl pit'al e sŏda (Trees on a slope, 1960), perhaps his most successful novel, deals with the effects of the civil war on three young soldiers. Irwŏl (The sun and the moon, 1962–1965) is a portrait of a paekchŏng (untouchable) in urban Seoul. Umjiginŭn sŏng (The moving castle, 1968–1972) is an ambitious effort to synthesize Western influence and native tradition in modern Korea.

Also in the 1960s and 1970s Hwang's short fiction became more experimental. Some of his most memorable and challenging stories date from this period: "Ŏmŏni ka innŭn yuwŏl ŭi taehwa" (Conversations in June about mothers, 1965), "Mak ŭn naeryŏnŭnde" (The curtain fell, but then . . . , 1968), "Sutcha p'uri" (A numerical enigma, 1974). Hwang's creative powers were undiminished as late as 1984, as the highly original "Kŭrimja p'uri" (A shadow solution) demonstrates.

Indeed, the length of Hwang's literary career, spanning seven decades, is virtually unparalleled in Korean letters. But it is his craftsmanship that sets

Hwang apart from his peers. It is safe to say that Hwang is *the* consummate short story writer of twentieth-century Korea. His command of dialect, his facility with both rural and urban settings, his variety of narrative techniques, his vivid artistic imagination, his spectacularly diverse constellation of characters, and his insights into human personality make Hwang at once a complete writer and one who is almost impossible to categorize. If there is one constant in Hwang's fiction, it is a humanism that is affirmative without being naive, compassionate without being sentimental, and spiritual without being otherwordly.

"The Mule" (Nosae), set in the author's native Pyongyang, was written in the late spring of 1943, at a time when Koreans were forbidden by the colonial Japanese government to publish in their own language. It did not appear in print until 1949, when it was published in the journal *Munye*.

O nce again young Yu saw a fresh pile of trampled-down dung where the mule had been tied up next to his house the previous night. And once again he reminded himself it was high time he gave the owner a piece of his mind and stopped him from bringing the mule there. That way, if his family ended up buying it, the owner could probably be persuaded to part with it dirt cheap. On the spot, young Yu sought out the old gentleman who lived next door, on the other side of where the mule had been tied up. As was his habit, the man was taking in the sun, pipe in hand.

"Grandpa, we need to do something. Either that damn little mule goes or my people go, one or the other. Irregardless, how come we got to put up with it? This very morning the neighbors come by and tell us to clean up the damn mess. We ain't said nothing to the owner, and the whole village is getting filthy. . . . You being an elder, the folks here won't speak up to you. Instead they come to us. How come we got to put up with it?"

The head with its horsehair hat liner nodded. The old gentleman seemed to have been put on the spot.

"Well, it's been an eyesore for so long, I wish we'd stopped it from being tied up there once and for all. The man who owns it keeps asking people to give him and his family a break and bear with them a little longer, until they can move it. . . . But he did promise to clean up the manure and all."

"Well, anybody can make promises. But I think the guy needs some convincing. You know, this cooler weather we been having is a luxury, but the dog days are coming, and that's when we got a *real* problem. Then that manure attracts every fly in the village."

"Yes sir, it does."

"I wish you wouldn't talk so polite to me, sir."

"Well, for the time being . . ."

"There's all sorts of diseases from Manchuria going around, and people say it's because of that damn manure. When it gets real hot, that's where they all start. Well, if he can't afford a place to keep that mule, the least he could do is tie it up in his own yard. Why the hell does he have to keep it next to someone else's house? It's a nuisance."

"Well, why don't we pay him a little visit this evening and tell him what you said?"

"Instead of going to his house, could you please tell him right here this evening when he comes to tie it up? See, it'll be harder for him to turn you down than me." So saying, young Yu, as if he had just thought of something, produced from his pocket a packet of Changsu tobacco he had bought for the old gentleman. "I just come across some of this—why don't you try it?"

As always, the old gentleman waved off the gift with the hand holding the pipe—"Now why are you always . . ."—but accepted it with the other hand.

"Grandpa, please tell him flat out to stop leaving his animal here. That mule owner feller won't get the message if you beat around the bush."

But the old gentleman, though he knew about the mule, couldn't bring himself to confront the owner at the scene. Instead, he gave the man enough time to return home for dinner, then visited his house, located in a hilly area some distance off.

The mule owner was taking his meal in the breezy room beside the front gate.

"I've caught you in the middle of supper," said the old gentleman, and he turned to go.

"No, no," said the mule owner, ready to rush out and lead his visitor inside. "You couldn't of come at a better time. We got a few odds and ends from the meal left over; how's about having 'em with a drink?"

"Now why are you always . . . ," said the old gentleman. How could he tell this man, who always welcomed him so heartily, to stop tying up his mule in the accustomed place? Feigning reluctance, he went inside.

"That's it, come on in," chimed in the man's wife with obvious pleasure. Knowing they had put the old gentleman and his family in a fix by tying up their animal next to his house, the husband had told her they should treat him to a drink whenever he visited. And so out she went, to return with a bottle in her arms. "Afraid there's not much for you to munch on, though. . . ."

With only kimchi and some scraps of dried pollack for snacks, the liquor soon took effect.

The old gentleman began to feel flushed. "You know, we have a problem," he ventured.

As if expecting this, the mule owner broke in: "I know I've gone and put you on the spot, but if you could give us a break and bear with us a little longer. . . . That mule is our livelihood. What else can we do? As you know, uncle, that little mule is all we have in the world. I've said this before, but without that little mule we'd of starved a long time ago."

No matter how drunk he felt, the old gentleman didn't have the heart to tell the mule owner not to tie up the animal in its usual place because of the mess it made. The man had said he couldn't survive without it. And besides, wasn't he himself always accepting warm hospitality from him?

"Well, sir, there's been all sorts of talk from the neighbors," he ended up saying.

"I figured as much. But uncle, sir, I wish you wouldn't talk so polite, me being just a young guy and all."

"Well, for the time being . . ."

"I'm no dummy. I know the neighbors for who they are. And I'll bet it's the one next to you that's making the most noise. . . . By the way, what does he do, that one?"

"Not much of anything, from the looks of it. Used to work at the rubber factory. . . ."

"Is that a fact?"

"From what I hear, his little sister's being sold off to a tavern, and with the money he gets it looks like he's going to start up something on his own."

"Is that a fact? Well, a man has got to do something for hisself, big time or little. How much do you get now, anyhow, for selling a girl into whoring?"

"Forty-six hundred *nyang* is what I hear."

"Forty-six hundred—that's four hundred sixty wŏn. Not bad. Though it wouldn't get you too far if you went and decided to blow it all."

"For sure. You know, you folks must have sank a good bit of money into that mule, and you have steady work to show for it."

"Yeah, else we would have starved a long time ago. Fact is, if you're young and don't mind a lot of legwork, you can make money. All you got to do is lead the mule on. Honest, uncle, you've given us a break so far—won't you give us a break from now on? As you know, uncle, we live in a rented house, and our yard's no bigger than a pussycat's face. Where are we supposed to keep a mule? There's not even room for a kitten."

"To be honest, it really doesn't matter to me. . . ."

"Uncle, sir, would you please explain our situation to the neighbors? Our livelihood depends on that little mule. . . ."

By now the old gentleman was nodding in agreement, but as he filled his pipe with the Changsu tobacco he thought of young Yu.

"Let's call it a night—I'm good and drunk," he said, refusing the drink that the mule owner was about to pour him.

"Just a couple more."

But the old gentleman rose.

"We don't mind it, you know, but in any event, if you could find some other place to keep it."

After the old gentleman left, the mule owner's wife cleared the drinking tray.

"Get the old fellow to sell the mule for you. We just can't afford to feed it anymore."

"Now hush up, woman. It's all planned out. If we just keep saying we'll starve without the mule, then we can squeeze out a good price for it." A smile played beneath his brownish beard. "In any case, I think we can sell that mule soon, and I got it all figured out who's going to get stuck with it."

The following day was the day young Yu's sister was to be sold to the tavern.

Young Yu left his house in the morning. On that particular day there came into view many girls of his sister's age. And, oddly enough, many horse carts as well. Yu tried to ignore them. But he was in no mood to go to a remote place such as Moran Peak, where you couldn't see a soul. Nor did he want to lose himself in a crowd watching someone hawk medicines. He could only roam the streets, where all sorts of people were going every which way.

Not until evening was near did young Yu drag his tired body home. As he had expected, his sister was gone. With trembling hands his aged mother silently held out a tightly wrapped wad of bank notes. And Young Yu silently accepted it. He went next door to see the old gentleman. Excitement had replaced his fatigue.

"How did it go?" Yu began.

"We have a problem. He kept giving me a sob story."

"I'll be darned. Didn't I say, sir, it wouldn't do to go to his house? You got to tell him no, then and there, when he ties up that mule of his."

"He begged me to give them a break. Said their lives depended on that mule. He asked us to bear with them."

"I'll be darned. There's a limit to what a feller can bear. How are we supposed to do that? The mule's been there day in and day out."

"He said without the animal they would have starved a long time ago. He just kept begging. What was I supposed to do?"

"I'll be darned. Grandpa, if your people or mine had a mule, we could put up with each other. But how are we supposed to put up with something belonging to a man we don't have no traffic with? And that mule's been there day in and day out."

"Well, sir, I guess you're right."

"I wish you wouldn't talk so polite to me, sir."

"Well, for the time being . . ."

"I'll be darned. Somebody tell me: how can a guy afford a damn mule when he don't even have a place to tie it up? If I was him, I'd sell that mule off real quick 'cause it's such a bother."

"I agree," said the old gentleman, the ever-present horsehair hat liner bobbing up and down. And then he was struck by an idea. "Mr. Yu, why don't *you* buy that mule?" He speared the air in front of Yu with his pipe for emphasis.

"Me? What am I supposed to do with a mule?"

"Why, you'll get a decent income from it. For a young buck with strong legs, it's the best thing you could hope for."

"I'll bet he'd want a bundle for that worthless animal, eh?"

"Well, since it's their lifeline, he may not want to sell it. Anyway, how about if I bring it up with him?"

"If you could please wait on that, sir, and instead, give it to him straight, one last time. See if he's going to take it somewhere else or not. And tell him if he don't, I'm going to turn it loose myself. At some point we got to draw a line."

Again that evening, instead of approaching the mule owner when he arrived with the animal, the old gentleman waited for the man to return home and then visited.

After the usual welcoming drinks, the old gentleman spoke up: "Why don't you just sell that damned mule and be rid of it?"

The mule owner gave him a look of dubious surprise.

"How are we supposed to get by if we just up and sell it?"

"Well, I guess you have a point there."

"And who's going to buy it?" broke in the owner's wife.

"Now keep still, woman," said her husband, pretending to scold her. "What do you want to know for when we can't sell it anyway?" And to the old gentleman, as if talking to himself, "Now I'm in a fix."

"I guess you have a point, but the folks in the village don't want that little mule kept there forever. Personally, I don't mind it at all, honest I don't, but everyone else does. One of them said if it wasn't moved this very day, he'd turn it loose."

"And honest, uncle, I knew you'd be the only one who wouldn't mind us keeping the animal there. When I think about how I can't take care of that mule, I feel like selling the damned thing off, come what may."

"Well, sir, I understand."

"I wish you wouldn't talk so polite, sir, me being just a young guy and all."

"Well, for the time being . . ."

At this point the mule owner again spoke as if to himself: "It's hard to get an honest price these days."

"What's the going price for a mule like yours?" asked the old gentleman.

"Well, let's see. Considering what I put into it, and throw in the cart, I wouldn't sell it for less than five hundred wŏn if they killed me."

"That's five thousand *nyang,* right?"

"These days no one in his right mind would sell a decent horse for less than seven or eight hundred wŏn. Grant you, mine's a mule, but five hundred is rock bottom. And it's a fact that mules carry more for their weight."

"Mr. Yu, why don't you buy that mule? You could make a fair living with it," said the old gentleman when young Yu visited him the following day.

"What am I supposed to do with a mule?" said Yu in a tone of surprise. And then, as if to himself, "I'll bet he'd want a lot for that worthless animal."

"He won't sell for less than five thousand *nyang*."

"That's five hundred wŏn!"

"Right."

"He's out of his mind!"

"Well, sir, I don't know. I hear these days you can't get a decent horse for less than seven or eight thousand *nyang*. In the case of a mule, they say five thousand is rock bottom. And mules always carry a lot for their weight."

"I really wish you wouldn't talk so polite to me, sir. After all I'm just a youngster. . . ."

"Well, for the time being . . ."

At this point young Yu again spoke as if to himself: "Five hundred wŏn? Damn, that's a lot of money!" At the same time, he produced a packet of Changsu tobacco and offered it to the old gentleman. "I got my hands on some of this—please help yourself, sir."

As always, the old gentleman waved off the gift with the hand holding the pipe—"Why are you always . . ."—but accepted it none-theless.

Again young Yu spoke as if to himself: "Five hundred wŏn? Damn, that's a lot of money!" Then, with the same hand that had produced the tobacco he squeezed the roll of bank notes in his pocket. "Well, if it was four hundred I might consider it."

That evening the old gentleman brought together young Yu and the mule owner at a soup-and-rice shop on the corner of the main street.

Sitting around a bowl of broth to take with their liquor, the men poured one another a couple of rounds of drinks.

Young Yu spoke up first: "I come along just to oblige grandpa here, but anyone'll tell you five hundred wŏn is pushing your luck."

"No way, sir. I come along just to oblige uncle here, too. Now if I take my time and a good buyer comes along, it's a cinch I can get six hundred—at least. And besides, if I sell it we'll be in a fix right away."

"Then why don't we call the whole thing off. It's not like I had my eyes on that little mule. I just thought I might do you a favor, you not having a place to keep it and all, and buy it off you if the price be right—"

"Just a minute," broke in the old gentleman. "Now Mr. Kim here is asking five thousand *nyang*, and Mr. Yu here is offering four thousand, so let's meet halfway and settle on forty-five hundred. And I'm not looking for a commission or anything, as long as you two gentlemen can put up for the drinks."

The old gentleman looked expectantly at young Yu and the mule owner in turn.

"Well, I don't know, but if you say so, grandpa," said Yu, whereupon he extracted the tight roll of bills from his pocket.

The mule owner just as deliberately ignored the money, and said disinterestedly, "I don't know either, uncle, but it's your say-so, and that's the way it's going to be, I guess." But then he began to gaze at the money as Yu counted it.

By now they were full of liquor, and at the old gentleman's suggestion they rose and left. The old gentleman walked uncertainly, more because of the alcohol than the darkness. Young Yu and the owner of the mule followed. For once, the drinks had no effect on either of them.

The old gentleman arrived at his house, but instead of going in he walked up to the mule. The other two followed him.

Standing in front of the mule, young Yu found himself thinking of his little sister. The former owner of the mule, for his part, clutched the roll of bank notes in his pocket, thinking that tomorrow he ought to buy that fancy pushcart with the rubber tires he'd been eyeing recently.

The old gentleman, scratching the mule's neck, congratulated himself for closing the transaction. He looked at the two men standing in the darkness. They should have made that deal a long time ago, he thought. In spite of himself, he chuckled in satisfaction.

The old man's had a few too many, thought the other two.

"One of you boys got a light?" asked the old gentleman after he had stopped laughing. And then he said, "From now on, I'm going to talk less polite to you boys. Hope you don't mind." Then he affected a series of coughs with an air of self-importance.

The next day young Yu set right to work with his mule and cart. He had decided to try West Pyongyang Station first. But several horse carts were already there in the station plaza. So he lined up with other carts on one of the main streets. But his turn never came. Have to be an early bird tomorrow, he told himself.

As he set off down the street he kept noticing the horse carts, as on the day his little sister had been sold. But the matter involving his sister didn't occur to him now. He was interested only in whether the horse carts were loaded or empty. Most of the carts he noticed were carrying loads.

He had turned toward Taedong Gate Boulevard when a middle-aged man hailed him. Could he haul a gravestone as far as Kambugi? Yes, said Yu. For how much? asked the man. Whatever he thought was reasonable, said Yu. Whereupon the man suggested one wŏn, eighty chŏn. The way the man talked, Yu gathered he had already bumped heads with several other drivers over the freight fee. Doubtless the offer was much too low. But he couldn't let this customer slip through his fingers, thought Yu.

The slab that was attached to the base was small, but then stones are often heavier than they look. By the time they gained Karuget Pass the mule was sweat-soaked and laboring. Young Yu felt as if he himself were carrying the burden. The owner of the gravestone complained that the "damned mule" was just being contrary and told Yu to give it a taste of the whip. But Yu didn't have the heart for that, no matter how slow they were going.

After delivering the stone, Yu followed the streetcar tracks back to the old Pyongyang Station, but found no customers. No matter, though, for he had a load to show for that first day.

The following day he turned out early at West Pyongyang Station. No other carts were there. Today might end up all right. But no sooner had he told himself this than a dozen horse carts gathered.

Noontime arrived, and with it the timber merchants. But it was the horse cart drivers appearing after Yu who negotiated the price, leaving Yu out, and half a dozen horse carts loaded up and left. Again it seemed useless to remain, and so young Yu headed toward the city center.

He stopped at the bank of the Taedong River, where he could see many horse carts carrying raft logs. But all of them were four-wheeled carts. The loads they carried were out of the question for a two-wheeled cart, and especially a mule cart.

While following the riverbank he looked back expectantly at the tombstone works, but no business offered itself there. Again he passed the Taedong Gate, then turned down a street. He took advantage of the mule's relieving itself to squat beside the street and rest his legs. The day had grown steadily hotter, and he felt more tired. All he wanted was to sit awhile. But then someone from behind shouted at him to get his cart off the street while he took his nap. Startled, Yu rose to see the procession of four-wheeled carts loaded with raft logs.

When they had all swaggered past, Yu left with his empty mule cart. He was drained of energy, legs and all.

The next two days young Yu was kept at home by rain. The third day he went early to West Pyongyang Station, and there he happened to meet a horse cart driver hired by a family moving to P'yŏngch'ŏn-ni. The man asked Yu to help him, and although the destination was several miles distant along a muddy road, Yu put all thoughts of hardship out of his mind. They had just arrived at P'yŏngch'ŏn-ni when it happened. Encountering a mud puddle, Yu's mule couldn't manage the sudden rocking and faltering of the cart, and sank down onto its forelegs. Yu and the horse cart driver managed to pull it up, only to see dark blood running from its mud-covered knees. The horse cart driver took some coal-tar axle grease from his cart and applied it to the wounds.

That night young Yu rose several times to apply axle grease to the mule's legs.

The next day the mule looked as if it had withered overnight. Yu decided to take the day off. He fed the mule bean fodder.

The next day he decided he had better earn enough to at least pay for the expensive fodder, so there was nothing to do but lead the mule out again.

The day was waning when young Yu managed to deliver a small load to a place beneath the Taedong Bridge. On his way back, as he was gazing absentmindedly toward the bridge, he caught sight of a horse galloping his way. Trailing behind it was a loaded four-wheeled cart. The horse's mane bristled and it gritted its white teeth; surely something was not right. Bits and pieces of the load flew out of the cart and onto the bridge. The horse, as if reacting to a murderous enemy pursuing it, kicked at the crosspiece. Again and again it kicked at the cart in annoyance as it galloped along. The horse had passed the Chosŏn Bank and turned toward Pyongyang Station when the cart's rear wheels came rolling off one at a time and crashed into the streetside shops.

The next morning the story of this horse came out among the horse cart drivers at West Pyongyang Station. To begin with, the animal was carrying a load it couldn't handle, and when it stopped cold at the foot of the hill leading to the bridge to Sŏngyo-ri, the driver and the freight owner, assuming the horse was being contrary, whipped the animal and with much effort got it up and over the hill. At that point the horse for some reason galloped madly off, kicking at the crosspiece, and though it broke one of its hind hoof joints in the process, it kept running and kicking at the crosspiece, and eventually it broke its other hoof joint. Even without the use of its hind legs it galloped a ways farther, finally collapsing dead in front of the courthouse.

The legs of young Yu's mule grew steadily worse and the mule itself seemed more haggard by the day. But Yu couldn't afford to keep applying ointment and rest it for a few days, or feed it bean fodder.

One evening Yu was passing West Pyongyang Station on his way home and thinking he should graze his mule when he encountered the horse cart driver he had helped before. The man had some short logs to haul and he offered Yu some of the work. Taking into account the mule's injured legs, Yu gave it a light load. But the animal hobbled no more than a few steps before kneeling down. The two men tried to pull it up, but the mule gave no indication of budging. Damned mule's up to its old tricks again! thought Yu, and he applied the whip. The mule stirred under the first few blows, but then lay still, only the area being whipped quivering. Yu finally realized the mule was not simply being contrary, but he nevertheless gave it a furious whipping for the first time. He had the illusion that he was whipping himself instead of the mule, and he kept thinking that even if the animal were to die a spiteful death, like the horse with the broken legs, he could at least hope to make it run free just once, as the horse had done.

A short time later young Yu led the mule and the empty cart home. He wept silently and tried to avoid looking at the mule's back where he had whipped it.

And as if that were not enough, at home his mother tearfully reported that his little sister whom he had sold to the tavern was sick in bed.

Young Yu was seized with a blind fury. He ran outside. For a time he stood there like a man possessed. A thought occurred to him. He found a club. Then he ran to the mule and began beating it on the back. "I'll kill you first!" he wanted to shout over and over, but the sound that escaped his lips was little more than a moan.

Someone grabbed the arm with the club. It was the mule's former owner, headed for home with his empty pushcart. The sad truth was, for several days he'd had nothing but a flat tire to show for his day's labor, and an inexplicable anger was eating at his heart.

"Where do you get off beating it like that? No animal deserves that kind of treatment."

His words were barely out of his mouth when young Yu screamed furiously, "You again? What do you want!"

Instantly the two men were tumbling about on the ground, mule dung and all.

The old gentleman next door had just finished dinner, and he emerged from his house patting down some of Yu's precious Changsu tobacco in his pipe bowl. Witnessing the fight, he rushed over, but didn't dare try to separate the two men.

"Hey, you two, what's the reason for this? If you have something to say, then out with it."

He began walking in circles around them.

"Talk it out, you two—huh? I said talk it out!"

About the Translators

KIM CHONG-UN is president of the Korea Research Foundation in Seoul and former president of Seoul National University. Educated at Seoul National University, Bowdoin College, and New York University, he taught from 1962 to 1991 in the Department of English Language and Literature in the College of Humanities at Seoul National University. A specialist in modern American literature, he has written extensively on Jewish American authors such as Saul Bellow and Bernard Malamud. He is the co-translator, with Richard Rutt, of *Virtuous Women: Three Classic Korean Novels* (1974) and the translator of *Postwar Korean Short Stories* (rev. ed. 1983).

BRUCE FULTON is director of publications of the International Korean Literature Association and a translator of modern Korean fiction. He was educated at Bowdoin College, the University of Washington, and Seoul National University. He is the co-translator, with Ju-Chan Fulton, of *Words of Farewell: Stories by Korean Women Writers* (1989) and *Wayfarer: New Fiction by Korean Women* (1997) and, with Ju-Chan Fulton and Marshall R. Pihl, of *Land of Exile: Contemporary Korean Fiction* (1993). He is the guest editor of *Seeing the Invisible*, a *Mānoa* feature issue on recent fiction by Korean women. The Fultons have received numerous awards for their translation work, including the 1993 Korean Literature Translation Prize (for *Words of Farewell*) and a 1995 National Endowment for the Arts Translation Fellowship.

CPSIA information can be obtained
at www.ICGtesting.com
Printed in the USA
BVHW030426271219
567910BV00001B/5/P

9 780824 820718